He Was Just Sittin' There

And Other Stories

By Paul C. Cline

Edited by Diane C. Cline

All stories written for our Family and Friends

Print ISBN: 979-8-218-37158-6
EPUB ISBN: 979-8-218-37159-3

Published by The Literary Spa

He Was Just Sittin' There

And Other Stories

Works by Paul C. Cline

Second Fiddles: Prime Examples of Strength in the Shadows

Co-author:

Practical Law

By the Good People of Virginia

American Democracy

To Our Parents, K. P. and Irene Cline
and Rex and Olga Chilcote

Contents

Introduction

Someone has said that writing can be rather difficult, but that having written is most rewarding. I would agree that completion of an assignment or a story is very satisfying, but the creation of the story can be pretty great, too. Let me give you some examples.

Say you're describing a person or a situation and the humor in what you are describing suddenly hits you. My appreciation and admiration of physicians is nearly limitless; however, the possibilities of a "serious" convocation of medical specialists, say gastroenterologists, are virtually boundless. (See "The Early Days of Gastroenterology" in "The Annals.") (All right, why not go after the lawyers, with all the "said parties" and Latin lapses. Not a bad idea—perhaps next time.)

I never tire of the theme of giving underappreciated persons their due. It may be a fifty-year cook to the college president ("The Old College Secret"), or maybe a little boy who makes a mistake in class ("Minus Four").

The reader has likely come from an interesting neighborhood, or a special place with interesting people. Our background is small town and mountains. Don't get us started on the characters and goings on in our little burg ("You're on Fire"), or on the peaks above ("Up on the Housetop").

It's also good to have some kind of system for writing as long as it is not overused. I often start with a name. Sometimes it is furnished by someone else ("Hortense Quito" and "Amelia"), and try to imagine what that person is like and might be doing. Or, a situation might just arrive from out of nowhere or maybe a dream ("Percy—66").

Another, but by no means last, possible source of a story, is something that one has witnessed; for instance, the revue that was the premise of "Between You, Me, and the Light Post."

In writing, as in many pursuits, one can get overly concerned with perfection, but that doesn't seem to get us very far. Better if we just try it—we might like it.

Stories of the City

He Was Just Sittin' There

Cousin Elsie and I were like sisters growing up in hard times in the Depression. But then, as often happens, we drifted apart for some years. She married Otis and stayed in Virginia while Irvin and I spent years in the Midwest and in California.

As Irvin was coming toward the end of his career in medical sales, his company transferred him back to Virginia and we were delighted to take up again with Elsie and Otis. It was as if we had not been apart, and that was a good thing because Elsie and I were nearby to support each other when our husbands passed away within a year of each other.

I'd have to say that I benefited the most from that mutual support arrangement, since Elsie was one of those people who you were drawn to because of her way of listening and understanding whatever it was that was causing you trouble at the time. She had been that way even when she was young and we were in high school. She was "there" for those who needed someone to be there for them.

Even though we were not so awfully old we decided to prepare for our "Golden Years" by moving into a facility that included independent living with health care provided in case we needed it. We were pretty independent individuals, so we each got our own apartment; however, we wanted to be close so when adjoining apartments became available, we moved in.

We had room for company, which in my case was usually one of my three sons and his family. Elsie and Otis hadn't had children, more's the pity because they would have been the best of parents. Elsie would talk from time to time about "Jimmy," almost as if he were their son. He had grown up near them and had experienced a troubling home life. He became a frequent visitor at her and Otis' home, ate there often, and sometimes slept over when his home was in particular turmoil. She admitted that some might think the arrangement strange, since he was a white boy and she and Otis were African Americans.

We talked of these young people and lots of other things when we got together, usually in the morning over our tea or coffee. "Other things" were often national and international happenings, since we lived in Northern Virginia, which is dominated by the presence of Washington, D.C. and all its goings-on.

One day, when they were doing some carpentry work in Elsie's apartment, she asked the carpenter if a door could be made between our apartments so that we could visit each other without going out into the hallway. He said that a moveable panel between our two walk-in closets would be the easiest, and when I agreed, the job was done. Because his workmanship was so good, you wouldn't even know it was there if you didn't know where to look.

We each had friends, but I'd have to say that most of our companion time was spent with each other. So it was especially difficult for me, when Elsie, much too young, passed away several years ago. I missed our morning chats and going shopping together, and even though we disagreed on some government and other issues, we never fell out over our opinions.

After Elsie's passing, I assumed that I would be getting new neighbors, but it was the strangest thing—the management said that they were going to leave the apartment vacant with all its furniture and things in place. The reason they gave was that there was an issue with "the estate." I had not heard of such a thing—very unusual in our facility. I didn't do anything about the panel between the apartments—that could be done when someone moved in next door.

Then I began hearing noises in the apartment that I knew to be vacant. It was always at night, usually well after dark and sometimes up until after midnight. The noises naturally disturbed me—what could make noise in a vacant apartment? Of course, it was none of my business and it was only occasional, but I was unable to come up with a good reason for it, except to consider that the noises might be from outside or above or maybe coming through the heating ductwork.

The sounds from the apartment became more infrequent, so I did not do anything about them for several years. Then one night I thought, I'm going to check this out. Maybe I've been imagining things—but I don't think so.

So I got my flashlight, turned off the lights, went to "Our Panel," and quietly slid it open enough to slip through. I silently went through the closet and into the bedroom. Under the bedroom door I could see that there was a light on in the living room. Why would that be?

I opened the door a crack and peeked in. I could not see anything at first, so I opened the door further.

And there, sitting in one of the living room chairs, reading some papers, was the President of the United States, James G. Grantley. He looked up and saw me, so it was too late to back out.

I stood there for a long moment, and we just looked at each other. Maybe he was as startled as I was, even if I didn't look much like a terrorist.

And then, something just told me, "You're Jimmy."

"That's right, and I'll bet you are Aunt Elsie's cousin, Florence."

"Yes. We lived here side by side for some years before her passing," I said.

"I know all about you and your husband Irvin. Aunt Elsie told me lots of stories about your growing up and your moving west. Aunt Elsie and Uncle Otis were always so special to me growing up. They kept me out of trouble with their welcoming me into their home. And they encouraged me to 'make something of myself'—and I guess I sorta did."

"I'd have to say you did that, Mr. President."

"I'd rather you'd call me Jimmy," he said.

"I guess I could do that—but what are you doing in Elsie's apartment? I guess it was you I heard from time to time."

"I'm sorry about the disturbance—I tried to be careful, but those Secret Service guys can't seem to check out things quietly. As to why I'm here," he went on, "this is the place where I am the most comfortable. I can sit here among the familiar furniture and surroundings of my earlier days—that sideboard there and that lamp and that china cupboard—and I can quietly consider the best way to handle some of the problems our country has to face."

"And," I said, "I'll bet it was you who arranged to have the apartment remain vacant."

"Yes, the manager of the facility here quietly worked it out, and I agreed to come and go as inconspicuously as possible, but you know those Secret Service people, they're so particular."

I said, "Well, I guess you want me to get our panel closed up, so I won't bother you anymore."

"No, that won't be necessary. Aunt Elsie told me all about that panel. There's no need to close it up, and you can visit when you want," he said.

"Oh, I couldn't do that."

"You know what, Aunt Florence—I can go see kings, and prime ministers, and presidents whenever I want, but here I have an opportunity to be with family."

Papa's Place

In order to save money for college, Buddy Brogan began working as a busboy at The New Century Restaurant when he was fourteen years old. He worked after school and in summers. He was so reliable and well-liked that he became a waiter when he was sixteen and even seated customers some evenings. He was soon to be eighteen, in his last year of high school, and had saved enough for three years of college.

Buddy was of average height, slender with dark brown hair and eyes. He was good-looking enough to charm the younger women restaurant customers and waitstaff, as well as being popular at school.

Although not especially athletic, he nevertheless was well-liked by the guys. He was friendly with everyone, but it was still a stretch that he often talked with Jimmy. Jimmy, an apparently homeless man in his forties, often showed up at the back alley of the restaurant. John, the manager, usually said, "Buddy, you go deal with Jimmy. I can't even understand him."

And it was difficult to communicate with Jimmy. His speech was halting and his sentences incomplete. He always talked about himself as "Jimmy did this" or "Jimmy does that." He was not unfriendly and seemed to appreciate the attention Buddy gave him. Buddy also gave Jimmy sandwiches and any other food that the manager would permit.

John said, "I don't even know where Jimmy lives."

"I don't either," said Buddy, "but I'll ask him."

When Jimmy came next to the back door, Buddy asked him where he lived.

"Jimmy lives at Papa's place," he said.

"Where is Papa's place?" asked Buddy.

"Jimmy lives over there," Jimmy said, pointing in the direction of the shopping mall.

This exchange got Buddy wondering whether Jimmy had a warm and safe place to stay, especially since the weather was turning colder. So one day when Jimmy came by Buddy left his job for a while and followed some distance behind Jimmy. Jimmy proceeded in the direction of the mall until he came to the back of the Fairall Furniture Store. There, after looking around and not seeing anyone, he went behind a hedge. Catching up, Buddy could see that he entered a basement door on what looked to be an earlier part of the huge building.

On his return to the restaurant Buddy told his manager that Jimmy lived in an apparently unused section of the Fairall Store. "His father must live there, too."

"Why do you say that?" asked John.

"Well, he told me that he lives in his papa's place."

"But we've never met his father," said John. "Seems strange."

"It sure does," agreed Buddy.

Nothing changed in the pattern of Jimmy's visits and Buddy's providing him with food until late in the summer before Buddy was to go to college. Buddy found Jimmy seated on a crate in the alley with his head down and obviously unhappy.

"What's wrong, Jimmy?" he asked.

"Jimmy's real sad."

"Why? What happened?"

"Papa died."

"Oh, Jimmy, I'm so sorry," said Buddy, placing his hand on Jimmy's shoulder. "Is there anything I can do?"

"No, just be Jimmy's friend."

"You know we're pals."

"Jimmy knows."

The summer ended and Buddy went to college and was very successful in his studies. He went during summers and was about ready to graduate. Even though he stayed busy he occasionally thought of Jimmy especially when the air turned chilly in the late fall. He hoped Jimmy was okay. One day just before graduation he received a registered letter from an attorney, Henry Golding, in his hometown asking him to visit his office the following Saturday morning. Although a visit home was not really very convenient, Buddy was so curious that he showed up at the lawyer's office at the time requested. From the rich polished wooden décor, he could tell that Golding was one of the most prestigious law firms in town.

The receptionist asked him to wait a few minutes and then took him back to the lawyer's office. Upon entering he was surprised to see Jimmy seated on a couch in the office. Mr. Golding was seated in an armchair nearby and rose as Buddy came in.

"Hi, Buddy," said Jimmy.

"Hello, Jimmy."

"I know that you two have known each other for a long time. And Jimmy says that you are friends," said Mr. Golding.

"We sure are," said Buddy, still puzzled about what was happening.

"Jimmy tells me he knows a great deal about you, Buddy," said Mr. Golding. "He says that you worked at the restaurant and were always kind to him. He says that you have gone to college, have done well, and are about to graduate. He knows about you, but do you know much about him?"

"Only that he and I have known each other quite a few years, and that he lives in the rear of the Fairall Furniture Store at the mall. He lived there with his father until his father passed away."

"Well, it's evidently true that you are good friends, and that Jimmy lived at the Furniture Store. But it's not accurate to say that Jimmy lived with his father," said Mr. Golding.

"No?" replied Buddy. "But he said he lived in 'Papa's place.'"

"Well," said Mr. Golding, "in a way that is true. Except that 'Papa's place' is the Fairall Furniture Store, one of a chain of two hundred thirty-seven highly successful stores owned solely by Francis Fairall—at least until he passed away several years ago."

"Oh?" said Buddy. "But..."

"Let me finish, please," said Mr. Golding. "And our local store is Jimmy's 'Papa's place' because Mr. Fairall was Jimmy's father."

"Oh," was all that Buddy could come out with, while looking intently at Jimmy.

"He was my Papa," said Jimmy.

"You probably didn't know that Jimmy is 'James R. Fairall.'"

Buddy couldn't speak.

"And," continued Mr. Golding, "that he is the sole heir to the Fairall Furniture Stores."

"No, I didn't," said Buddy. "I had no idea, Jimmy."

Jimmy just looked at Buddy and nodded.

"You may be wondering why we asked you to come here today," said the lawyer.

"Well, I've learned a lot already," said Buddy.

"There's more, Buddy," said Mr. Golding. "You see, at Jimmy's request, we placed the entire furniture chain in a trust at the death of his father. He said he was waiting for something to happen before making any further changes. And he came to me last week and told me that he was ready for a change. And that change involves you."

"Me?" was all that Buddy could come out with.

"Yes," said Jimmy. "Jimmy wanted Buddy to graduate from college. Then Jimmy wants Buddy to be COE of Papa's business."

"CEO," corrected Mr. Golding.

"Yeah, CEO," said Jimmy.

"But..."

"Our firm has looked into your background, your work ethic in and out of college, and your character, and we feel that, with good staff support, you will be able to guide this firm," said Mr. Golding.

"And you're Jimmy's friend."

After a number of meetings with Jimmy and Mr. Golding, and after Buddy had graduated from college with honors, Buddy assumed the reins of the big furniture firm. He had much help from associates at the company and steadily grew more competent in his leadership role.

Through it all he remained close to his friend Jimmy. And Jimmy moved out of "Papa's place," and into a very nice apartment, that Buddy helped select for him.

And, thereafter, he referred to his new home as "Buddy's place."

Silver and Tin

Hard times had struck while they were young. Both were blinded early on, She in a car accident that had taken her family and He by machinery on the old failed farm.

They occupied nearby spaces on a busy street in the city banking district. He sang and played the guitar behind an old tin pie plate, and She sold flowers from her stool set up behind a small silver bowl.

They talked and She laughed through the warm summers and cold winters of their northern city. He talked readily, but even a smile was too much for him—just as the misfortune of his affliction never really left his mind. But He was capable of still enjoying one luxury—her being nearby. So gradually the sidewalk spaces they occupied came closer until they were side by side. If She had to leave for a time, He sold her flowers, and She guarded his guitar in his absence.

A Stranger came by daily on his way to and from work and always greeted them with "How are things today?"

She: "Just fine, thanks."

He: "Terrible."

The seasons changed, but the greeting and responses remained the same until, at the sound of the Stranger's footsteps, She would simply say, "Fine," and He, "Terrible."

Time passed and the association of the sidewalk occupants remained the same, friendly and supportive—until a "bad day" overtook each at the same time. The "little things" that had occurred to upset each over the years culminated in an explosion over the disdain She had for the thud of coins hitting his old tin pie pan, and his similar critique of the sounds given off by her silver bowl.

In the aftermath of this event the Stranger found that He had moved just beyond the range of noise from the coins, but the Stranger did notice that He did not set up until He was satisfied She was present and all right for the day.

The separation lasted for the period of a long peeve, until one morning He gave the Stranger a different answer to the Stranger's greeting. He said, "I need to go shopping."

So shopping they went, and on their return He and the Stranger waited nearby until she counted her morning money. She did this counting each day when noontime toned on the nearby church clock.

The Stranger accompanied him to her stand and guided his hand as He dropped a small diamond ring into the silver bowl.

She moved her head quickly and listened as He and the Stranger walked away. She reached out and retrieved the ring from her silver bowl.

The Stranger hoped for some change in responses when he next approached them, but received the usual "Fine" and "Terrible" for several weeks. Until—she said to the Stranger, "I need your help."

She walked with the Stranger to where He was entertaining and waited until He stopped singing.

He heard them approach and was puzzled at hearing footsteps that accompanied those of the Stranger. Nevertheless, He gave out with his usual "Terrible." He also thought he sensed movement and heard a noise nearby. He reached down into his old tin pie pan and found lodged there a silver bowl.

Win or Lose

He was a giant to us kids. Not a big, over-bearing young man, but rather tall and thin and very flexible in his striding toward us and in his motions while telling us his magnificent stories. You might say it was just that he was so much bigger than we were.

We were kids on the block in the early nineteen-forties. The War was there, every day. It was on the radio, in the newspaper on our way to Dick Tracy or the Dagwood and Blondie, and in conversations of our parents. World War II was there also in more powerful ways, as when one day a week we bought our War Stamps, or "Victory Stamps." Or when we brought in balls of metal foil and newspapers for the war effort. Even when we thought about our missing Milky Ways, missing because of rationing.

But powerful wasn't a big enough modifier when we heard of the casualties, saw the blue and gold stars in neighbors' windows, and ultimately when we learned when we were in the upper grades that the husband of the teacher we had had in first grade, the beautiful Mrs. Finley, was killed in Europe.

Still, we listened to our favorite radio programs, not all of which featured war things, sled-rode on the slope behind the school, created or found hideouts, raided fruit trees at dusk, played kick the can in the street by the school, and managed to push the war away, at least for a time.

Just as there were stronger contact-points to the war, there were greater levels of diversion from that conflict. And the highest pinnacle of escape for us kids occurred when we were in the early evening occupied with some serious game in front of the neighborhood grade school and someone would say, "Winston is coming over."

All action stopped. Right then. By everyone. We all mustered on the four steps on the outside of the school. Sit down. Everyone. All eyes front. No need to give demerits for tardiness or unruliness. No need for *esprit de corps* building to have order prevail. Just have some advance observer say, "Winston is coming over."

Also, not need to ask, plead, or cajole. We knew what we were to do—listen. And we and Winston knew that he would do what he did so well—stand before us in the growing darkness and tell us a story.

The stories were his, at least as far as we knew. Maybe he had read some of them or altered some of what he had read to fit his audience. Didn't matter—partly because we just liked what he chose to relate to us, but mainly because he put us in the stories.

Put us right in the heart of the action of those action stories. "Cappy, you are going with Carolyn into the library of that old house that looks like the big old dark Duncan place down on the corner. And while you and she are looking at the many books, Carolyn moves one forward and the bookshelf spins around and you two find yourselves in a tunnel that is very dark and seems as if it is headed down to the next level of the house. And suddenly you hear footsteps in the distance and you stop and wait. They come closer and closer. Until they are almost upon you. But you are afraid to run or even to move. And then you hear, 'I believe someone else is here,' and you suddenly know that it's Nancy who just said that. And you say, 'Nancy?' and Nancy bops you on the nose while screaming her head off, and even in your pain you are glad to know that you have run into Nancy and Gloria, rather than someone else who you didn't know..."

In succession we were all placed into the thick of the story of the spooky old house or of the odd clearing over the hill that we would not dare venture into at night, or of the on and off light in the window of the old lady who was described by neighbors as bedfast. No one was left out. All were scared or challenged, but all performed admirably in the story. And all were named.

Persons on the home front do not suffer as greatly as the fighting men and women, but it is still difficult to live anything near a normal life when battles are being lost and won. And even though the children are protected by efforts to shelter them from the realities of conflict, persons who study the effects of disruption on the lives of youngsters contend that these young ones are affected nonetheless.

So, when a young man interrupts his usual pattern of activity to share a tantalizing tale with smaller ones than he, his attention to them may do more for them that he would ever know. At the very least the impression Winston made on us has lasted for most of us for going on eighty years.

The House on Eighth Avenue

"Why would Pete Willis do a thing like that?" Marian said as she and husband Lonnie walked by the Old Burns Place just before dusk on Halloween.

"He always was a little strange," Lonnie said. "I've known him since we were kids. Since my house was just a block over, we ran with the same group of kids. One thing, though, he was always close to his mother."

On their evening walk Marian and Lonnie were passing the cream-colored two-story frame house with green trim, in the style of days gone by.

"There it goes—the living room lights just came on. Guess they're on a timer," said Lonnie.

"I can see the old furniture, and pictures on the wall, just as it must have been in his mother's time," said Marian.

"More like Pete's grandfather's era. The old man had a gravestone business. Did very well and was a good saver. Tight with their money, was that whole family," said Lonnie. "Pete never goes into the house. A handyman maintains it—no one else is let in."

Just then they saw Cliff Ridge walking their way. "Better not hang around Pete's place long," Cliff said. "The ghost might get you."

"You're kidding," said Marian.

"No, I'm not. I don't necessarily believe it, but neighbors say they've seen something moving about in the house."

"That's a little scary," said Marian.

"Yes," said Cliff, "And some kids were trick or treating there last October and a light flashed in their eyes as they rang the doorbell. They ran off in all directions screaming."

"Let's move on, Lonnie," said Marian. "No reflection on you, Cliff, but it's getting a little too creepy here for me."

The next visitors to the home were a young couple and their little daughter on her first dress-up for the big night of trick-or-treat. But, tonight at this house, neither treats nor the opportunity for tricks, as the family moved on in search of joy in candy confections and appreciation for how cute the little girl was.

Treats and lots of them were pressing three visitors to move swiftly through their neighborhood. Cappy, Bill, and Nancy, who had been together on Halloween since kindergarten, were now mid-teens and having one last fling at this fall ritual. They had made a significant haul and were heading home.

"That's that creepy old Willis house," said Nancy.

"Yeah, left just as it was when my grandfather was a boy," said Cappy.

"Wonder why?" said Bill.

"Nobody knows," said Cappy.

"Let's take a peek," said Nancy, proven braver than the boys in times past. "No one's there."

"Someone might call the police," said Bill, the cautious one.

"We'll go around back," said Cappy.

"Good idea," said Nancy.

So, with Bill reluctantly following, the young friends walked the edge of the house around to the back.

"Hey, no lights in the back rooms," said Bill.

"Wonder why?" said Nancy.

"Mystery house," said Cappy.

Nancy headed for the steps to the wide back porch.

"We'd better not go up there," said Bill.

"Just a little peek in," said Nancy.

In their usual order Cappy went next and then Bill.

"It's too dark to see anything in there," said Cappy, disappointed.

"There's just a little light—looks like an old office or study—desk, file cabinet, chairs," said Nancy.

"Let's go," said Bill nervously.

"Can't see what the pictures are," said Nancy.

"Let me look," said Cappy. "Yeah, even a fireplace—wait a minute—no one ever goes into this house?"

"That's right," said Nancy.

"Well, something just moved over by the desk," said Cappy.

"Naw," said Bill… "Can't be."

"Can too," said Cappy, "and it's coming this way."

Just then a face appeared in the window.

The three pals leaped off the porch, nearly running over each other as they headed for the front street and all the way home.

Next morning, Saturday, they met at Nancy's to talk over the past night's experience.

"Was I seeing things?" asked Bill.

"Well, I know I saw someone looking out that door," said Cappy.

"Me, too," said Nancy, "and it looked like a girl."

"Strange," said Cappy. "I'd like to know more."

"You weren't so interested last night," said Bill. "You outran us in getting out of there."

"Yeah, well, I don't mean I want to go up on that porch again, but maybe we could watch the house. Whoever it is has to come and go sometime," said Cappy.

"I'm game," said Nancy. "How about starting this afternoon?"

In late afternoon they took up secluded positions where they could observe the old house from various angles. Time passed slowly, as it does when one is not moving and just watching and waiting. They waited until dark.

Cappy saw something first—a shadow—someone coming toward him—along the back alley that had been his post. The form moved on toward the house.

By then Nancy and Bill were alert to the movement. Nancy, either braver or more foolish than the boys, moved forward, removing a small flashlight from her pocket—and shining it directly on the dark, moving person.

That person turned but would not be identified in a dark hoodie and jeans. The boys had come to Nancy and the stranger and caused that person to stop.

"What are you doing here?" asked Bill.

"You have no right to stop me."

"Why, it's a girl," said Cappy.

"Nice work, detective," the girl responded.

Bill said again, "What are you doing here—and who are you?"

"Let's sit on the back porch and I'll tell you."

After taking places on the ancient porch furniture the girl of about fifteen, brilliant red hair, tall, serious, told her tale.

"I'm Carrie Willis; my dad is Arthur Willis."

"The same last name as Pete Willis, who owns this house," said Bill.

"Pete Willis is my uncle. And there's the problem. He has said for years that my grandparents left the house and all that was in it to him. But my dad knows better—that the home was willed to him and not to Uncle Pete."

"What's the problem then?" asked Cappy.

"The problem is that Uncle Pete used my grandparent's old wills to show he owns the house."

"And there is another will?" asked Nancy.

"My dad says there is, and that it is hidden some place in the house," said Carrie.

"And I'll bet your Uncle Pete won't let your dad search for it," said Bill.

"That's right, and my dad won't do anything about it. He just says, 'Let Pete have it.'"

"So...," said Nancy.

"So I've decided to come to the house and search for the will. I come at night because Uncle Pete would never give his permission for me to search," said Carrie.

"Any luck so far?" asked Cappy.

"No, and I've searched attic to basement. I'm about to give up."

"We could help you," said Nancy.

"But what good would that do?"

"Maybe fresh eyes," said Cappy.

"And working together," said Bill.

"Well, it can't hurt, I guess. But you'll need flashlights."

"We'll meet you here tomorrow evening, ready to go," said Cappy.

As promised, the three friends were waiting for Carrie the following evening. They were quietly approaching the back porch of the house when a sound caused them to halt.

"Rodney...oh, Rodney, is that you? You've been a bad boy! There you are, you bad dog—running away from me while I was walking you."

Only a neighbor with a bad dog—and a loud voice, but it caused Bill to say quietly, "Whew," when neighbor and dog went into the house next door.

Carrie used her skeleton key to open the old kitchen door and they went in. "Shall we search in teams?" she said.

Nancy said, "Good idea. I'll go with Cappy—so he won't get lost."

"Yeah, right—I'll end up finding that will, and then you'll see who is lost," said Cappy.

"Nice start—but nothing new between those two," Bill told Carrie, and they all laughed.

Carrie said, "Bill, let's you and I start downstairs, and Nancy and Cappy can go upstairs."

With that suggestion the search began. A long description of the search and its thoroughness might be given here, but the result would be the same—no result, a complete strikeout.

After the usual questioning, such as "Did you look...?" "Did you search...?" the friends sat on the steps going upstairs, wondering what to do next.

"I'm just sad, thinking about my dad and how close he was to his mother and father, and then being left out of their..." Carrie paused. "And they were awfully nice and considerate. I loved my grandparents."

"I know what you mean. I had the greatest grandmother. She...oh, my," said Nancy.

With that she jumped up and said to Cappy, "Come on."

Naturally, Bill and Carrie followed their two pals up to the stair landing halfway up the steps and began tapping on the paneling at the turn of the stairs.

"What are you doing" asked Carrie.

"During the Civil War, some men in this area refused to go into the army," said Nancy.

"Conscientious objectors," said Cappy.

"Right—and when authorities came by, it is said that one of these men went into a hiding place behind paneling just like this," said Nancy. "So my grandmother told me."

"But no luck here," said Carrie.

"Nope—this is solid. No hiding place," said Nancy.

Dejected, the friends headed back to the porch. They just sat quietly.

Cappy suddenly looked up and said, "I was just thinking about my Granny. She made the best cakes, and cookies, and..."

"So?" said Bill.

"So, one time when the family was visiting, she said, 'Want to see something?' We said, 'Sure,' and she told us to follow her to the basement. She went to the shelves where she stored her jars of fruit, pickles, and vegetables for the winter. We said, 'That's nice, Granny,' and she said, 'No—wait...'"

"What then?" said Nancy.

"Then, she went to one side of the shelves and pulled, and they moved. We couldn't believe it. Even my Dad, who grew up there, was surprised. He helped Granny pull the one side the shelves clear around, and guess what?"

"What?" asked Carrie, as everyone was interested in Cappy's story.

"There was a little hidden room behind the shelves. It had bunkbeds on each side and a little table between the beds."

"Wow," said Bill. "But what on Earth for? Why was the room there?"

"Granny told us that during the Civil War the home was a station on the Underground Railroad. Enslaved people who had escaped and were heading from the South to the Free States were given safe housing there until they could proceed further north."

Carrie said, "Do you think...?"

Nancy finished her thought: "...that maybe behind those shelves downstairs in the basement...?"

"Only one way to find out. Let's go see," said Bill.

With that they all got up and went down the basement stairs. The shelving looked heavy and built to be permanent.

Cappy reached for one end and pulled. No movement.

"Let me help pull," said Bill. But both fellows pulling together could not make it move.

"Try the other end," said Nancy.

Bill pulled on the other end, and the shelves began to slide outward. "They move easily," he said, as the opening grew big enough for all to see inside.

They found a small room, still big enough to contain a set of bunkbeds on either side. Between the beds was a small table on which stood an old kerosene lamp.

"Wow," said Cappy. "Who would believe this room existed?"

"And," said Nancy, "that it was part of our country's history?"

"And there's more," said Bill, turning with a grin, to Carrie. "In this little drawer in the table—is a legal paper. I'll bet it's the will you've been searching for."

Where Have I Seen This Before?

Will's favorite author—Martin Levant. Rainy evening. Bad day at work—all problems, no solutions. Ruth and their two children at Granny's. Now, to check out what Ol' Martin had to say.

Chapter 6, where Will left off. Detective Zoe Linder and Sergeant Mario Antino were investigating the theft of the jewels that the crown prince of a wealthy Middle Eastern nation had brought with him for his month-long tour of America. The prince had stayed in the finest resorts and hotels on this trip and was now visiting the wealth of history in Philadelphia. Unfortunately, his stay at the William Penn Hotel was marred by the loss of not only a fortune in some of the most precious national gems, but also the Regent's Emerald. This was the ultimate keepsake of his land's fabled heritage, and the prince knew that his Daddy, the king, would kill him over its loss.

But, not to worry, Philadelphia's finest crime solvers, Linder and Antino, were on the job. In Levant's prior twenty-six books featuring this potent duo, all mysteries had been solved and the unjust had been placed safely behind the walls of the stoutest Pennsylvania prisons. Linder and Antino were national treasures, too.

Will had read nearly all of Levant's thrillers, which lined the most prominent shelf of Will's new walnut bookcase. Reading these books gave Will his finest form of relaxing. As he read on, Will sensed that he had read this book before. He was sufficiently troubled that he looked at the copyright and found that it had just been published. Still, certain words and phrases and descriptions of persons and places were somehow not entirely new. Of course, after writing twenty-six novels, Ol' Martin—Will considered that they were on a first-name basis—could be forgiven for occasionally repeating something.

Following various leads, the Philly sleuths came upon an address of a remote property just inside the legal limits of the city. It was dusk by the time that the detective's duties finally permitted them to leave headquarters to check it out. They could see that the old home, while at present rather run-down, had been imposing and even luxurious in its day, likely the estate of a prominent Philadelphian.

One could tell from the condition of the brick exterior that the house was a century or so old and had been built solidly enough to tell that no cost had been spared in its construction. High enough to indicate two stories and a full attic, and wide enough to accommodate a broad porch, the police pair knew that a search would take effort and time. Walking around the house, passing apple and cherry trees and a large covered grape arbor, they discovered various outbuildings. The most imposing was an old two-story carriage house which had been converted into a garage. Mario Antino, who was nearing retirement, recalled seeing some of these relics of the past and pointed out the door to the front of the second floor where hay for the horses could be hoisted up.

"Interesting," said Linder. This was her usual phrase to respond to Antino's lectures of the past, in which she had virtually no interest. To be fair, in several of the pair's past adventures, it would have paid dividends had she shown a greater interest in what her partner had to say.

"Okay, okay, I see what you are doing. Still, it wouldn't hurt to listen to wiser heads when…"

"What say," said Zoe, cutting off another Mario

mini-lecture, "we come back tomorrow and go through the house and these other buildings."

"Now, that's the best idea that I've heard from you in a long time. We have the key to the old house, and it's not occupied, but I don't suppose there is any electric service for lighting."

"Now, that's one of the best conclusions..." And both chuckled at the latest back and forth mild insults that they had never allowed to get out of hand in their past many years' association.

The detectives returned the next day and went through the house from top to bottom, from the widow's walk above the roof, into the attic, down through bedrooms, and the first floor with its large living room, library, and dining room. The search took a long time because the heirs to the property had left the home as it was in years gone by, with all the furniture in place.

As "Ol' Martin" precisely described the house, both outside and room-by-room inside, Will could clearly see the property. He sensed that he had seen houses like it, or maybe one house, in his past. And maybe even such a "carriage house." But this was in Philadelphia, and Will had been there only once, when he and Ruth had taken the children to see the Liberty Bell and the other well-known historic sites.

After a fruitless search of the several dark and damp rooms of the basement, the pair headed for their favorite bit of detective work, finding the best pizza place nearby. They each paid for their own lunch, as they had done ever since that episode in book eleven when the question had arisen over the cost of the meal. Each thought the other had been so childish in their handling of the disagreement, which, if Will remembered correctly, amounted to sixty-three cents.

"I want to check out this carriage house first," Mario said upon their return to the grounds.

"Garage."

"No, Zoe, it's a carriage house."

"Well, Mario, you are much older than I, so have it your way."

The pair of dueling detectives entered the side door of the building and found themselves in a huge room that hadn't housed carriages for years. There was barely room for a car because the room was wall-to-wall with the discarded, unused, or out-of-date furniture, clothing, games, appliances, and other evidence of lives of generations who could afford to buy—and put aside—the rest. In fact, the room was so piled up that one could not see from one end to the other.

"What was that?" said Zoe.

"There's someone in here—over there." Mario pointed to the other side of the large room.

They attempted to work their way toward the sound, but the passages were few and the aisles narrow. Initially finding nothing, they conducted a thorough search with no results.

"Where did they—or it—go?" said Mario, looking up to the ceiling for some clue of the disappearance.

Will blurted out, "I know! I know!" Then he caught himself. "Good grief, I'm getting carried away with this story. But how do I know where the intruder went? Because I've been there before. That's where…" Will began skipping through the book until he reached nearly the end where the intrepid investigators discovered every crucial clue and solved every lingering question.

"I was right, by golly, I was right," Will said out loud. "I've got to quit that talking to myself. There, I've done it again." But he had to admit to himself that he was excited and couldn't wait to tell Ruth about the coincidence.

Ruth and the children came in shortly after. While Ruth fixed cocoa, Rob and Evie told their dad about the accident they saw on the way home, with a car turned upside down on the side of the road. Will had trouble concentrating on their tale, thinking all the while about the part of the story in the old carriage shed.

Will saw the children to bed, relented to their pleas for a story with one of his shorter creations, and firmly told them it was time for "beddy-bye." This seemed to work, and he went quietly downstairs to where Ruth was still sitting at the kitchen table.

"Mom was so happy to see us, especially Rob and Evie. She had made cookies and had ice cream..."

Will interrupted her. "I want to tell you something," he said.

"Oh? Is it serious?"

"Well, not exactly. It's more—eerie," he said.

"Woo-ooo...," Ruth said, smiling.

"Give me a chance to tell you."

"Okay, shoot."

"Well, I was reading old Martin's latest book."

"I've told you—you get too wrapped up in those detective stories," she said.

"This is different." And Will went on to tell her the story set out in the book he had been reading and the setting of the old house and its garage—carriage house.

"And, as they were checking out the large, cluttered room, they heard what sounded like someone moving on the other side of the room, but when they investigated, there was no one there and no way that someone could get out of the room."

"Hey, slow down," Ruth said. "There's got to be an explanation here somewhere. There always is."

"Yes, there is," Will said. "But I knew that explanation without waiting for it to be revealed later in the book. And I was right."

"How in the world...Okay, you've read so many detective stories that you probably...By the way, how was the escape made?"

"Through a trapdoor in the floor. The trapdoor was covered by an old rug and went down to a crawl space under the building," Will said. "And you're right, I might guess the answer, but I could see the trapdoor. And, I could see the crawl space, and where it exited in the back of the property."

"That is weird," said Ruth. "How could you know all that?"

"It's like I've been there…and I have!"

"No way—where?" Ruth said.

"Back in my home town—Oakmont. There was this old house that fronted on what we called Quality Row, where the finest homes were located. It was a very large home, and it had the same big old structure that is described in the book—and, by the way, there were cherry and apple trees and a big grape arbor. We used to raid the cherry tree."

"Raid?"

"Yeah, we'd sneak over at about dusk when the sweet cherries were ripe and eat a few. Once in a while the maid would catch us as we were there under the tree."

"Who was we?"

"Me, Cappy, and Nancy, my pals."

"Nancy?"

"Yeah, she was okay—you know, for a girl, when guys are about twelve.

"I see," said Ruth. "I guess now we have to figure out how what you remembered from those days turned up in a book by a popular writer."

"Yes," said Will, "we have a detective story of our own that we need to solve."

Will stewed about the solution to why a scene in a recent detective novel would be so similar to an episode in his young life. Ruth watched as Will "dropped out" of their conversations, seeming to have something on his mind—and she knew it was this remarkable coincidence.

After several days she finally said, "How about if you would call one of your old friends who were with you in your neighborhood adventures."

"I've been thinking about that. I've lost track of Nancy—I believe she is in California—but I know that Cappy is still running the family bakery business in Oakmont," said Will.

"Hello—Is this Oakmont Bakery? I'm an old friend of Cappy. What? There's no Cappy there? Do the Strongs still own the bakery? Well, who is the manager? Oh, Wade Strong. Yes, that's who I want to speak with."

"Hi, Cap. This is Will Finley. I guess they don't call you by Cappy anymore. I had forgotten that your name was Wade. How have you been?"

After chatting with his old friend about their lives since their early days, Will asked about his discovering the event of their early childhood in the recent book by Martin Levant.

Ruth sat listening to the phone call, hoping that Will could learn something that would ease his puzzlement over what he had read. When Will finally ended the call, Ruth said, "Well?"

"Cap knew about Martin Levant's book, and he knew about the coincidence. In fact, he inquired around town as to how to contact me, because he knew I would be wondering about it if I happened to read Levant's book."

"Did he give you any answer to your questions?" Ruth said.

"No, he didn't. He said he wouldn't go into it with me, but that I should talk to Nancy."

"That's strange—Why would she be able to help you?"

"And why wouldn't Cap talk to me about it?" said Will.

"So—Call Nancy," said Ruth.

"Guess I'll have to if I want to get any answers. Cap gave me her phone number."

Will dialed the number he had been given. "Nancy? This is a voice from your past. It's me—Will Finley. Yeah, for real. How have you been?"

Will went on with the call, but his end of the call consisted mainly of "Uh-huhs" and an "Oh, my," and a "No kidding?"

When he completed the call, Will simply sat staring off into space.

Ruth said, "Did you find out what you wanted to know?"

"Yeah."

"Well, what was it?"

"You'll never believe this," said Will.

"Well, try me."

"Nancy reminded me of her last name," Will said.

"Is that all? Okay, what is it?"

"Martin."

"Yes, she was Nancy Martin. I had forgotten."

"So..."

"Yeah, so all of these years she had been writing these detective stories using Levant, a name she made up, and—her real last name, Martin," said Will.

"Well, this will give new meaning when you tell me about the latest story that "Ol' Martin" had been writing," said Ruth.

"A lot of new meaning," agreed Will.

Percy—99

It may have been the lasagna. It may have been the peach pie. But it may have been something more.

Irv was restless that night. He had had too much to eat at dinner at the Italian restaurant with his wife Monica on her birthday and with two other couples who were their best of friends. Then they had returned to Irv and Monica's for dessert. But he had gone to sleep right away and had slept soundly—until the dreams started.

Irv and Monica kept active with walking, riding their bikes, and exercising. So they usually slept soundly. Irv had vivid dreams, but they were usually, to him, nonsensical and so not remembered in the morning.

Until this dream, or maybe it was a nightmare. Or maybe even as they said in his childhood home, a "nighthorse." A nighthorse was a major sleep-disturbing event. He seemed to be at a party. As it often happens in dreams, it took place in a strange building, something like an apartment house or condo that was new and bright. The rooms connected strangely so that he was surprised at the angles and the turns as he went from one room to another. The furniture and fixtures were ultra-modern and emanated an unnatural glow.

Pretty standard dream-stuff. He grew tired of the standing up, cocktail party routine, so he selected a chair that had offered some comfort, in contrast to most of the seats in the room. He sighed as he sank down in the soft chair and began his favorite party pastime, watching others as they chatted, laughed, and moved from group to group.

His chair was alone with an end table beside it and a lamp on the table, so no one was seated nearby to converse with him. He just sat there in the "lap of luxury," another old family term, and worked at keeping his eyes open. He was so drowsy, but it wouldn't do to conk out at such a nice social function. But he wasn't fully attentive, either.

In this state of half-and-half he spent possibly fifteen minutes without interruption from any of the partiers. Then the words hit him: "Percy 99." The voice and tone was so close by that he looked around himself. There was no one close to him; at least, no one who was not occupied in conversation with others.

Okay—funny acoustics in a funny room configuration. Or a chatterer in one of the standing groups who was making a point loudly to their fellows. Or he may have momentarily dozed off even though his eyes were still open and, he thought, he was completely conscious.

No matter. Just sit there in calm and comfort for a few minutes more.

It came again. "Percy 99." Clear as a bell. Forceful. A waker-upper. He looked around again. He observed everyone near him. No one whom he saw could have said those odd words to him. And yet the voice had been just a little bit familiar.

His agitation must have awakened him. Instead of being in the chair at the party he was in his bed beside Monica in his home. He was perspiring and addled. More disturbed, for some reason, than would usually be the case when he awoke from a bad dream.

But it wasn't really a bad dream. It was not one of those drops from the sky, near accidents, or bouts with wild animals that cause one to wake up in a frantic state.

But the experience had a power over him that he could not ignore. He felt he must record it. So he reached over in the dark to the nightstand and felt for a pencil and book. In the pitch dark he opened the front cover of the book and, as best he could, wrote "Percy 99." With that effort completed he lay back and went to sleep.

The next morning, he had his breakfast without a thought to his night-time experience. He showered and dressed and reached for his watch on the nightstand. He saw his book there and his memory was jogged to the extent that he picked it up and looked at it. Still not having a clear recollection of anything except that there was something about that book. He opened the cover and saw there P (or D), a (or e), r (or c), another letter, v (or y), and what looked like 99. The 99 brought him to alertness about both the word and why it was scrawled in the book.

"Percy 99," he said to himself. Then he had a bare recollection of having a dream or some kind of revelation with that word and that two-digit number. And, as bare as his recollection was, his comprehension was even slimmer.

He put the book down, shaking his head, and went to work.

Occasionally, he would open the cover of the book and look at Percy 99 and try to recall any connection to the word or the number. Nothing came to mind. He tried for an anagram of Percy that would make sense. He tried 66. Still nothing. He mentioned it to his wife, and to his son and daughter, and to his friends. His son likened it to a major league ball player. His daughter said she had made a 99 on a test at school. His friend Leon said it had to do with a rather strict school principal named Percy Jones whom they had experienced as youngsters. Nothing anyone gave as a theory seemed plausible to him. Gradually, he lost interest in the spoken word and number of his dream, and chalked it up to its being what it was—just a dream.

Irv was an engineer with a specialization in water—everything from dams to pipelines to conservation measures. He took his job seriously—too seriously, according to his family when he worked long hours and was pre-occupied about some problem from work. Monica was a fire-fighter.

She had gained enough seniority to apply for and get the daytime position of public spokesperson for the fire department. She gave out information about serious fires, visited schools, and publicized fire safety measures. Irv was proud of her achievements, especially because she had done so well in a field largely populated by men. He hoped his daughter would be able to gain success in any arena she chose.

Monica especially enjoyed her school visits. While visiting the Waterman Elementary School to put on her safety demonstration, she went into the teachers' lounge for a cup of coffee. She took a magazine from the table and sat down. Three of the teachers who were seated at the opposite end of the lounge nodded pleasantly to her and she smiled back. She knew Jane, one of the teachers, very well because Jane had taught both Monica and Irv's children.

As Monica sat there, she began to go over in her mind the outline of her presentation to the children and to check whether she had all her equipment with her. She liked to show things as she spoke, because she felt that too much talking caused the children to lose interest in her important topic.

She did not mean to eavesdrop on the conversation of the teachers. In fact, she ignored them for the most part—until she heard a certain word. She wasn't sure at first, but they seemed to be using the word over and over. The word was "Percy."

While she was still mulling over what the word might mean as they were using it, the teachers finished their break and left the lounge. It was time for her to go to the auditorium, so she immediately became involved in her work and put the teachers' conversation out of her mind.

That evening, after dinner, Monica said to Irv, "A strange thing happened today at Waterman School." Then she related to him the teachers' repetition of the word "Percy" while she had been seated nearby.

"So you couldn't have been mistaken about what they were saying?" Irv asked.

"Hardly. I was not that far away, and it seemed to be an important term to them, judging from the way they were repeating it."

"Could you tell what it meant?" Irv asked further.

"No, but they were very serious during that part of the conversation. There was no laughing or even smiling."

They were silent for a moment or two, each taking in the unusual coincidence of Monica's revelation.

Then they both began to speak at once, with Irv saying something like, "How about..." and Monica saying "I think I'll..." After laughing about their sudden joint inspiration, Monica continued, "I think I'll call Jane. You remember her, don't you?"

After Irv indicated he remembered Jane well, Monica called her, first apologizing for interrupting her evening and then telling her about what she had overheard.

Jane immediately sounded serious. "Yes, we were talking about the assistant principal, Tish Rexrode. She has been off work for several weeks and is very ill."

Monica then asked Jane what Percy had to do with the illness.

"The Percy test is a new blood test, as I understand it. It measures certain characteristics of the blood that give an indication as to whether the heart is in danger of becoming weakened."

"What did that have to do with the assistant principal's illness?"

Jane replied, "I understand that if she had had this test earlier, the treatment would have been more likely to succeed. Now, it seems that she has severe loss of heart function."

"That is a shame, when there is a way to detect a health problem, and it is not used."

Jane said quickly, "Oh, I don't think it's anyone's fault, because the Percy test has just been fully approved for use."

After Monica told Jane that she hoped her colleague got better and that she appreciated the information, Monica returned to sit with Irv. She told Irv what Jane had said, and both were silent again. This time, neither continued the conversation about the Percy test, but rather turned to their reading.

Irv especially was intrigued with the news of the new test for heart symptoms. He saw that the fact that the word had been used in a dream did not connect it in any way with what Monica had learned. But the dream was so real. And what did the "99" mean? He found it difficult to put the matter out of his mind.

He regularly played softball after work on Thursdays. While he was playing shortstop and batting, he put most of the day's concerns out of his mind. Then, while sitting on the bench waiting for his turn at the plate, Jim Simpson sat down beside him. He did not know Jim well, but he knew that Jim was a doctor.

"Jim, do you have a few minutes after the game for us to talk." He could almost sense Jim's here-we-go-again feeling that Jim was about to be cornered for free medical advice.

But Jim said, "Sure," and after completing the game, they sat down on the bleachers.

"What's on your mind?" Jim asked.

"I know you're a doctor, but I don't know what your specialty is."

"I'm an internal medicine specialist. Now, what's that got to do with anything?"

"Well, I want to tell you something very strange that has happened, and I'd like for you to tell me what it means."

"Sounds pretty weird, but tell me about it," said Jim.

"I had a dream..."

"Uh-oh."

"Now, hear me out. In this dream the words Percy 99 were spoken clear as a bell. I told my wife, Monica, about the dream, and by coincidence she overheard "Percy" mentioned by some teachers. They were referring to an ill associate of theirs. When Monica asked one of the teachers what Percy meant, the teacher said it was a test for detecting a form of illness. What about that?"

"I don't know much about dreams, but I am well aware of this new Percy. We use it to determine whether there exists in the patient's blood an excess of a certain type of cells that may attack the heart and other organs of the body."

"Then, what does the '99' mean?" asked Irv.

"The scale for the Percy test runs from zero to 120. Anything up to ninety is in the normal range," answered Jim.

"So a 99 is pretty high."

"I would say so—very high. It would indicate that something is definitely wrong."

"But why would it come up in my dream? And how does it apply to me?"

"I can't say, Irv, but one thing we can do is to have you tested. All we need is a blood sample."

"Let me think about it, and I'll let you know," replied Irv, and with that the two men got up from the bleachers and walked to the parking lot.

"I think you should have the test," said Monica with conviction after Irv had told her that 99 was a high test reading.

"None of this makes sense, but I guess you're right. I'll call Mel's office." Mel Price had been their family physician for ages.

Irv went to the lab as directed by the nurse in Mel's office, had a small amount of blood drawn, and awaited the results. He wasn't exactly worried, but he was more than merely interested in the outcome.

Mel called Irv at dinnertime. "Your reading is 67. That's well within the normal range."

"Thanks, Mel. I guess this was just a wild goose chase."

"Don't mention it. It's certainly a different scenario from what we are used to in practicing medicine. But I'm glad you don't have to worry about this blood condition. It can be pretty serious."

That night Irv went to bed much relieved. He went right to sleep and rested well until just before dawn. Then he heard those words again. "Percy 99." He was prepared this time for the words, but not for what else he had discovered. He knew the voice that spoke the words. It was the voice of his old friend John Walker. He was certain of it. He and John had grown up together in their hometown of Oakmont. They had been close as boys and had gone to the same college later on. John had gone on to become a physician.

Yes, he knew John's voice well—but the thing that caused Irv to bolt wide awake was that John had died in an automobile accident two years before.

"What's the matter?" asked Monica, now at least partly awake, too.

"Just a dream. I'll tell you about it at breakfast."

"Okay," and back to sleep she went.

But Irv didn't sleep. He couldn't sleep anymore because John's words had been so real, and so sincere, and so urgent.

Irv told Monica about the repetition of the "Percy 99" as they sat over coffee at the breakfast table. Monica appeared to be a little shaken at the mention of John's name. She had known him for as long as Irv and had felt a loss when John had died.

After pondering Irv's revelation for a moment, she said, practical as always, "Well, we know now about what Percy means and what the 99 might signify, but what does it have to do with us? You were tested and the results were very satisfactory."

"Yes," noted Irv, "but what about someone else who might have an elevated reading and is in need of a physician's care? What about you?"

"Me? I'm feeling fine. Maybe a little tired, but it's a little tough with my work schedule, the home, and things we are involved in."

"Would you have yourself checked?"

"Irv! I think this has gone far enough. It's you who is hearing things—things that might be explained from your overhearing something about the Percy test at a doctor's office or someplace else. You know how people talk about their physical exams and illnesses today."

"Just the same, think about it," Irv replied evenly, although he was a bit discombobulated by it all.

"I will…think about it," promised Monica, without conviction.

That evening Irv pressed Monica into agreeing to be checked with the Percy test. She made the appointment the next day, although she knew the doctor's office staff were rolling their eyes at this one.

She went to have the test, and, telling Irv she hoped he was satisfied, put it out of her mind.

Then came the phone call from her doctor. "I have some bad news and some good news, Monica," he said. Mel was such a good friend of Monica and Irv's that he could get away with phrasing his information in such a way.

"Bad news first," urged Monica.

"Your Percy test reading is high—too high."

"Now some good news, I hope," she requested.

"I've compared your Percy test results with the routine blood tests from your last physical examination. This high Percy is apparently a recent elevation. We can deal with the problem very effectively with treatments now available."

"Will I have some lasting impairment?" she asked.

"No, you shouldn't, since we have found this out so early and can go on the attack right away."

"I'm relieved and thankful. And I know Irv will be, too."

"What I really would like to know is why you requested this particular test to be performed. We have scads of tests for this and almost every other ailment. Why the Percy and why at this time?"

Monica countered with an offer and a question. "I'll have Irv tell you all about it if you will tell me just one thing."

"What's that, Monica?"

"What was my reading on the Percy test?"

"The reading on your test, Monica, was 99."

One more thing:

This story was suggested to me in a dream. The voice was that of an old friend of my wife's and mine, Michael John Reilly, a physician (John Walker in the story. Mike's mom's maiden name was Walker). In my dream, Mike said two words, "Douglas 99". Douglas is Mike's son, and was a pilot in the Air Force. Mike has been deceased for a number of years.

One more thing No. 2:

I went to my family physician, Dr. Grimms, and asked him if there is a Douglas test. He indicated that there is. I asked him what the scale is. He told me that it goes from 1 to 100. I requested that he give me the test, which is, like the Percy, a test of certain conditions with respect to the heart. I am awaiting the results of the Douglas.

The Lincoln Project

Lincoln Louden was a window washer—high rise—big buildings. He spent his days in a descending cage suspended at varying heights from the ledges of structures all over the city.

He had a few good friends, but the thing was, he had grown tired of their comments to him about his job. "Watch out for that first step; it's a doozy." "Come up and see me sometime, big boy." "Don't look down!" And his personal unfavorite from a trying to be funny friend, who quoted: "The optimist fell ten stories, and at every window bar, he shouted to his friends within, all right so far!"

For his work was dangerous. He had to triple check his ropes, ledge clamps, and cage every time he started down. And he had been told never to get completely comfortable as he let himself over the ledge in his swinging cage.

But what sights he observed...and it wasn't only the distant scenery. He didn't mean to look in windows, but what could he do? He was peering all day into either offices or apartments.

His co-worker Rodney, on the other hand, took those inside views as a perquisite of his employment. That told you all you needed to know about old Rodney.

It was a summer Monday and not a good day. Foggy in early morning. The ledge of this particular building didn't inspire confidence. He nearly dropped his squeegee while trying to maneuver from the ledge to his cage. So Lincoln was glad to see four o'clock—quitting time—approaching.

But then, intent on the panes of the fourth-floor apartment, *she* came into view as she entered the door of her flat. In the course of his day, he saw humanity in all shapes, sizes, and descriptions, but *she*—she was dressed head to toe in white—a nurse, attired in the manner Lincoln had seen in only old movies. Uniform, hose, shoes, even cap—all white. A by-stander might have noticed an additional sway of his cage, as he found himself staring intently inward.

She—young, dark hair, very attractive—was not amused. She marched over to the window and with a hefty pull closed the draperies, shutting Lincoln out. He continued to stare—to no purpose—at an expanse of the reverse side of window drapes.

Lincoln finished his shift but did not stop thinking about the vision at the fourth level. All evening he pondered. Why the white uniform? Who was she? How did he get so lucky? And finally, how to learn more?

Lincoln had been a Green Beret in the Army and what he liked best was studying and drafting tactics. Why not use some of the same skills for another type of campaign?

By the next morning he had an idea for his first strike. As he descended down the next column of windows he swung dangerously to the side, permitting him to reach *her* window. At his second swing he taped on the window a yellow rose that he had preserved ever so carefully on the way down. He assumed that it would be easy for her to guess who had left the rose for her.

He carried that assumption until the next rainy day when the crew washed the inside of the windows. He—the tactician—saw to it that the fourth floor was his, and that he was performing his task at just the time she had appeared the first day.

His well-developed multi-faceted assumptions were sundered, however, by her reaction to his presence. "You!" she said in a tone that even the most unbiased observer would deem unkindly.

"Yes, it's me," was his unplanned pathetic reply.

"You were the one who was spying on me," she said.

"No. I was washing your window, and your drapes were...."

"You didn't have to look so hard. You should just do your job, and...."

"Wait a minute. You think I like hanging on the side of a building?"

"Well...."

"And that I do it just to catch a glimpse of irritable people?" he said.

"Irritable?" she said.

"Did you see the rose I left?"

"Yes, that was a pretty nice surprise."

"Well, I wish I hadn't."

"Maybe you should just leave."

"I will just as quickly as I can finish this window."

She went into the other room and he completed his work and left. He did linger a moment in the lobby on his way out to see the name on the mailbox for apartment 407—Lisa Abraham.

Now, normally Linc knew when to retreat and was tempted to do so—but he was smitten and had to do something about it.

Next tactic: He made a neat sign and placed tape upon it and attached it to a long telescoping pole used to wash windows. He carefully centered the sign on the outside of Lisa's window. It said, "Coffee after work at Smitty's Diner?"

Linc sat in the Diner for forty-five minutes, and showing that he could take a hint, left.

Same tactic, new sign: "Come to the Little Cottage Tea Room at 4 on Saturday?"

This time Lisa showed. She came in as if on a counter-offensive, maybe a Blitzkrieg. She gave forth with a barrage of words, among them, "Leave...alone...not...going out... window washer...good-bye for good."

After that defeat in battle Linc went about his business. His offensive was over, leaving him a little sadder, a lot wiser.

Fall came and Lisa showed up for her regular shift in the surgical recovery room at the hospital. The nurse on the prior shift gave her report about the cases on the floor, and Lisa began making rounds.

As she entered Room 202, she saw a young man in scrubs speaking with a patient. He turned toward her.

Her first words were, "Are you an orderly on this floor now? How very annoying."

"Actually, no, I'm a third-year surgical resident here at the hospital."

"But…."

"I was just helping out my Dad this summer; he owns the window-cleaning business."

"Oh."

Linc continued, "And, I'd like you to please check this patient's bandage every three hours."

"Yes, Doctor."

In spite of what some may hope, Abraham-Lincoln was not to be. For, while Lisa might have been willing to go beyond even a truce, Lincoln had already met, and was devoted to, a schoolteacher by the name of Rhonda—Rhonda Ford.

The Millian Dollar Doll

My younger sister, Elaine, spotted it first.

"That's Granny," she said, looking at the picture that had graced the logo of the Millian Department Store chain for the past half-century. We were seated at a table at the student union, I to give and she to receive her share of a package from our folks.

Elaine, dark-haired and slight of size, in her first year of university, would not be dissuaded. "It is, Pete, it is."

"But," I challenged, "how can you tell? That picture is so small and it was taken so long ago." I was a senior at the university we both attended, and, if I didn't know it all, what I didn't know was not worth knowing.

"It has Granny's features, even if you go back to the years when she was young. Besides, I've seen pictures of our grandmother as a young girl."

I looked more closely and could see what she was talking about, but I was not going to give in quickly.

"Let's ask Mom," I said.

"Okay, let's just ask Mom," Elaine agreed.

We both whipped out our phones and called Mom. Elaine got through first, and, naturally, presented the question in a way that was nearest to her view of the matter. I was forced to place my ear close to her phone, but it was worthwhile to hear Mom say that she was not the "Millian Dollar Doll."

"Ha." That's all I said, short and adequately to the point.

I should have known that would not be the end of it for our Elaine. Tenacious, perseverant—you get the idea.

The next day Elaine called and left a simple message, "Ha. Ha. Ha."

I reluctantly called back, knowing that she was renewing the rivalry of information, opinion, and declamation that had been a major feature of our growing up in the same household.

"What is it?" I asked when I got through to her.

"I looked up the history of the Millian Dollar Doll on the Millian web site, and it clearly, clearly, clearly...."

"Okay, get on with it," I interrupted.

"...states that the Doll was a Miss Oliver, the picture was taken in 1950, and it was taken in Wilmington, Delaware," she concluded.

"Good grief," I said. "If that's correct, it describes Granny. Her maiden name was Oliver, she lived in Wilmington, and she would have been in her late teens in 1950."

"I'm calling Mom," said Elaine.

"I'm calling Granny."

What Elaine said next I never expected to hear—ever. "Good idea."

"Hello, Granny," I said, picturing her picking up the receiver of her ivory rotary phone which she said was still "plenty good enough" for her.

"Is that you, Gerald?" she replied.

Gerald is not what I answer to, to anyone but Granny and Grandpa.

"It's me. I have a question to ask you."

"Of course, Gerald. Go ahead and ask."

"Were you the Millian Dollar Doll?"

Silence. More silence.

Finally, she said, "Why do you ask?"

"Elaine noticed the resemblance, but Mom said it wasn't so, but Elaine found that the Doll was Miss Oliver of Wilmington, Delaware."

"I see."

"Well, is it you?"

"What are you and Elaine doing this weekend?"

"I'm okay, but I don't know about Elaine," I said.

"How about your coming to see Grandpa and me?"

"Sure. I'll check with Elaine."

I told Elaine about the way Granny evaded answering our question, and Elaine said she would not miss visiting our grandparents. The old couple lived only a couple of hours from the university.

We arrived just before lunchtime on Saturday, well-calculated for having a lunch that Granny "had not gone to any trouble with."

Sitting at the kitchen table in their older, two-story, rather old-fashioned home, we talked about family, earlier days, how school was going. When we finished Granny's sumptuous meal complete with apple pie a la mode, Elaine could not hold back any longer.

"Is it you, or not, Granny?"

Granny looked at Grandpa, who nodded back at her.

And then, she simply said, "It's not me."

"Are you sure?" I asked, in one of my more brilliant moments.

"I guess I would know," Granny replied.

"Of course, you would," I quickly said.

After a pause in the conversation, Elaine brightened and asked, "Do you know who it is?"

Again, Granny looked over at Grandpa and answered with a drawn-out "Yes."

"Well, who is it?" I asked.

"It's my sister," she said quietly.

"But, but—you only have brothers, Uncle John and Uncle Will," said Elaine.

"And," still very quietly, "Esther."

"Esther?" said Elaine. "We've never heard Mom talk of an Aunt Esther."

"She doesn't know anything about her," said Grandpa.

"I don't understand," I said.

"Might as well tell them the whole story, Gwen," said Grandpa.

"Yes, it's been unspoken for too long, I guess," said Granny.

I said, "Tell us about it, Granny."

"Well, besides John and Will, there was Esther. She was two years older than I and grew to be a very beautiful young woman."

"You were a looker, too, Gwen," interrupted Grandpa.

"That's nice of you to say, Arthur, but Esther was especially attractive. So attractive that she was urged by her friends to enter the Millian Dollar Doll contest. It was a national contest to represent the Millian Department Store chain. It was a major event because Millian was such a well-known national chain."

"And she won," said Grandpa.

"The whole family went with her on the train to New York City for the festivities that included the picture-taking, a round of dinners, and an orientation of her responsibilities as good-will ambassador for Millian. We were overwhelmed at the reception she received from the company and important clients of the company."

"Then it began to get interesting," said Grandpa.

"Yes," continued Granny, "she traveled throughout the United States, escorted of course. It was an education in itself, seeing the various parts of the country and carrying out her responsibilities to the firm. Well, around the beginning of the second year of being the Millian Dollar Doll she was at a New York party, and there she met an older man who said he was an Austrian count."

"The plot thickens," said Grandpa.

"Hush, Arthur. Anyway, this relationship did not sit well with our folks, particularly Dad—that's your great-grandfather. He told Esther to come home for a while and stay away from Count Rudolph Ackermann. She refused, and after several months, she married the Count and moved to his estate in Austria."

"That was the last time we saw her," said Grandpa. "Her father was so opposed to her marriage that he forbade any future reference to her in the family."

"It was unfair, I guess, but we went along with it," said Granny, almost in tears. "Esther and I were very close growing up, and I have missed her all these years. But she was very hurt by Dad's rejection of her husband, and she has not made any contact with us."

"Have you told Mom about this?" asked Elaine.

"Yes," Granny replied, "I called her last evening and told her everything. She was shocked and asked a number of questions. I'm not sure that she still fully understands."

"It's a lot to take in," I said.

"Yes, I've known about it since the time it happened, and I can hardly believe it," said Grandpa.

We talked more about this new topic in our family, sometimes just shaking our heads. Our grandparents wanted us to stay overnight, but we declined, saying we had studying to do. As we headed back to the university, we were alternately silent and talkative, always thinking about what we had learned from our grandparents. About the only conclusion we came to was that we didn't want to let the matter drop right away.

Elaine called me a few days later and started the conversation with "Let's go to Austria."

I said, in my usual quick-on-the-uptake mode, "What?"

She went on to say that she couldn't help thinking about our Great-Aunt Esther, that she would like to meet her, and that she had written her a letter."

"What?"—at least consistent.

A week later, Elaine called again. "I've got a reply. Meet me at the Union."

At the Student Union Elaine showed me a letter, postmarked Salzburg, Austria, and written in the beautiful handwriting of our Great-Aunt Esther. The stationery was embossed with the address "Schloss Ackermann."

"I looked it up: Schloss means castle," explained Elaine.

"Okay."

"And, read this."

After reading the part of the letter she was pointing to, I said again, "Okay."

"You mean, you would go?"

"No, I just mean, I'm trying to take all of this in," I replied.

"You're real quick, Pete. She says she would like for us to visit. I think we should. How about spring break?"

"Not so fast—what about Mom—and Granny. What would they think?"

"You call Mom and I'll call Granny," said Elaine.

This is what we did, and, even though neither our mother nor grandmother were altogether committed to our going to Salzburg, neither one said they would totally object.

On this modest go-ahead, coupled with Elaine's blatant pleading, we began making plans for a trip over spring break in our classes at the university.

The States to Vienna and then to Salzburg. A driver was waiting for us in a luxury car of the type seldom seen in America.

The driver, Karl, welcomed us to Austria and said that we had about an hour drive to Schloss Ackermann. When I commented upon Karl's good English, he said that it was required for his job, since the Ackermanns had so many visitors who spoke English.

The mountains were beautiful and the new green of spring made the drive enjoyable. After going from major highway to lesser roads, we entered a winding tree-lined lane. From there, all the trees and shrubbery we saw were well-planned and well-cared-for.

After a mile or so we saw on a distant hill a stunning sight—an old stone castle with a large center section and immense wings on each side. It had fancy parapets and numerous windows composed of small panes that shone in the midday sun.

Karl drove us to the front of the castle where he tooted his horn. Immediately, a man, Ernst, and a woman, Lisle, each dressed in servants' garb came out to greet us and to take our bags.

"It's like a movie set," Elaine whispered to me.

"Yeah, for sure," I whispered back.

We entered a great hall and went with Ernst to a nearby large, bright sitting room. After a short wait, a virtual double to Granny appeared. The only differences were in dress and carriage, each more formal than we had ever observed in our Granny.

But the same warmth was felt immediately—no stand-offishness, but rather enthusiastic hugs for my sister and me.

"I am so glad you are here," said Great-Aunt Esther, her tears showing her to be overcome by our arrival. "Rudy will be here soon. He's tending to some problem with one of the horses."

Because of Aunt Esther's welcome, Elaine and I both wanted immediately to talk of home and of Granny and our mother. We had to wait for our turn since Aunt Esther had much to say and more to ask about her sister and brothers and other family members.

Presently Uncle Rudolph joined us—a tall, imposing man, overflowing with charm and good nature. He was curious about our family, our university, and our lives in general.

The conversation was carried on into the large dining hall, complete with a massive fireplace. A large fire was roaring, giving warmth to a room that had its walls covered with ancestral pictures and ancient swords and armor.

In order to make conversing easier, we sat with our aunt and uncle at one end of the large banquet table. We were served a marvelous lunch on beautiful plates and handsome crystal.

After lunch Elaine and I were shown up the main staircase to our adjoining bedrooms. My room had a large bed with wrap-around curtains, huge dresser and chest-of-drawers, and rich wall-hangings. I could not believe that we were guests in such an opulent home, but at the same time had been given such a warm welcome.

After a time to ourselves, we went downstairs to find Aunt Esther in the sitting room.

Elaine asked, "Would you like to see some pictures, Aunt Esther?"

"Oh, yes," was about all our aunt could manage for a time, as she was caught up in the memories brought back by the pictures of her close relatives and her homeland.

She asked about each person in the pictures, where the photos were taken, and what the occasion was. It seemed that she couldn't get enough of news about our family.

Uncle Rudy came in after a time and offered to show us about the estate. Karl had the car warmed up, and we took a ride that seemed to be endless through pasture, woods, and small villages; yet, Uncle Rudy said, these were all part of his land holdings.

He told us some of the history of his family which had lived on these lands for centuries.

Growing very serious, he also told us how grateful he was that we had visited our aunt. He said that he could tell that she thought of here earlier life in America, and that this renewed relationship completed her life here in Austria.

Elaine said that we were just as pleased about meeting both of them and I agreed.

On our return from our trip around the estate we had tea and cakes. We spent the evening at a dinner of many courses and constant conversation.

During the next few days, we attended a musical performance in Salzburg, rode horses on the estate, and visited a salt mine.

In spite of the many activities, we still had me to spend visiting with Aunt Esther. Near the end of our five-day visit, she made a statement that surprised us. "You know, I envy my sister Gwen more than ever since you have come to visit us."

"What?" I said.

"He means," Elaine interpreted, "why would you envy Granny when you have everything that most people only dream of?"

"Oh, yes, it's been an ideal life here with Rudy these many years. But we have not been blessed with children and grandchildren—something that is so apparently part of Gwen's rich life," she said with some sadness.

"Pete hasn't always made our parents' and grandparents' lives richer," said Elaine, attempting to lighten Aunt Esther's mood."

Aunt Esther was amused at that, and soon we were laughing at Aunt Esther's describing the antics of herself and her sister and brothers when they were youngsters at home. I could tell that she often thought of those times, and she must have frequently wondered about their lives today as they had grown older. So I was not surprised when, as we were ready for Karl to drive us to the airport, she made the announcement, "I am going to America."

"You are?" said Elaine. "That would be great."

"I know Granny and our uncles will like that a lot," I added.

"You really think so?" asked Aunt Esther, apparently somewhat relieved.

"I know so," said Elaine, in her usual emphatic way, leaving no room for doubt.

After good-byes to our aunt and uncle and the members of the household staff, we rode to the airport and flew to the United States.

Upon being met by our mother and father I guess we "gushed" with descriptions of our aunt and uncle, their home, and their way of life.

However, we saved back one bit of critical information until we visited Granny. After re-telling everything we had described at home, we sprung it on her.

"Aunt Esther is coming for a visit," Elaine said.

"To the United States?" asked Granny very slowly.

"Yes," I said, just as slowly. "And, oh yes, she's coming here—to see you and the uncles."

"Here?" was all Granny could get out as she looked over to Grandpa for the nod that she knew was coming.

Elaine and I also knew what was coming next.

"Well, we just have to clean this house from top to bottom...and we need some new pieces of furniture, especially in the guest bedroom...and the yard needs a lot of work... and...."

This time Grandpa's nod might not have been as vigorous as usual.

Macadamia

Marmaduke Zambower had grown tired of ruling Macadamia, a nation not large but with a proud history located just adjacent to Austria and Hungary. Great-Great-Great Grandfather Zambower had been granted this enclave by the Empress Maria Theresa, for as long as there was a male heir to the throne named Marmaduke Zambower. Marmaduke was the first in that long line to have only daughters, very beautiful and talented daughters, of whom he and Queen Lovina were exceedingly pleased and proud.

But, weary of ruling or not, his choice of giving up the throne was blocked by his wife and daughters, and he had never been able to say no to any one of them, much less to all of them together.

At the same time, Marmaduke's subjects had grown exceedingly restless under his rule, for various reasons. First, they were a little concerned with his name, thinking Marmaduke was a bit dated for their modern nation. After all, Macadamia had social media, national debt, and dissention, just like every modern land. Second, Marmaduke required the national anthem, Make Macadamia Great, at every national, town, and village function, before movies, on the hour at the national television station, Wuhu, and at the beginning and at the end of each school day. Several other exceedingly tedious economic, political, and social reasons added to the unsettling of the population.

In addition to all these stresses on Marmaduke, another situation was the one causing the immediate problem. Though small, Macadamia had a corner on the growing, marketing, and profiting from the nut that bore its name. As such, larger nations and their macadamia nut sellers feared the land of Marmaduke. The domestic nut growers and marketers liked the situation just as it had been for generations.

Enter Spyder McGee, the dominant nut producer, marketer, and profiteer in the country. Rich, handsome, confident, ruthless, and mustachioed, McGee assessed the situation in this war: It was necessary to keep stability for the sake of nut production. If Marmaduke couldn't keep stability, he needed to be pushed aside. Nut production was the competing power center in the nation. Why shouldn't he who dominated that seat of power also hold the reins of government?

So, Spyder worked diligently to gain the support of a rebellion by the nut millionaires, their workers, people sick and tired of Make Macadamia Great, and those folks who were just always unhappy with everything. With this support Spyder and his leadership team formed an army, dressed them in the latest camo, furnished them with weapons, and headed for the Castle.

Marmaduke was not caught unawares. He had studied the defense of Marmaduke the Second, who had withstood a much earlier attack by pulling up the drawbridge and heading for the turrets. Marmaduke did this and was surprised when Spyder's army placed a pontoon bridge over the moat, set fire to the raised drawbridge, and advanced inside the outer walls of the Castle in eighteen minutes. The defenders on the walls, in the turrets, men and women in service to the King and Royal Family, cooks, and bakers, who had not been entirely committed to combat, threw down their weapons, mops, and spatulas, and made just enough show of disappointment toward the invading personnel, who were, most often, their siblings or cousins.

Marmaduke, humiliated before his subjects and all the world, knew that he was beaten and demanded that the ceremony of rendering his sword to the victor be held privately between him and Spyder McGee. McGee agreed and the two of them, Marmaduke in crown, Spyder in the uniform of a Five-Star General, sat alone in the Great Hall of the Castle.

The formal ceremony began as it always did in that nation, with the King making the initial offer, "Have a nut?" to the visitor. The standard reply was given, upon the acceptance of the proffered macadamias, "Don't mind if I do." Then the King's turn: "I thought you'd at least take an hour or so to broach the Castle, Spyder." The visitor's reply: "I told them and I told them, 'Now, don't be in too big a hurry,' but you know those young folks when they get excited and...." The King: "Oh, well, it's over, and now I have an excuse to get off this throne and finally get to travel and enjoy life without worrying about these aggravating citizens and their problems." McGee: "Yes, and we can now settle the country down and go back to peacefully growing and marketing...." The Deposed King: "And making sure that I continue to get my share of the profiting—from those marvelous little macadamia nuts."

And with the Formal Surrender over, Marmaduke and Spyder McGee emerged into the Royal Courtyard, to be met with the roar of the jubilant crowd and the Royal Chorus in a balcony singing, "It's Great to Be a Macadamian."

The City Zoo

Drury McCormick worked in the City Zoo feeding the snakes. Not that he liked snakes that much when he was assigned to their care, but after a time the job grew on him. He certainly respected them, even from the first, especially the dangerous ones. But, then again, he noticed that they had separate characteristics, even distinct personalities.

For instance, Beverly, the old Boa, was a loafer—just lying there catching as much of the sun's rays as she could. Edith, the little garter snake, was a rover—constantly exploring every corner of her cage. Rodger, the rattler, waited until he had an audience to shake his tail, as if to threaten, or maybe, as Drury believed, to show off.

Even if some of the snakes' traits were only in Drury's imagination, their actions, or in the case of Beverly, their inaction, made his job more interesting. Something else, even more importantly, made his life interesting—Gloria, Keeper of the Big Animals, whom he eyed from his "lower" position with the snakes. He would have to admit that he was envious of her superior position in caring for the large animals. He thought, what a great day she put in—exercising elephants, feeding giraffes, and even doing some sign language with Oscar, the Great Ape.

Oddly enough, Drury's charges, the crawlers, were a bit upset, too. Percy Python, who had the very top cage, could see over into the large animal domain. He reported regularly to his pals about the elephants' walking about freely, the giraffes' running if they wished, the Great Ape's climbing as high as he wanted. Much unhappiness in snake country.

Because of their own dissatisfaction the snakes must have sensed Drury's attitude toward the Big Animals. Not a two-way street, however. Drury didn't have a clue as to what the inhabitants of his cages were thinking.

And then, one evening just after feeding, Beverly raised her head just a little and said, "Hey, Drury."

Drury whipped around and looked into space.

"No, down here. It's me—Beverly. I need to talk to you about something."

Drury came out with a hesitant, "Oka-a-ay." (All right, what would you come up with if a snake suddenly spoke to you?)

"Here's the thing," said Beverly. "You're upset and so are we about those Big Animals, the sweet job of their caretaker, their lack of cages, their special meals...."

All Drury could come up with at this point was to go along with the conversation, even though he still couldn't believe he was talking to a snake.

"Yeah," he said, "and that bunch gets all the attention, and the visitors ask Gloria all those questions, and she looks like an expert, and..."

"What I'm saying, Dreary, is that we and you think alike, and we've been working on a plan."

"A plan?—and it's Drury, not Dreary."

"Whatever," said Beverly. "We'd like to pay a little visit to Big Animals tonight and have a little chat."

"A chat?"

"Yeah, our crowd has elected me leader, and I'm supposed to talk things over with their hot-shot mouthpiece, Hugo Giraffe," said Beverly.

"All by yourself?" Drury was still in a daze and still couldn't believe this conversation, but he added, "How do you plan to do that?"

"Our gang will go along to back me up, and our plan involves you."

"Me?"

"You need to leave the door to this heaven for snakes open tonight."

"But how do you get out of your cages?"

"Oh," said Beverly, "We can get out any time we want. It's just that everything has been alright up until now."

"I can't believe I'm doing this," said Drury, shaking his head, "but the door will be left slightly ajar tonight." He was unconvinced anything could, or would, happen; however, Drury did as he promised when he left that evening, still trying to imagine what would follow.

What followed was the slight rattling of cage doors at dusk and a silent procession between the snake's cages and the nearby great open area of the Zoo where Hugo Giraffe was eating leaves from high up in his favorite tree. A voice from nearby said, "Hi there, Big Boy."

Hugo looked all around.

"I'm right here," came Beverly's voice from the limb just above his head. "We need to talk," she continued. "In fact, let's get comfortable." With that she dropped from her limb and coiled herself gently around Hugo's long neck. "That's better," she said.

"What? Who?" was all Hugo could come up with.

"Just settle down, Stretch. This won't take long," she said.

"I don't have to stand here and listen to some night crawler," said Hugo.

"Yeah, you kinda do," said Beverly, gently engaging her length a bit more firmly round Hugo's neck.

Hugo then got the message and replied, "What do you want?"

"Well, my friends and I," and at that there was a clamor down below of "Hi there, I'm Percy," "Hey," "How ya doin'," and the like.

"To continue," said Beverly, "my friends and I feel that the time has come for you to share your vast area with us.

If someone would just suggest this to Gloria, maybe with just a slight hint that you all might cause some trouble if she refused...."

"Oh, we couldn't do that," said Hugo.

"Yes, I believe we could," said Oscar, the Great Ape, who had discovered that big old Percy Python had grasped his right leg in his rather substantial mouth.

At that, with the effective way the other snakes had established themselves in a threatening manner on the other animals, the lowly creatures won the day. We should ever be aware that when snakes are united, and are very serious, and have a plan, snakes can get their way. And they did.

City Zoo was alone in the country with the added, very popular feature of a combination in one place of both lowly and lofty creatures, living in peace and harmony.

And it came out that another purpose of Beverly and her buddies was to get Dreary, that is, Drury, to capture Gloria's attention. Gloria readily admitted Drury and friends had done just that.

Gloria returned the attention toward Drury, and they became a fine team. They eventually married—in the Zoo—with lots and lots of witnesses. Their three children loved to hear the story of how their parents met and fell in love with the help of certain inhabitants of the City Zoo.

The Horse Up a Wall

"Horse" Lockery had been there a long time. "There" was the Peninsula University for Professional Scholars, located in upstate New York—good school, good reputation, poor set of initials for those who had not mastered short and long vowels. "A long time" was fifty-seven years counting his time as a student there, now retired but still coaching defensive line for the intermittently successful team that he had coached in their years of dominance in their league. "'Horse,'" because he was very big, and he had a way of looking even bigger to his teams over the years, especially considering the reputation he had gained in his several years in the pros.

He was not what he "used to be" by any criterion of outside reckoning, and even he, who had stared down pain and discomfort and aggravation through his lifetime, had to admit that the chill of fall was getting to him. He was hurrying home from looking at films for the upcoming game—home to Martha, called by generations of students as "Miss Martha," about the only force that subdued the Horse. She had a way with him, and he with her, except his way was, typically, capitulation.

He was passing Graham Hall, named for Professor Thadeus Irvington Carpal Graham, who had led the Math Department in Horse's early years at PUPS. Talented but odd, Prof Graham had been walking home when a student stopped him at just after noon one day and asked him a question about a problem in the morning's class. Graham took chalk from his pocket, got down on the sidewalk, and began writing out the problem. A crowd gathered, to the embarrassment of the student, who quickly said, "Yes sir," when Graham asked if he understood. When Graham got up, he asked the student which way he, Graham, was going when the student stopped him. When the student pointed in a certain direction, the professor said, "Oh, good. That means I've had lunch."

The Horse was chuckling about the many stories about Old Graham when he heard what sounded like a sniffle. He was walking beside the high wall that surrounded Graham Hall. Coach Horse never understood why that wall was there, very high and very narrow at the top. He soon discovered that the sound came from above, the top of the wall.

Perched there was a young woman who, even though it was late dusk, could be seen to have dark hair, usual college attire, and an unusual amount of distress.

The Horse stopped and looked up. "What are you doing up there?" he demanded. Horse didn't just speak when he spoke—he added an element of growl that had been developed over the years to keep in line those who most needed it and even those of little need.

"It's just a mess," she said.

"A mess?"

"What do you mean, a mess?" Horse was a loss at what else to say, having three grown daughters, who, through the years, had managed to remove any essence of good judgment that he might have had toward young women.

"It's just..."

"What?"

"...I flunked Professor Klingle's Chem test..."

"Oh, that's nothing. Everybody flunks a test or so of his. Our guys...."

"...And Stone and I broke up..."

"Stone Yarber, our quarterback?" Stone—great football name, father and grandfather had played for the PUPS, but would never go anywhere where good decision-making was even a minimal requirement.

"What else?" Horse asked.

"Isn't that enough?"

"I don't know. I'm not sure that boy is worth..." At that the young woman changed from sniffle to low wail, so that even Horse knew that he needed to back off a little. "What's your name?"

"Rosalee," she managed to say.

"Well, Rosalee, you come on down—by the way, how did you get up there?"

"Walked."

"You mean you walked along that high wall all the way from the front of the building?

"Yeah."

"How do you plan to get down?"

She said, "I don't. I'm going to stay here all night."

"Aren't you cold?"

"Kinda."

Horse had a dilemma. He couldn't leave her there in the cold on a high wall with a good chance of falling off. But he had no way of getting her down, and he knew his powers of persuasion wouldn't carry the day. So he said, "See ya," and headed for home.

"See ya," she said.

Walking on, all he could come up with was one thing—need a ladder. And he had a twelve-footer in his garage only a block away. When he got home, he yelled into Martha and told her he had to go back and get someone off a wall. Martha, being used to sudden changes in plans, in this case, their dinner, grabbed her coat and scarf, and with a "What?" followed him to get the ladder.

Putting the ladder on his shoulder, Coach grabbed Martha's hand and off they went to that miserable Graham's miserable wall.

Rosalee was still on her perch. Right away Martha started in with her two-front offensive, that Rosalee was going to catch her "death of cold," and that "She shouldn't let any boy...," but quickly saw from the higher pitch of Rosalee's distress that the second front was not a winner.

While Martha advanced and retreated, Horse had set up his twelve-footer near to Rosalee and stepped on the first rung.

"What are you doing?" said Rosalee.

"I'm coming up," said Horse, with his usual iron-clad conviction. And he did make it up to the second step. A small crowd had formed and shouted encouragement.

On the try for the third step, however, Coach's foot went through the rungs, he veered to the side, and it was all he could do to hang on to the sides of the ladder. A second try was not only just as awkward but also as unsuccessful.

Then Martha began her admonishing Horse with "You're going to hurt yourself, Ludlow," and similar helpful comments, before turning her attention to Rosalee with the opinion of "Do you see what you have caused here," and "The Coach is too old for this sort of foolishness."

Horse was having a hard time getting his leg back over the second rung, let along making any upward progress. After the leg came out and with lots of arm-strength the third rung was attained, but, at that point, the top of the ladder began to slide along the wall.

Rosalee hadn't minded both Horse's and Martha's stern talking-to, but she was getting tired of seeing the coach's pathetic attempts to get up that ladder. She quickly used her rather substantial analytical powers to calculate costs and benefits.

With a broad sigh, she called down, "Okay, Coach, just untangle yourself and get off that ladder. I'll come down."

By this time, the small crowd had grown larger around Horse, Martha, ladder, and wall. Various comments had been offered as to possible solutions, but, considering the strong feelings made evident by the actors in the drama, none of the congregation came forth in any forceful way.

Martha held the ladder as Horse untangled himself. He moved the ladder over closer to Rosalee and held it as she quickly came down to earth to the cheers of the onlookers.

"I guess I should thank you and your wife for trying to help me," said Rosalee, "but I was so upset, and..."

"Don't worry about that," said Martha. "We all go through difficult time, especially when we are young."

"Especially to you, Coach. I'm grateful."

"Nothing to thank me for, Rosalee—but I knew I couldn't get up that ladder, and I thought you'd never give in and decide to come down."

Just then a voice belonging to a young man, possibly on the football team, came out of the crowd: "Hey, Coach—is your name really Ludlow?"

Go, Wally, Go

"I'm tired of standing in one spot," said Wally Washer. He enjoyed his life of washing clothes, rinsing them, and spinning them around. Pretty exciting, but the reason he wanted to move was to visit the new dishwasher that he learned (through the clothesline) had come to the kitchen.

One day when he overheard the family leave for a vacation and the radio had turned itself on to some fast music, he started to rock a little. And when he rocked, he moved! One inch, two inches, half a foot, a foot . . .

"Where ya goin'?" asked Donald Dryer, his laundry room pal for so many years.

"I gotta get out of here," said Wally.

"Why?" said Donald. "We have it nice here, not too many loads. Could use a window, though."

"Oh, sure, you're content with your heat and spin, heat and spin, heat . . . ."

"Don't get personal, Wally. If you'd spin better, I wouldn't have to work so hard."

"Not going to miss you much, Donald," said Wally, as he continued to edge toward the door to the hall.

That door proved to be a little tricky. Not extra wide, it caused Wally to move sideways. Likewise, the door to the kitchen caused trouble—and some chipping of the paint.

"Got to figure out how to get that repainted," said Wally to himself.

He didn't worry long because he was near his goal—a visit with the shiniest, most beautiful appliance he had ever seen—Dreama Dishwasher. She, with her many colorful buttons and shiny door handle, was breathtaking. And, smart, too, capable of handling every form of dish or cutlery, from delicate crystal to pots and pans.

"Hi there, Beautiful," said Wally.

"Oh, hello," said Dreama. "Who are you?"

"My name's Wally."

"Where are you from?"

"I'm in the laundry room."

"Oh," she said.

Wally could sense that Dreama thought him to be a second-rate appliance because he lived outside the more upscale kitchen neighborhood.

"Where are you going?" asked Dreama.

"I'm going back to the laundry room," said Wally, as he started inching away, "since you seem to think I'm not good enough to . . . ."

"Don't be in such a hurry to leave," said Dreama. "You have some nice features. Those big gold push buttons really go well with your settings."

Wally began to feel warm; warmer even than when he was on his hot water cycle. "I can stay a little while, I guess."

And so, with their matching burnished metal exterior and companionable digital settings, Wally and Dreama became the talk of both the Kitchen and Laundry crowds.

None of their friends were surprised when, at the time of the next family vacation, Manny Microwave hosted an extravagant party and announced that the two were engaged. Wally even coaxed Donald to be his best—er, man.

Time Out

NB: Well, it could happen—

It is well known that Cal Ripken, Jr., was the owner of the Charlotte (FL) Stone Crabs. The Stone Crabs were an affiliate of the Tampa Bay Rays baseball team and were in the Florida State League. It was not so well known that Ripken is also in charge of personnel matters for the Stone Crabs. These player issues might involve anything from hiring and firing to various employment conditions and actions.

Ripken, who played for the Baltimore Orioles in the American League, has been around baseball all his life. His father was a big-league coach and he had a brother who also made the majors. So Ripken knows baseball, baseball rules, and baseball players.

It is very well known that he also holds the record for the longest playing streak during which he went for years and years without missing a game. In setting his record he bested the "Iron Horse," Lou Gehrig of the New York Yankees.

With this background we might have found Cal Ripken in his Charlotte Stadium office looking over the won-loss record and other statistics of the Stone Crabs when his assistant "Whiz" Bang, enters.

Cal says, "Have you seen these latest figures, Whiz?"

"What figures?"

"Our stats for the past month."

"I never look at those things," says Whiz.

"How come?"

"I don't like to look at them, Cal."

"Why?"

"They're hard to figure out, that's why," says Whiz.

"They're just hits, runs, errors, games won and lost, and such."

"Too many numbers," says Whiz.

"You're a real whiz, Whiz."

"Yeah."

"By the way, why are you here?" asks Cal.

"Let me see," says Whiz, furrowing his brow. "Oh, yeah, that young right fielder wants to see you."

"Don Kare."

"I said you wouldn't see him."

"What?"

"I told him you said you wouldn't care if you saw him or not."

"Wha—oh, no, Whiz. You see, his name is Don Kare." says Cal.

"Oh. Can I send him in?"

"By all means, Whiz. You can stay, too."

Whiz ushers in young man in a Stone Crabs uniform, cap in hand.

"Hello, Mr. Ripken."

"Hi, Don, what's up?"

"Oh, not much."

"You getting along all right?"

"Getting along?"

"Yeah, with the team and all," says Ripken.

"Oh, sure, I like to play baseball and I like the guys and..."

"So what can I do for you, Don?"

"Well, it's my back."

"Your back?"

"Yeah, I kind of pulled it last evening when I was batting in the third inning."

"You pulled your back?"

"Yeah."

"I'll bet it hurts."

"Yeah."

"I'll bet you had trouble sleeping last night."

"Yeah."

"I'll bet you could hardly get out of bed this morning."

"That's right."

"So," Cal asks, "why are you here to see me?"

"Well, I thought it might help if I took a night off from playing."

"A night off, eh?"

"Yeah, maybe two."

"Two, eh?" asks Cal.

"Yeah."

Cal looks past Don, then to the left, then to the right, and finally up toward the ceiling in the corner of his office.

Keeping his attention focused into that corner, he says, "What do you think, Lou?"

Don now looks up toward the same corner.

"Say what, Lou?"

Don looks back at Cal and back to where Cal is staring.

"Say, you heard him tell me about his back, Lou?

(Pause) "Yeah—sounds pretty bad, Lou."

"You say you heard him say he had trouble sleeping? And getting out of bed."

Don is now looking back and forth from Cal and where Cal is devoting his full attention. Don seems to be getting less and less comfortable.

Cal asks, "Ever feel that way, Lou? I mean, ever feel kind of tight in the shoulders, strained in the lower back, arms hurt, knees achy, real tired?...You did, eh?"

Don is moving back toward the door.

"Well, what did you do? Oh, just played ball, eh?"

Don, to Whiz, "Tell Mr. Ripken I am feeling better and I have to go now."

"I'll tell him."

As Don leaves, Cal looks down and around at Whiz. "Anyone else to see me, Whiz?"

"Nope."

"Okay."

Rules: Senior Softball League

Rules Developed by Les Mobile, League Founder

Eligibility. Minimum age will be 75; maximum age is dependent only upon the ability to show up.

Any bat length is permissible as long as 15-ounce maximum weight is maintained.

Any size glove that a player can manage to carry is permissible.

Bases will be flush with the ground to minimize tripping.

Bases will be moveable. Distance between bases will be determined after surveying capability of the least competitive player.

Two bases will be utilized at first, second, third, home. A screen will be placed just beyond home plate to prevent a player from just keeping on going and never being seen again.

Pitchers will be hired from the Young Senior Softball League, as designated by Mo Mobile, Commissioner of that league.

A screen will not be needed, since the 15-ounce bat is standard.

No catcher will be needed as pitcher will simply throw a new ball on each pitch. Note: This rule may be changed for any team which can furnish a catcher capable of throwing the ball back to the pitcher.

No rover will be utilized since "rover" implies some degree of ability to move.

A defibrillator is required in each dugout and at each base. (Optional between bases.)

Use of oxygen during play is permitted for only outfielders. Oxygen tank will be conveniently placed on outfielders' chairs.

Hearing impaired players welcome.

Players who have had their driver's licenses removed because of age will be picked up at the Home by limo.

Game rules: One-three inning game. Count—up to 3 balls and 7 strikes. Ball hit past infield—game over.

Use of snuff not permitted for fear of corrupting "younger" players.

Finally, representatives of rehab facilities, hospices, and undertakers will be asked to leave.

Enjoy Your Prunes—
Be a Regular Person

Written in the Public Interest

Author's Note: While the original intention behind this seminal article was to have it published as a ***Bulletin*** by the United States Government, this plan was scuttled by an insensitive bureaucrat who claimed, erroneously, that it would exceed the "threshold of revulsion test" declared in a Supreme Court case. When the author finds a lawyer who will accept his case, this Government claim will be unceremoniously overturned.

When one perceives the OAP (Ordinary American Prune), does one even for a moment stop and think, where does this fruit come from? Likely not. We are so busy these days that, even with the "Jewels of the Earth," as the OAP has become uniformly known, we do not do it justice but rather ignore all that goes into its cultivation, cross-culturing, fertilization, and harvesting, let alone its distribution. In all fairness, scholarly treatment has been given to its benefits and contraindications. This treatise will finally give the OAP its due.

Historically, Prune cultivation began in the Far Eastern regions of our globe; to be specific, very far out in Outer Mongolia. The lofty regions of the southward-looking sides of the higher mountains, with their favorable west to eastern breezes, supported in a unique way the development of the first Prune. Sadly, no one has been able to identify the grower of the first Prune tree, but a noted Wuhan laboratory has, after extensive testing, postulated that the first Prune was derived from the natural cross-fertilization of the crabapple and the pawpaw. (The alternate theory that the Prune came from the persimmon plus the pawpaw was debunked by serious researchers who found the proponents of that theory just liked the rhythm behind persimmon plus pawpaw.) Development of the Prune moved enthusiastically both east and west, reaching both United States coasts just after the Revolution. This has caused some historians to lament that the Revolution might have been over much more quickly if the Colonists and the Brits could have settled their well-documented Prune-haggles.

(For an extensive historical treatment of the Prune, see this writer's acclaimed article, "The Prune through American History," in *The Journal of Delectables*.)

A word about Pitted and Non-Pitted Prunes. The first known version of the Modern Prune, was, of course, the Non-Pitted Variety, known then as simply, the Prune. Then along came Sir Archibald Pit, a descendant of the noted Pitt family that had so much to do with the Commonwealth of Pennsylvania. Incidentally, Sir Archibald's line of Pitts shortened their name during the Shorter Rebellion. At any rate, Sir Archibald re-cultivated the Non-Pitted Variety over many years until he developed the Pitted Prune, for which he was knighted and given the Order of the Garter. Incidentally, Sir Archibald has frowned on the version of his monumental efforts that dwell on his "graft" of successive plants to reach the Apex—the Pitted Prune, especially since revelations linked his efforts to the receiving of illicit profits derived therefrom.

A word about the lowly plum. In some spurious sources the Prune has been related in some vague way to the lowly plum. This claim was put to rest in this writer's modest three-volume treatise, *The Prune: Not Even Vaguely Related to the lowly plum,* for which this writer received the much-coveted Capone Award. Incidentally, this writer received that prestigious award on Valentine's Day.

Military Stories

The Sarge

Our family Sunday picnics were no picnic. Too many hard-headed guys in the family. Too many positions taken along the political spectrum over the years. Too little inclination to move from those positions even as times changed, everyone got a little older, and the women of the clan continued to agitate for less agitation.

But there was one thing the generations agreed on—the Army. Mention the Marines and you had our attention. It was just a question of who would answer the challenge and make the equalizing remark.

"Marines?" Grandpa would ask. "Who are they?" Grandpa, Andy Crenshaw, was large, ruddy, with the slightest remnants of red in his white hair.

"And what did they ever do?" Pop would chime in. Pop, Tom Crenshaw, was tall and spare, and had little gray in his trimmed, dark hair.

Then they'd both look at me, and maybe both had just been all over me for my new, weird, strange, goofy ideas, but not that they expected me to add to the confusion over what earthly worth that leather-necked branch of the service represented.

So I would say, "Nothing I know of." I am Bob or Bobby, kind of fair, and not as tall as either my grandfather or father.

Then we'd be real quiet for a few minutes as we just sat and considered. Then one of us, usually Grandpa, maybe Pop, and sometimes me would make a positive comment about the Army or reminisce about some service-related experience.

Maybe it was because I was still a little riled about their recent abuse directed toward me—I decided to start it off this time.

"I think even an old Army guy could take on a young Marine."

Grandpa: "Yeah."

Pop: "Yeah."

Grandpa: "I could take on some young guy in that outfit."

"I'm sure you could, Grandpa, but I wasn't thinking of you. I was thinking of an old-timer that they sent to our outfit just before going to Iraq. He was in good shape, but he was pretty old. Age didn't stop him from drilling us until I thought we'd drop in our tracks. Another thing old Mac did was to warn us of lots of situations where, if we didn't use our heads and our training, we'd be sure..." I noticed then that Grandpa was looking off into space with a frown on his face, as if he was thinking real hard. I looked at Pop and he was kind of doing the same thing.

"What?" I asked.

"Don't you be complaining," Pop said. "He was doing you a favor."

"I know," I said. "What he told us saved me more than once. But why were you looking so strange just then?"

"Well," said Pop, "it reminded me of a staff sergeant I served with during Viet Nam. He was even a little bit old for that scrape, but he knew his business. And, funniest thing, he was Mac, too."

"How about you, Grandpa? You didn't have a sergeant like that with the name Mac in WWII?"

"As a matter of fact..."

"No way," I said.

"You're making things up again, Dad," said Pop.

"Now why would I do something like that? Old Mac McClintock was a buck sergeant in charge of our squad in the Battle of the Bulge."

Now it was Pop and my turn to silently look off into space, frown, look another way, frown, and just sit there.

"I gotta tell you something strange," said Pop, finally. "Our Sergeant Mac was short for Sergeant McClintock."

"I'm leaving," I said.

"Why would you do that, boy?" Grandpa asked.

"Because I guess I somehow had his son, or cousin, or something, because our sergeant was also McClintock. Roscoe McClintock."

"But you'd better not call him that," said Grandpa.

"Or he'd make you pay," added Pop.

"I knew better than to ever even try," I agreed.

"Had to be a junior, or like you said, a relative," Grandpa said. "And he had to be better-looking. That cut below Mac's eye sure didn't help his appearance."

Pop and I spoke at once, and the gist of what we both said was that our Roscoe McClintock had a cut under the right eye.

"Right it was—and I saw him get it. Hand-to-hand combat with a German soldier who used a rifle butt on him."

"Coincidence," said Pop. "Maybe the same one for you and me, Dad, but not the young soldier here."

"No," agreed Grandpa, "too long, too long, too long."

"But..."

"What?" asked Pop.

"He did show us a picture of his family once. And he was in dress uniform."

"And?" urged Grandpa.

"And he had hash marks all up and down one sleeve."

"How many?" asked Grandpa.

"Too many to remember. And Combat Infantryman's Badge, medals galore, and rows and rows of ribbons."

"But he'd be too old to serve with you, Son," said Pop.

"I know."

"Let's figure this out," said Grandpa. "Mac was about twenty-four when I knew him in 1944."

"And he would have been about forty-eight when I knew him in Viet Nam," said Pop. "Which, come to think of it, might not have been far off."

"And," I said, when I served with him in Iraq, he would have been—whoa, not possible."

Granny stuck her head in the room just then and said that it was time for her and Grandpa to go home. She wasn't very large, and not very loud, but we knew who was still in command when she spoke. We all said our good-byes, but I'd have to say we were still shaking our heads.

During the next week I couldn't help but think of Mac McClintock. I still couldn't call him Roscoe. So, on Wednesday I got on the computer and checked his name through Army records. I got a hit, a single hit on a Roscoe McClintock. And he was retired, living in the next state, about a day's ride away.

So I called Pop and simply said, "Road trip."

He quickly picked up on what I told him and said he'd get Grandpa set for moving out smartly on Saturday to visit "The Sarge."

We argued only a little on the way to see Roscoe McClintock—maybe it was the anticipation, or maybe the wonder over several things, including how he had been a part of all of our Army experiences, and how in the world he had survived in the Army for something like sixty years.

"Who are you guys?" was the greeting, looking us up and down in inspection mode.

We told him.

He followed up with "What do you want?"

Grandpa told him of our conversation that led us to believe we had all served with him.

"I don't remember, but you might as well come in the house. Tell me more about who you are and when you were in the Army." His home was a one-story brick Cape Cod on a quiet street, about as far from any fighting or confusion as could be, and, as we might expect, neat as a pin. He said that his wife Erma was at the beauty parlor.

So each of us gave the dates and places, some of which we had tried to forget.

"Well, maybe."

"Surely you remember at least one of us, Sergeant-Major," I said.

"Well, maybe, and call me Mac, or Sarge."

"Sure, Sarge," said Pop.

"Of course, I remember you guys. I remember you and me about freezing to death, Andy, in the Battle of the Bulge. And I remember you, Tommy, in Viet Nam. Bad duty. And Bobby, I couldn't believe it when I somehow learned who you were when you came to Iraq."

Then he sat back in his armchair and roared with laughter. He was very close to letting us know that he was pleased at our visit.

"Okay, Roscoe..." began Grandpa.

"I told you never to call me Roscoe."

"Okay, Sarge, how in the world did you ever spend such a long career in the military? Seems pretty unusual."

"You're right about that, Corporal, er, Andy. But it just happened. I stayed in the service after World War II, and it was tough going to peacetime duty. Korea came along and I re-learned how bad war can be. I got to misbehaving myself in bars and taverns and I ended up getting busted. I was almost asked to leave the service when Viet Nam came along. They seemed to want me more in the fight than at home in the US, so I got my rank back, and Tommy, you know how it was over there."

"But that only takes us up to about forty years ago," I said. "You were just getting a good start on your career then."

"That's right, but, Andy, you remember the second lieutenant who commanded our platoon?"

"You mean Pickles? His name was John Dillon, which was shortened to John Dill, and then Pickles," explained Grandpa. "I remember you had to give him a lot of, shall we say, support, to get him to make a go of it."

"That's him," said Sarge. "Well, in spite of how pitiful he was at first, he got better as time went on, and maybe it was because he looked good in dress uniform, he started going through the ranks. By Viet Nam he was a general, if you can imagine that, and somehow he found out I was still hanging around. To make a long story short, he got me on his staff to sort of advise on weapons and tactics. I had seen lots of both. He kept me there as he went on up."

"How high up?" I asked.

"Member of the Joint Chiefs-up."

"Good grief, Pickles Dillon," said Grandpa, shaking his head.

"He made a good officer and he treated me very well," said Mac. "But I told him I couldn't very well help him much in evaluating the new weapons unless I got a chance to use them. I got plenty of chances in Desert Storm and Iraq."

"How did you keep up with the young guys," asked Grandpa.

"It was very tough. They were in great shape and had good training. I guess it was when you came into my outfit, Bobby, that I finally figured it was time to quit."

"Was I that bad of a soldier?"

"No, you're a good soldier, but when I found out who you were, and I realized how long ago I had served with your grandfather. It just became too much for me to handle any more."

"Guess you were getting pretty rickety," said Grandpa.

"What do you mean, rickety? I can still handle the carbine, er, I mean the M-1, I mean the M-16, and move out with the best of them."

That was more like the Roscoe McClintock that I remembered. And I'm sure it was more like the man Grandpa and Pop had served with.

All I could think to say was, "I'm sure you could, Sergeant-Major."

"Call me Sarge."

Not a Walk in the Park

He didn't belong there; maybe he didn't belong anywhere—anymore.

"A good day for the concert" was the uniformly accepted greeting of the several thousand lawn-chairists who had come to hear the town's very accomplished symphony orchestra. It was a warm sunny March day, to be reveled in by not only the permanent Florida residents but also the snowbirds who were escaping temporarily the northern chill.

The orchestra was seated in symphony fashion on a movable platform constructed even with a canopy to ward off either sun or rain. The leader for the day was a young man who was a temporary replacement for the older, recently retired conductor. The new conductor's credentials included both attainment of the appropriate degrees and the creation of his own musical scores.

The park was located in a triangle among three intersecting avenues and featured representative palm and other trees and greenery. Just in the middle was a white gazebo with a red tile roof. On the periphery of the park were swings for the children and benches and picnic tables for any who wished to use them.

In order to please the variety of musical tastes of the assembled crowd, the orchestra had selected some classical, some movie themes, and some marches.

If the selections leaned in one way, they were probably toward the tastes of the oldsters who constituted the majority of attendees. Gray hair abounded in the audience, often husband and wife, but also included were children and college students on their spring break. Almost all seemed happy to be there, seated and attentive.

Attentive but standing, however, was a man who did not fit the mold of the other people in the large crowd. He was on the on the right edge of the audience. He stood quietly and erectly for the National Anthem, and slouched through obligatory classical overture. But when a medley of Duke Ellington tunes began, he pulled a harmonica from his shirt pocket and began to play along with the orchestra. Soon he was lost in his musical accompaniment with his head tilted to one side and his hand vibrating in enhancement of his instrument. He continued his playing during the next several numbers which included a movie score, a march, and some Broadway tunes. From a distance, at least, it appeared that he kept time with the music and was able to follow the orchestra effortlessly.

After twenty-five minutes or so, however, he stopped. Perhaps the selection being rendered turned him off. Perhaps someone near him complained. Perhaps he grew tired of standing and playing. Or perhaps something had affected his ability to concentrate for an extended time.

He pocketed his harmonica, turned about, and made his way from the crowd to the outer grass of the park. Then he turned and walked along the concrete pavement that bisected the majority of the crowd.

He was close enough to see that he had refrained for some days from shaving, bathing, or washing his clothing. Jeans and denim jacket covering a plaid shirt were his uniform of the month. His shoes were shapeless and had a hole at the right little toe. His hair was long but insufficient for a ponytail.

As he walked along, he looked to his right at the orchestra which was playing a classical number. Just as he came to where he was directly in front of the conductor but some distance away, he shouted something that was unintelligible but had the feel of encouragement for the efforts of the musicians. He then moved on, disappearing to the side of the assemblage.

The harmonica player was nowhere to be seen for the next several numbers. Then he reappeared with two other men of about his same age, dress, and demeanor. They were leaving the performance, walking as if they had no particular place to go and not in any hurry to get there.

Then came the orchestra's playing their "Salute to the Services" medley which included the Army, Navy, Marine, Air Force, and Coast Guard songs. People who had been a member of any of these branches of the military were asked by the conductor to stand and be recognized as their song was being played.

When the strains of "From the Halls of Montezuma" were first heard, the three men in denim turned quickly around and faced the music. They came to attention as best their present condition would allow and remained at attention until the Marine Hymn ended. They then turned, and as the harmonica player made a dismissive motion of the hand, slouched on to their next non-appointment.

Figure Head

The oldest boats had figureheads—carved images, often of women's heads, that extended out from the front of the boat. And this boat had another kind of figurehead—only it was not a boat but a ship, and the figure was Captain Roy. He was alive, alert, and well; he was just old. He'd sailed since his youth, beginning as a cabin boy and working through the ranks. He'd sailed war, merchant, and passenger vessels, much of the time in charge as captain of the ship.

His earlier ships had been fueled with coal and then with oil. Truth to tell, he wasn't at all up to date on the workings of his ship, or the details of its organization, or personnel issues with the "Company." He was here because he was old—and he looked like a Captain of the Line should look—straight and trim, clear-eyed, with a white beard reminiscent of the sea captains of the early twentieth century.

He had a nice stateroom, meals were good, pay wasn't bad, and all he had to do was memorize some facts about this great cruise ship, stand and receive passengers as they lined up for teas and other formal activities, and host some of the travelers at dinner.

Piece of cake. Easy-peasy, as his granddaughter (great-granddaughter?) said. Nothing to it.

Except he felt a fraud. He wasn't in charge of anything and he thought it a travesty and a shame and an offense against his long line of former mates to be simply posing.

And not being in charge was a new experience. He had been in charge—captain—for decades before retirement. He knew his ships, his men and women, his missions, which ports were hard to maneuver and thus required him at the helm, and when to be firm and when to relax his grip a bit.

But now, handshakes, teas, lines of people, tables, table talk. Good duty and bad duty at the same time. Oh, well, fulfill his contract and return to Molly. He didn't do much at home, but at least there he didn't pretend to be more than he was—Molly wouldn't let him, calling him off his "high horse" as often as necessary.

While on the ship, he did have a good deal of time off, and he did still love the sea. He'd watch out from the little balcony off his room, or sometimes go to the bridge. There, the "real" officers of the ship were unfailingly kind to him, showing him due respect for his long record of command.

On a clear morning, sitting on his balcony with a cigar, Captain Roy was watching the removing of the ship from its moorings at this latest Caribbean port of call. All the passengers were back on board, having taken the tour of the island, visited the bars and shops, and purchased lots of souvenirs. Just like most of the other stops.

But this channel back out to sea was a little trickier than most, in Captain Roy's estimation, so he was saying under his breath such admonitions as, "Careful, careful, more to port, good, good." "No, no, not so close to shore."

He felt a bump. Rather slight, but it caused his coffee cup to move.

"We've hit something," he thought. "Not a hard hit, but something. I wonder..."

He got up and made his way to the bridge.

"Did you feel it?" he asked the officer in charge.

"Feel what, sir?"

"The ship hit something as we came out of port."

"I didn't notice anything," said the officer. "Did any of you?" he asked others on the bridge.

All replies were either "No" or a shake of the head.

"Well, there was something." After looking out at the water for a bit, he said to the officer in charge. "I'd like for you to find a passenger for me."

"A passenger, sir?"

"Yes, John Richardson."

"He's probably still having breakfast now, sir."

"No matter, just get him. Bring him here," said Captain Roy.

"Aye, aye, sir."

Soon, an older man about the Captain's age came onto the bridge.

"Captain," he said.

"Master Chief."

"I was going to come to see you, but, you know..."

"I know, I know," said the Captain. "This assignment is a far cry from the old days."

"Don't worry, Captain. By the way, you're looking good."

"No time for that. Did you feel it, as we came out of port?"

"Yes, sir, I did. And right away I thought..."

"Clock Rock," said the Captain.

"Clock Rock, sir? Never heard of it," said the First Mate, who was second in command. "Why is it called Clock Rock; and who is this man who has been admitted to the bridge?"

The Captain said, "First, it's called Clock Rock because, regular as clockwork, somebody comes too close to a very large rock outcrop as they come out of this port. Second, this is Master Chief John Richardson, who sailed with me forty some years."

"Forty-three years, sir," said the Chief.

"Back to the issue at hand," said the Captain. "We could have a serious..."

The Commander interrupted, "With all due respect, sir, I don't think..."

"As I was saying, this could be serious. What do you think, Master Chief?"

"I agree, sir."

Rolling of eyes and shuffling of feet by the bridge crew.

"We can check it out at the next port, sir," said the First Mate.

"Not good enough. Here's what I want you to do. Turn this ship around and head back into the port we just left."

"But, sir, the Company will be very upset, sir," said the First Mate.

Captain Roy went on, "Our first duty is to the over two thousand passengers on this ship."

"But…." said the Commander.

"In the turning of this ship back to port, I want Master Chief Richardson included in the maneuvering."

"He's not…"

"Yes, he is. Do it. And somebody get him a uniform. You can leave off the hashmarks. You won't have enough, anyway."

Seeing no alternative, the bridge officers, with the Master Chief watching closely, began turning the big cruise ship around. They also passed on word to the passengers, by way of the crew and staff, that the change in schedule was routine, the reason being that more fuel was needed to be taken on.

But the Captain maintained an anything-but-routine command of the movement back to port, hoping that any damage was not threatening to the ship and its cargo of so many people. The Chief shared this concern and kept a careful eye on all the efforts made to return to port.

Their luck held as the ship eventually was returned to its former moorings. Once there, the Captain, again much to the disfavor of his immediate subordinates, ordered all passengers ashore. He did rely on his staff to see to an orderly disembarkation, now with little panic since the ship was securely moored.

Company engineers were immediately flown into the port. They found a large hole in the starboard side. A sister ship had been speeded to pick up the passengers and get them safely onto the remainder of their cruise.

The Captain congratulated the crew on their prompt actions that possibly saved lives and the ship. He also gave a nod to the Chief and received a nod back.

The Captain seemed to take on "new life" throughout this episode, much to the pleasure of his old fellow seaman, the Chief. Both were recognized in the weeks following for their effective handling of a situation that might well have led to a disaster at sea.

And, when the Captain performed his duties at dinners, teas, and other functions, he was recognized by his crew and the Company as being firmly in command of the ship.

“Old Folk” Tales

He sat down and glanced at his program. Good, there were listed two Sousa marches, one midway through the first half and “Stars and Stripes Forever” at the end. He liked that. That’s what he had ventured out for; and that’s what it was for him, a venturing from his home, almost an adventure, something he seldom did except for shopping for food and an occasional baseball game during Spring Training for the major league clubs.

The conductor came out to applause and conducted the opening number, a fanfare dedicated to Korean veterans. They deserved it, he thought. Then the color guard presented the colors, they said the Pledge of Allegiance, and sang the National Anthem. And the program got under way.

He was enjoying himself, even tapping his foot inconspicuously on the floor to the beat of the patriotic selections. The band was good. The leader in one of his introductions to the musical numbers told of the professional backgrounds of some of the band members.

Then came intermission. He had to stand for a moment to relieve the soreness from sitting so long. Just then the three older ladies to his left excused themselves and passed in front of him. The second woman smiled at him for an instant too long. He was embarrassed. (“Oh, great, she might want to talk later.”)

He wasn’t used to this kind of contact. Various friends and relatives had attempted to match him with very nice women, but he hadn’t done well in these encounters, at least by his own reckoning. He hadn’t pursued any relationships on his own. On their way back to their seats the women simply went by with a quick “Pardon me.”

More good music. Then the "Salute to the Armed Services." The conductor said that persons who had served in the military should stand and be recognized when the band played their service song.

Big decision, whether to stand or not. It was so long ago, and he was not used to any recognition.

At nearly eighty, tall and spare with snow white hair, he wore a cap, base-ball type, which said "China-Burma-India". This indicated his service with the air veterans who had flown "over the hump," the high Himalayas, during World War II.

The Community Band always drew a crowd. He'd see the cars filling the parking lot. Until this evening, he always passed on by.

The attack on the New York City Twin Towers had affected him, however. That violent act brought back memories of the extreme chaos of war. He became fearful for the first time since, ten years prior, he learned that his wife Marie's condition was severe and he would likely lose her. He had been alone for a long time.

The 9-11 attack also brought back a longer-existing fear of what terror could accomplish. He did not worry so much for himself in his small Sunshine State community with its older population and its streets that rolled up at sundown. But he did worry for his son and daughter and their children who lived in built-up areas on the east and west coasts of the United States.

The uniform had been put away, actually, had decayed well in the past. Marie had said she wished that he would put it on for her, but he knew he probably could not get into it anymore, so he never did. Let the past, at least the war past, take care of its own self.

Coast Guard song. Lots more former Coast Guard people in Florida than in most places in the country. The crowd applauded those standing. Oh, boy.

Then the Air Force service song. At least he recognized it. He wasn't sure he would. In front of him a young couple were nudging each other for the one to stand and be recognized. After a couple of elbows each the young woman stood. A surprise, but it shouldn't have been, when he thought about it. Women were serving even in the "old days" when he was in uniform.

Watching the contact between the couple up ahead evidently got his mind off his hesitance to rise, because he found himself getting up. He stood during the playing of his service's music, looking around to see who else was on their feet. Several of the other veterans waved at him, and he nodded back. It wasn't as bad as he had expected.

In fact, it was kind of pleasant. He felt some of the old camaraderie that had existed in his unit so many years before. He took pride in that. And he took pride in his being among the senior members of those being recognized. It was pretty good.

Then the Navy song. Lots of getting up, and waving, and applauding.

Only one left—the one for the Marines. He liked that one and wanted to hear it. This was kind of fun. People started getting up here and there. Same waving. Same applause.

He'd been looking mostly straight ahead. As his eye swept to the left he was amazed to see that the woman beside him was standing. Not only standing, holding herself straight and tall. He hadn't really noticed her in his preoccupation with the crowd and in his avoidance of contact with her and her friends.

He was "into it" by now and applauded heartily. She noticed and smiled at him. That didn't seem too unnatural. Guess she had applauded when I stood. He nodded back.

She sat down with the rest of the Marines. At least he guessed she did, because he was now looking straight ahead. The moment, with its pomp had past. Reality again.

The performance went on for another couple of numbers. During this time he glanced to his side, barely moving his head. She was a little younger than he, but not by much. She was attractive, yes, good-looking, and not just "for her age." Gray as he was, but neat "as a pin," as they used to say. She started to turn her head slightly his way, and he quickly went "Eyes front."

Then the Big Finish. The audience was used to the drill where they clapped to the beat of the last measures of the "Stars and Stripes Forever." Everyone standing. He liked this. He thought the piccolos set up the final stirring moments in a fantastic way. He was clapping, too; maybe a little off the beat, but still joining in.

He looked around and saw the Marine clapping. She looked at him and either smiled at him or laughed at him. Give it the benefit of the doubt—they were sharing the joy.

The music ended. Big applause. He was looking straight ahead again, now looking forward to just leaving. But the person to his right was talking with someone in front of him. He couldn't get away. But neither could she.

They smiled at each other. She put out her hand. "Madeleine Thomas."

He took it. "Rodney Sirk."

Still no movement. "They call me Maddie."

"I'm Rod."

They could tell that her friends were getting anxious to leave.

"Would you go with me for coffee?" he asked.

"Yes, I'd like that."

One thing had led to another, and on a fine morning in the next year they were sitting on the screened balcony of their condo overlooking the Gulf of Mexico. They had read the newspaper and were just sitting back studying a couple of sailboats as they moved farther out in the Gulf.

"Maddie?"

"Yes."

"You remember the night we met?

"Yes, Rod."

"You remember I asked you to go with me for coffee?"

"Yes, I do remember that."

"Weren't you worried about leaving there with me that night?"

"A little."

"So, what made you have courage enough to do that?"

"Well, after all, Rod, you must remember—I am a Marine."

"Yes, Maddie, I do remember that."

Small Town Stories

Ikey Crump and the Middlebury Fair

Ikey Crump was a lot of fun—not. He was a contrary old bachelor who lived on the edge of town on a couple of grown-up acres. His dress was bib overalls, complete with change purse in the bib where he kept his money, an old, old baseball cap tilted to the side, and clodhopper shoes.

His conveyance was a riding lawn mower with implement trailer behind. Sometime in the past Ikey had lost his driver's license. No matter, he never went anywhere, anyway—just to the store to get his provisions and to his mowing jobs.

He seldom talked to anyone. His jobs were on a schedule, and everyone knew what he charged and paid him without a word.

Kids were frightened of him, and parents told their youngsters to stay out of Ikey's way. Some parents threatened kids with a visit from Ikey if they misbehaved.

There was an exception to his accustomed home-bodiness. Once a year he went to the Middlebury Fair. Middlebury was a small town with not much to recommend it, except the Fair. Years earlier old Judge Joshua Hampton had said, "Let's have a fair in this backwater place." Judge Joshua was so influential, having kept the citizens on such a short rein by his heavy-duty sentencing that some of those citizens thought it might please him to name the town Backwater—but didn't.

Ikey got to the fair by virtue of his brother's taking him in his big Mercedes automobile. Before you say, "Isn't that nice?"—forget it. Brother Irvin, who somehow managed to inherit the whole of his father Isaiah's large estate, transported twin Ikey because of Pop's will. It said, "It is required, necessary, demanded, and altogether appropriate for said Irvin to do something for Ikey once a year." So that was it, pick up and deliver to and from the Fair once a year. The pair spoke no words except when they arrived at the fair, Irvin would say, "Here we are." And Ikey, "Yep," as he got out of the car.

In addition to the corn dogs, barbecue, and country music, Ikey especially liked the competitions. High on his list were the pickle judging, especially bread and butter—his mom had often entered her exhibits and had often won. He liked the tractor pull, being a tractor man himself—small scale, of course. And the calf judging, as he had shown a number of young steers when he was a 4-H member.

He first had to look over all the calf entrants with his practiced eye and bet with himself as to the winner. No way would he open that old coin purse of his to let escape betting money.

Part way through his calf critique, he noticed in the adjoining goat pens, a young girl sitting on a hay bale, holding the halter of a beautiful young female goat. Strange that she had her head down and her shoulders were shaking—she was crying. She was about eleven or twelve, with auburn hair and a healthy, outdoor look.

No one was near to look after her or to comfort her, and this posed a problem for Ikey. Back home, he had sometimes seen youngsters who were in distress, but because of his reputation as one to be feared, he gave these situations a wide berth.

But here with no less sadness for the youngster's distress, he ventured into unfamiliar territory. "You okay?" was his opener.

She looked up, and then back down.

"What's the trouble?"

She finally looked up. "It's all ruined," she said.

"What's ruined?"

Sniffling—"Got here too late."

"What?"

"Too late to enter Ikey," she said.

"That's Ikey?" he asked.

"Yes, Ikey," she said forcefully.

"Ikey?"

"Yes, sir. Short for Isabella," she said.

"Oh—Isabella?"

"Now don't you laugh, mister—it hurts Ikey's feelings."

"No, no, I'm not making fun. It's just...Ikey's my name," he said.

"Oh—How about that?" she said. "Funny—both the same."

"Yeah, kinda funny. You were too late, eh?"

"Just by a little bit. I got a ride with a neighbor and he had trouble rounding up the sheep he was entering."

"Well, here's what I'm thinkin'," he said. "We can't let an animal with a great name like Ikey be disqualified. Gotta do something about this."

"Yes sir, but what?"

"You and Ikey just wait here. I'll be back."

Ikey set his baseball cap perfectly straight, hiked up his bibs, shined his clodhoppers on the back of his overalls, and purposefully headed for the Fair Office. There a clerk waved him on into the manager's office.

The manager, appearing harried and tense, checked out Ikey top to bottom before speaking. "Well?"

"We got a problem."

"We?"

"Yeah, me, a young friend of mine, and a goat," and Ikey went on to explain the young girl's dilemma and disappointment.

"But we have rules," said the manager.

"I know," said Ikey, "and I've seen lots of rules, but what's fair is fair, especially at the Fair." (That last just came to him.) "What can we do about it?"

"She can come back next year," said the manager.

"Nope."

"Let her have free food and drinks while she's here?"

"Nope?"

"You just go away??"

"Nope."

It was an impasse. Both sides were dug in.

After a long mutual stare Ikey pulled his cap bill to the side, hiked up his bibs, and took off to the door, mumbling not nice things about the Middlebury Fair.

On the way he picked up a soft drink for himself and the girl. When he gave hers to her, he explained how he had failed at his mission. He said, "Sorry. By the way, what's your name?"

The girl replied, "Ronnie."

"Ronnie?"

"Okay, it's short for Veronica."

"Oh."

"What about it, mister?"

"My name's Ikey—I got nothin' to say. Except—can I give you some money for rides, and corn dogs, and ...?"

"Can't you come with Ikey and me? It's no fun going on rides alone."

"Nah, you don't want to go around with an old fool like me."

"Well," she said, "you did your best for Ikey and me. You were great."

"Now, don't...say too much, but I'll go see the sights here with both of you."

So Ronnie and the two Ikeys toured the Middlebury Fair to the exceeding joy of Ikey (the man). Farewells that evening were difficult for the unlikely fair-goers.

But the story doesn't end there. Some years later, Ronnie, a Pre-Veterinarian student at State University, discovered while talking with Mitzi, a fellow student, that Mitzi was from Ikey's home town. Ronnie inquired if Mitzi had known of an older man named Ikey Crump.

"Oh, sure," said Mitzi. "He was that funny old guy who used to go around town on his riding mower. Us kids were scared of him. People said he was weird."

"What's really funny about that 'weird' old man..." said Ronnie.

"Yes?"

"He was my best friend—and every summer, until he passed away last year, we would meet to spend a wonderful day together—at the Middlebury Fair."

Uncle Jim's Treasure

"Your Uncle Jim must have liked you a lot to leave you this house in his will," said Gwen, as she and Marty went up to the front door of the old, run-down structure.

"I used to come over here and see him, even though he and the rest of the family didn't get along. He was okay, though. We talked and he liked to show me old pictures and things that he had."

"But he must not have had very much of value, from the looks of this place. It hasn't been painted in years, there are boards missing from the porch, and some of the windows are broken," said Gwen. Gwen was as dark as Marty was fair; she was more of a risk-taker, but Marty was quick to "get with the program" and stayed on task longer; they were both seventeen.

The house was later than Victorian, but earlier than modern, two stories, wide front porch with banister, shutters—some here, some not—and lots of vines, weedy flower beds, and untrimmed bushes all around. It was not quite spooky, or if it was, it didn't matter because hardly anyone would have been attracted to it enough to care.

"You know what we would always do when I came to see him?" asked Marty.

"No, what?"

"He'd always lead me around to the back to look in his garage."

"Why did he do that?"

"I don't know. It was as if he was proud of the accumulation of stuff that the garage held. He'd open the door and there it was. A mass of tools, furniture, garden equipment and supplies, and who-knows-what-else. It extends clear to the door.

There's not room for another thing in that building—and it's a two-car garage. And, lucky me, it's all mine now."

"I guess it's not much of an inheritance," suggested Gwen.

"Maybe not in money, but it was precious to Uncle Jim, and so it means a lot to me."

Marty produced a skeleton key and unlocked the front door. To the right of the entrance hall with its large old hat rack and library table was the living room. It was just as his uncle had left if—the old lounge chair sat across from the ageing television and was surrounded by piles of newspapers and other reading material. Along one of the outer walls were floor to ceiling shelves loaded haphazardly with books. On the walls were family pictures—one of these was very large.

"That's his mom and dad and his brothers and sisters when they were young. The boy on the right in the front row is my dad," explained Marty.

"He never married?"

"Once, when he was twenty or so, but it didn't last long."

"That's sad—to live your life alone."

Marty reflected on this, saying only, "Yeah," but thinking that he wouldn't want to spend a solitary life. This led him to glance at Gwen, with whom he might do the sharing. But he knew that she considered him only as a best friend. Anyway, he was glad that she had agreed to come to Uncle Jim's house with him. They differed on many of the things they talked about. But they at least talked about them, and Marty was grateful for that and believed Gwen to feel the same way.

"The family called him 'Uncle Dub,'" Marty said, "but not to his face."

"Why on earth did they call him that?" questioned Gwen.

"He's forever doing things double. He would have identical old cars. He was proud of his load of stuff in his double-car garage."

"And I saw the two TVs, one on top of the other."

"What are you going to do with all his things?" Gwen inquired.

"I might get a second-hand dealer to make an offer and take it all away."

"Or you could go through it."

"Why?"

"There might be some valuables among all this clutter."

"I find that highly unlikely."

"I could help you."

That changed everything. Marty didn't answer too quickly, but he had already made up his mind. "Yeah, we might do that."

"What else is there to know about Uncle Jim?" asked Gwen, for she was growing to feel that the old gentleman was a relative of hers.

"Well, he liked puzzles."

"Crosswords?"

"No, little poems or situations where you were supposed to figure out the answers. He always was delighted when I could get the answers."

"Maybe there could be a mystery here," suggested Gwen, looking around Uncle Jim's house.

"Could be, but job one is to go through all this stuff. I'll talk to Uncle Jim's lawyer, and if he gives the go-ahead, maybe we could start."

"How about Saturday?"

"Suits me," answered Marty.

On Saturday morning it did not take long to see how big the task was going to be. Uncle Jim saved everything. The valuable was piled next to the junk, and sometimes it was hard to tell which was which. They began in the dining room since it was the least cluttered, and they could make the most headway. They had a clipboard and carefully logged the furniture, dishes, silverware, and other objects in the room.

"I brought sodas. Want one?" asked Marty after a couple rather tedious hours.

"Sure."

They went to the refrigerator and Marty got out the pop cans.

"He surely kept a lot of clutter on the refrigerator door," noted Gwen.

"Yeah, those are pictures of me when I was little and as I grew up."

"And lots of sayings."

Marty responded, "He liked little funny lines, like this one: 'Growing old ain't for sissies.' He'd say that and laugh and laugh."

"What's this mean? 'Double, double, boil and bubble.'"

"I don't know. It's obviously a corruption of 'double, double, toil and trouble' from Macbeth," suggested Marty.

"He must have put that there for a reason."

"Yeah, probably; who knows?" said Marty, rolling his eyes.

They worked through the dining room and took time out to go to Gus's Hot Dogs for lunch. There they were greeted by several of their friends and ignored as usual by Gus.

On their return to Uncle Jim's, they tackled the living room, which consisted of mostly furniture, a piano and lots of old sheet music, and a floor-to-ceiling bookcase.

"I guess we should go through each book," said Gwen. Now it was her turn to roll eyes.

"How about if we just looked at the interesting ones now and went through them later?"

"And maybe we could take a picture of each shelf for a kind of inventory," added Gwen.

So she started at the top, standing on a small step ladder and Marty began at the bottom. Soon they were showing each other the various volumes that appealed to them.

It was Gwen who noticed it first. "You know, there are

some books behind the ones on the front of the shelves. Not behind every book, but only here and there. Should we pull them out and look at them?"

"I think we should," answered Marty, and soon they had a collection of twenty-odd volumes.

"Why would your Uncle Jim put these in back of the others?"

"He ran out of room?"

"No, there're gaps in the front rows. He didn't need the space."

Marty and Gwen began searching through the back-shelf books, noting that they were older than the others.

"We should have Mrs. Tomlinson from Second-Hand Books look at these. They may be valuable," suggested Marty.

"Good idea." Gwen paused, "What's this? It's a note in your Uncle Jim's handwriting. It was taped to the shelf. It says, 'Yew best git out of Dodge, pardner.'"

"That's what it says all right," said Marty, reading the note. "But what does it mean?"

"Well," said Gwen, "my dad likes ancient cowboy movies, and that sounds like a typical line from one of them. Do you think it means we shouldn't be here?"

"No way," replied Marty. "That wouldn't be like Uncle Jim at all. He always wanted me to visit, and I know he would have liked you." Marty turned away as he thought of how personal that sounded.

"Right, everyone likes little old me," stated Gwen, making light of the moment.

"But it's got to mean something. Does 'Dodge' mean anything to you?"

"Only the old Dodge trucks Uncle Jim told me he has stored in his garage."

"Let's go there next," said Gwen.

"Okay, but you're in for a real treat. Uncle Jim always wanted to show me his two garages when I visited him, but all you could see was the stuff just inside the door. They were piled full of everything imaginable."

They went out the back door to the garages. Marty opened the door of the first one. "See what I mean?"

"I can't face all this right now; it's getting too late. How about tomorrow afternoon?"

"Suits me," agreed Marty.

So the next afternoon they began taking Uncle Jim's prized possessions from the garages. They frequently looked at each other, affirming that one person's treasures is another's trash. After much lifting and lugging they made their way to the cab of the old relic of a Dodge pick-up.

The Dodge was something to behold. It had never been washed in its over seventy years of existence. It was a candidate for a "scratch and dent" sale, except these blemishes were the rule rather than the exception. Since they had reached only the driver's side, tried that door and after much pulling, caused it to creak open. The packing and springs were exposed in the seat. A pair of lock-on pliers served as a window handle. The age of the vehicle was affirmed by the turning knob affixed to the steering wheel.

But the pick-up was pretty clean inside, indicating that its former owner had valued it. Marty eased over to the passenger side and Gwen climbed in behind the wheel.

"Well, this is 'Dodge,' I guess; wonder what's here that might cause Uncle Jim to make reference to it in the note we found on the bookcase?" asked Marty. He opened the glove box and found it bare, except for a piece of paper with his uncle's writing.

"Wrong Dodge," read Marty.

"Good grief," sighed Gwen. "Where to now?"

"Think there's another car buried in the other side of the garage?"

They piled out of the truck, opened the other garage door, and began working their way through the fondly collected debris of Uncle Jim's lifetime. This time, they focused their moving of things and soon came upon the back fender of an old blue car. With further effort they managed to sit in the front seat of a Dodge sedan that was even older than the truck—pre-World War II. Something else was different, also. The car was well-preserved inside and out.

"This is a treasure in itself; maybe this is what your uncle was pointing us toward," suggested Gwen.

"But we would have found it anyway."

"True. What's in the glove compartment?"

"Nothing. It's been cleared out."

"Here's something. It's down in the pocket on the inside of the door," said Gwen. "It says, 'You stay in the car while I go in the bank.'"

"That sounds like it's from an old gangster movie of about the same era as this old car."

Gwen pondered the message. "This is surely something that Uncle Jim wanted us to follow up on, and the key words seem to be 'car' and 'bank'."

"Yeah, let's check out the car first."

Good idea, but no results. Two hours later, after moving the collection of things from around the car, looking into all the openings of the vehicle, and even looking under the old Dodge, they came up empty. And they still had to move the ton or so of items back into the garage.

"I'm getting tired of this," muttered Marty.

"Me, too. Let's go to Gus' Hot Dog Stand for a couple of hot dogs with everything."

Sitting quietly in the booth, tiredly pondering Uncle Jim's messages, they suddenly looked at each other. "But what bank?" they said together.

"That's a problem—there are lots of banks and branches in town," lamented Gwen, "but maybe Uncle Jim didn't mean it to be so very difficult."

"Okay, what would make our search of all those banks easy?"

"I don't know. Maybe it's something we know already."

"Well, the first clue was 'Double, double, boil, and bubble'."

"Something with 'double, boil, or bubble' in it."

"Double might mean 'two'."

"Or 'Second,' as in Second National Bank," said Gwen.

"It's worth a try. Tomorrow morning?"

"Okay."

The next morning at nine Gwen and Marty entered the main branch of the Second National Bank and approached the middle-aged woman at the inquiry desk.

"May I help you?" she asked.

"Yes, I'm Marty Varner, and I was wondering if my uncle, James Varner, banked at Second National."

The receptionist looked at Marty very seriously. "Just a moment," she said. She picked up the phone, made a call, and quietly said to the person on the other end, "He's here."

Marty and Gwen were taken aback when they heard this.

"Go into the office on the other side of the lobby," the receptionist said.

They proceeded to the office and stood at the door. The door was marked, "Anne Ware, Vice President."

Ms. Ware, a rather tall red-haired woman in a business suit, rose from her desk and beckoned for them to come in and sit down.

"You're Jim Varner's great-nephew?"

"Yes," said Marty with some hesitation because he didn't know what was going on.

"Your uncle banked here for many years. He was a good friend to many of us. And he talked often of you."

"Me?"

"Yes," said Ms. Ware. "He thought you were a good young man with a good future. He even bragged some about how well you did in school and in sports."

"How about that," said Marty to Gwen.

"He must have been really fond of you," said Gwen.

"And he loved games and puzzles," said Ms. Ware. "He often asked us riddles on his visits to the bank. I guess that's what led him to make an agreement with us."

"What kind of agreement?" inquired Marty.

"He asked us to hold something for you."

"Wow," said Marty. "I never knew he had anything in mind for me."

"That's just what he wanted you to think. He pledged me to secrecy, until you showed up after his passing on," explained Ms. Ware. "Your coming to the bank would indicate that you had followed his clues. I'll be right back."

After she had left her office the two young people just looked at each other as if in mild shock.

Returning, Ms. Ware handed an envelope to Marty. He looked at the front of it. "It says, 'To my Pal, Marty, who can figure stuff out.'" Marty, thinking about his favorite uncle, could hardly speak.

"Well, open it," urged Gwen.

"Okay, okay."

Marty carefully opened the envelope and took out a sheet of paper, on which was written:

Dear Marty,

Because I never had any children, I was real glad when you came along and was even more glad that you came to visit me and even tolerated going to look at all the "prizes" in the garage. Ha-Ha. (Marty smiled.)

I am happy to have you inherit my possessions. I believe you will know which ones to prize and which to discard.

Also, I wanted to do something else for you. I thought and thought. Then it came to me. Travel. I knew you liked to talk about foreign places.

So I am enclosing a gift that I hope you will use in good health for a long time to come.

Much love,
(Signed—Uncle Jim)

Marty looked again into the envelope and took out another paper.

"It's a pre-paid certificate for two persons from World Airlines for an annual trip for twenty years to any destination that the airline flies. All I have to do is contact the company each year and they will send me my tickets."

"What a great gift," said Gwen.

"And a surprise," noted Ms. Ware. "Your uncle did not even tell me what he had planned. And it's very generous since the present is for two."

"Well," responded Marty, "Uncle Jim was like that—he always liked to do things in twos."

Daisy, Daisy

Daisy, Daisy, give me your answer do.
I'm half crazy, all for the love of you.
It won't be a stylish marriage,
I can't afford a carriage,
But you'll look sweet, upon the seat,
Of a bicycle built for two.

"Daisy Bell," by Harry Dacre, 1892

"I hear you're getting married," said Tony, to his friend, Jerry.

"Yeah, that's right."

"You know she's too good for you," said Tony, as they sat around with the guys on their break at the brewery. Their fellow workers jumped in with loud laughter, taunting Jerry.

Jerry was well-liked by the brewery crew, made up of a variety of immigrant families—German, Italian, and Irish, among others. He was easy to kid, however, and his occasional slip-ups on his job of delivering brewery products in the city made him an easy target. He was also the driver of the oldest and smallest of the brewery wagons. His team, moreover, consisted of the oldest, most decrepit old nags, and was only two in number. The other drivers drove the big painted wagons with teams of four matched horses with polished harness.

It didn't matter—much—to Jerry. He needed the job to help support his mother and father and their large family. Besides, Jerry was very bright and also good-natured, so the jibes did not stay with him long.

It was a different matter with regard to Daisy. He was worried. While he was looking forward to his marriage to

Daisy—He still couldn't believe his good fortune that she accepted his proposal—he had little money and she was planning a pretty big wedding, complete with a weekend honeymoon. He had his suit for the wedding and was all set, except for transportation. Daisy wanted, really wanted to honeymoon at the beach, and he had no buggy, no horses, and barely enough money to get by on for a weekend. He could work extra for the money, but what about getting there—all he had was a bicycle.

The best offer he had was from his buddy Otto—a bicycle that was made for two persons. Sure, good to go if he were going across town, but even still, leaving the church on a wheel, as it was called in this early twentieth century, was not something he liked to think about, and he knew it was not going to be a very good plan in the eyes of Daisy. And, more than anything else he wanted to make her happy.

Daisy was talking with her friends, too, among them Ginger. Ginger saw right through Daisy's apparent good humor at the anticipated departure from the church on the biggest day of her life.

"But please do not let on to anyone about this," she said. "I want to marry Jerry more than anything, and he is working hard to move on up at his job. Someday . . ."

So the couple went through the events leading up to the wedding, some to be enjoyed and some to be merely endured, until that Saturday in June not long after the nineteen hundreds arrived. They had anticipated their new beginning together at the same time as the new century.

The church was beautiful with candles and flowers. Finely robed clergy complemented the well-attired family and host of friends who came to celebrate with the bride and groom. The bride was radiant in white with appropriately gowned attendants. The groom was eager though uncomfortable in being "dressed up," really well-dressed in the company of his groomsmen. The ritual of the ceremony was beyond the parties' expectations, running smoothly with up-lifting sentiment.

When it came to the part of the ceremony that Jerry wished for more than other parts, the kissing of the bride, the new couple embraced just long enough and headed for the door. A fleeting thought of the transportation that awaited might have occurred to Daisy, but it did not show and cast no shadow on her day.

The double doors opened as they approached and the sight on the street outside the church was a little more than a surprise, just short of a shock. There, parked squarely in front of the church, was a finely painted wagon, not too large, with bright trim and dazzling wheels. Steps led up to a wide padded seat in the front. On the seat were draped the reins leading to a pair of matched white horses, complete with well-oiled finely crafted harness.

When the story of this wedding was told, the elegance of bride and groom leaving the church in their fine transportation, complete with fringed canopy, was always featured. Also mentioned was the joyous smile of the bride and some smugness of satisfaction that the groom could not fully contain.

Alert readers have likely guessed that the beautiful conveyance was actually a transformation of the smaller beer wagon that Jerry used day to day in his work, and that the secret project engaged in by himself and his friends were celebrated not only on that wedding day but also in the lore of their community for generations.

Pray for the Race

There's a lot one can say about the Reverend Doctor Herkimer Henderson. There's also a good deal to tell about just his name. First, he likes it when he is called the full Reverend Dr. Herkimer Henderson. Second, he likes the Reverend, as he is a leader of a flock of "his people," known for both their goodness and for their devotion to their said leader. Third, he really likes the Doctor, ever since it was bestowed upon him by a rather small college led by his cousin, Dr. John Bob Henderson. Fourth, he doesn't mind being called "Herk" rather than his given name when he thinks it makes him approachable, and it is also, in his estimation, a classy name.

He is right thin, even to the point of his learned friends, comparing him to Ichabod Crane. He is right proud, as indicated by the attention he gives to what he is to be called. He is saintly, as will be attested to by his congregation and by those citizens of the town of Oakmont who have come into contact with him. His wife Ruth supports Herk in all his pastoral duties and in as many congregational pursuits as she can manage. Their children Herkimer, Jr., and Eldora are the best that PK's (Preachers' Kids) can be.

But Herk has one tiny vice that no one in the church or the town is aware of. He likes, really likes, to take off once in a while and go to the racetrack. The track of his choice is some seventy-five miles away, and, given the tendency of Oakmonters to stay put, a safe place for Herk to indulge without fear of being discovered. And, so far it has worked admirably, covered of course by his story of his being required now and then to attend a conference useful to the work of the church.

So Herk has gone off to his June "pastoral conference" and is about to put down a small bet on a long shot, Jonas Whale, in the sixth race. It is a small bet because he has about reached his spending limit. The reason he has about reached that self-imposed, seldom violated limit is that he bet big on the fifth race Trifecta in which scriptural terminology was so prominent in the names of the horses that it would have been a sin to resist. He is pretty disgusted, maybe as disgusted as he gets. While he had bet correctly on the first two horses to come in, his pick for the third horse, Revelation, came in fourth. He had hurled his ticket to the floor with all the other losing bets, as he went up to bet on the sixth.

As he offered his two dollars, an announcement came over the loud speakers, "Visitors should hold their tickets to the fifth race as the horse that had come in third had been disqualified." That meant, thought the happy Herk, his Revelation was the third winner of the Trifecta. Whoopee!

But wait—the ticket. Good news—he didn't tear it up. Bad news—it was on the floor, among hundreds of others that looked just like his prize pay-off.

Nothing to do then but to estimate the spot on the floor where he had hurled down that vital piece of paper and to descend on his knees to sort his ticket from its mates. His descent was an easy one physically because of his usual prayer posture, but emotionally he was as distraught as when that hypocrite, the Reverend Doctor Hector Plodder, had been called to the big congregation that Herk had contended for.

As he was making his second run through the tickets in his selected search area, he heard a voice—a familiar voice. It was old Jake Schwartz, who had a farm outside Oakmont, and who was a member of his congregation. Even more, Jake was the most prominent pocket-watch clicking, amen-chanting, sermon-judging leader of his congregation.

"Well, well, Jake, what are you doing here?" he croaked as he looked up.

"Bringing in a load of hay for the horses. I grow the best kind of hay for these thoroughbreds. Thought you knew that, Preacher."

"Slipped my mind," said Herk, rising to his feet.

"More like, what are you doing here, Reverend Doctor Henderson?" said Jake, drawing out the name as far as its syllables would permit.

Sweat was pouring down Herk's back in rivulets as Herk tried desperately to think of a way out of his dilemma, at least partly attributable to his eloquent sermons over the years on the evils of gambling. "Well, I'm, I'm—praying. That's it, I was down on my knees, deep in prayer—for those poor souls who are addicted to this evil pastime. Yes sir, I come here, and to other racing establishments, and try to save as many . . . ."

"I don't believe it," said Jake.

"Wh-what?" stammered Herk.

"Yes sir, I knew you were a good preacher and a good man, but I had no idea that you actually practiced what you preached. I might have known you would go all the way in trying to help these fellers who can't stay away from temptation."

"Why, thank you, Jake. I always have appreciated your support."

"Well, I have to be getting back now," said Jake.

"How about a cup of coffee?"

"No, thanks, Reverend. You know how it is—always farm chores. See you back in town," said Jake.

"Sure, Jake, I'll do a little more praying before I go. See you in church."

Jake walked off and Herk knelt again and was soon again sorting tickets. Had he not been so desperately examining these scraps of paper, he might have seen at a distance, at the last ticket booth, his loyal parishioner, Deacon Jacob Jeremiah Schwartz, offering a similar scrap to the man in the booth, and saying, "Yeah, I got lucky with that fifth race."

The Snowman

Hiram Hottle was a loner as a kid, very bright, not bad looking, but glum—real glum. He was second in his class at Bigelow High, but, as was noted in the high school yearbook, he was "the most likely to enjoy working alone in a lab." He finished his college chemistry degree, in three and a half years if you please, and was offered a scholarship to Cambridge University for the following fall. He was on his way.

Despite his kinship for the lab, he decided to do something else during the intervening spring. Something real different. How about this for different? Due to the severe teacher shortage in his Georgia hometown, his mother learned of an opening in the high school science department. She told Hiram about the temporary job, but he dawdled for so long that the high school position was filled, as well as the other openings—except one.

Are you ready for this? It was in the third grade at Bigelow Elementary. No way—right? But when Hiram learned of the townspeople giggling at the thought of his glum presence with third graders, he said sure. That was in 1973. He stayed right there.

If you had concluded, as did one hundred percent of those who were even slightly aware of the situation (even his mother), that it wouldn't work, you'd be wrong.

And he didn't ever lighten up. "I've never seen him smile, even toward any of the youngsters in his classes," said Becky Starling, who was in Hiram's—Mr. Hiram's—class of 1983.

"No, me neither," said George Putnam '87. "And I'll bet he didn't call you Becky."

"Oh, no, it was always, always 'Rebecca.'"

But the thing was, Mr. Hiram's students learned, and what's more, they were noted for other things. When they came to the cafeteria for lunch or went onto the playground, they went in an orderly fashion—not military, but still orderly. And, strangely enough, they were happy. Sometimes, one heard laughter and clapping from behind his classroom door.

It was when Mr. Hiram began teaching his third generation of Bigelow kids that talk began regarding his retirement.

"He's been at it a long time," said Shirley Himmelfarb '92.

"Some might say too long, but my grandchildren have thrived in his class," said Harry Goldsmith '87.

When Georgia State Department of Education officials were checking records for Cobalt County Schools, they noticed that a Hiram Hottle had been teaching there forty-eight years. They sent a memo to the Superintendent of Cobalt County Schools, saying that it "might be in the best interests of the students of your County" if retirement were required of "said Mr. Hiram Hottle."

County Superintendent Bill Kennedy, Hiram Hottle's class of '82, called Ernie Kowalski '92, Bigelow Elementary Principal, and told him the situation.

"That is a real problem, Bill," Ernie said.

"Yes, it is. Now, Ernie," said Bill, "what I'd like for you to do is...."

"Oh, no, I'm not going to tell him—you tell him."

"I thought you'd say that, and I guess I don't blame you," said Bill.

So the situation has remained unchanged, with all involved parties deciding to risk insubordination charges rather than face Hiram Hottle. All has been calm and quiet at Bigelow Elementary School, with Mr. Hottle still in charge of the third grade.

By the way, there was that incident this past February. It snowed in Bigelow for the first time in years. Old-timers allowed that there might have been a little covering of the ground in the '90's, but it didn't last. The present February snow was a real doozy, however. It began about 9:30 in the morning and just kept coming down. Principal Ernie issued a notice to teachers to keep the children inside through the school day so there would not be accidents or complaints from parents.

The students, who had never seen snow or played in it had difficulty focusing on schoolwork that day. Naturally, they wanted to go out in the snow, but the teachers denied their requests as tactfully as they could. The only allowance made for the anxious students was to permit them to go to the window from time to time to watch the snow accumulate.

About two o'clock, Principal Kowalski was also looking out his window. He was thinking about his early days "up North" and the good times he and his friends had in the deep snows of his youth, when he noticed movement below outside the main doors of the school.

Third grade students were filing out of those doors. These students were followed by Mr. Hiram Hottle. The students gathered around Mr. Hottle who gave them instruction on how to make a satisfactory snowball and how to throw it with accuracy at the nearby flagpole. Then Mr. Hottle led the youngsters in making a very respectable snowman. It might be noted that Mr. Hottle still didn't smile during the play, but he didn't seem to mind when the students turned his way and tossed snowballs at him.

Upon observing all the illicit activity below, Mr. Kowalski's first words were a frowning, "Oh, my." However, he shortly changed his demeanor to a smiling, but very forceful, "Yes!"

Great Grandfather

Jamie was dreading the first day of school. True, he had a lot of things going for him. He was entering the ninth grade, his first year at Oakmont High. He had worked hard in middle school, earned good grades, and so did not worry *too* much about the schoolwork that he would have to do in the coming year.

And he was looking forward to participating in sports in the coming year. He was a good runner and was turning out for cross country in the Fall and probably for track in the Spring. Also, even though there were few Black youngsters in his part of the county and so there were few of his race at the high school, he got along well with both the boys and girls and was looking forward to seeing his friends from his middle school years.

All in all, he shouldn't be worried about anything. But he was. The problem was his grandfather; wait, he was really his great-grandfather, Earl. Now, he loved Pop Earl, and they were the best of buddies. Pop Earl had taken him fishing, timed him in his running, and had even showed him how to play Pop Earl's old trumpet. They would just sit on the old man's front screened-in porch and talk or not talk as they felt like.

Pop Earl was always interested in what Jamie was doing and even more importantly in what Jamie thought about things. And Jamie liked to listen to his elder's stories of earlier times "up North."

What Jamie was worrying about was that Pop Earl was a custodian at the high school. He was not even the head custodian. He was just a janitor who mopped and dusted and emptied trash cans. And there he would be, every day, while Jamie was in high school. He would be everywhere Jamie turned. And everyone would learn that Pop Earl was his great-grandfather. And what would that do to Jamie's chances of making new friends and fitting in? It surely wouldn't help any.

He didn't dare talk to his mom or dad about this because the whole family thought the world of Pop Earl, who was his mom's grandfather. They put much stock in respecting older people, especially relatives.

He did say something to his buddy, Oscar, who was a year ahead of him in school. Oscar said, "The kids like your great-grandpa, Jamie. They even call him 'Pop Earl'."

Still, Jamie couldn't shake off the fear that some of his classmates would make a big deal of having his great-grandfather as a school custodian.

In the first few weeks of school Jamie found that he didn't run into Pop Earl all that much. Pop Earl showed up only when there was a spill to be cleaned up or rooms to be cleaned at the end of the school day.

Most of his friends did not know that he was related to Pop Earl. And he surely didn't spread it around.

So, life was good. He was running well on the freshman cross country team. His test grades were fine. He liked most of his fellow students. All was well.

Until...one day in the Fall, Patricia, who sat next to him in English, leaned over toward him and whispered, "I heard that the old janitor is your grandfather."

Jamie didn't know what to say, so he made a "sh-h" sound, since they were in the midst of the class period. At the end of class, he took off before Patricia could quiz him further. He was shaking because of his quandary. What should he do? He loved Pop Earl. Pop Earl had always been loyal to him, even when he had made mistakes and other members of the family criticized him.

But this was different. His success in the whole time he was to be in high school depended upon the acceptance by other students. And he knew that some of those students, including Patricia, came from families who might not associate with janitor's relatives. What should he do?

In the next few days, he could tell or he thought he could tell that some of his classmates were looking at him in a different way. Not his close friends and not his fellow cross-country runners, but some, like Patricia, who were sizing him up as a person to be friendly with—or not.

His solution to the dilemma was to avoid as much contact with other people at school as he could manage. It was hard to do because he had to be in classes, in the halls, and on the walkways with them. He began to be in a constant hurry to get someplace else. It was a very difficult time.

A school assembly was coming up. A performing arts center had been added to the high school. It held the entire student body. This was a good thing for him since it was one place where he could be anonymous.

The notice of the program informed the students how lucky they were to have the Versalaires, a legendary jazz orchestra, to perform for them. The Versalaires were in the area for a major concert, and the music director had asked them to make a special appearance at the school.

Jamie was sitting with the rest of the freshmen in the balcony when the curtain went up. The twenty or so members of the band were seated on the brightly lit stage behind large old-style fronts that obscured their music stands. These fronts were painted with a large stylish "V." The members were dressed in white dinner jackets, and the leader, "Tink" Mason, was attired in a tux. Even if they appeared much different from the bands Jamie had seen before, it was still pretty spectacular.

The leader introduced the band by reminding the audience that they were viewing history, in a way. He said that this band played the music that his father and an earlier version of the orchestra had made famous in an earlier time when swing was the style of both the music and dancing. He told a little bit about that era and concluded, "Anyway, don't worry about any lessons now; just enjoy the music."

And Jamie and his schoolmates did enjoy. Pretty soon they were applauding not only at the end of the numbers but also at the end of solo pieces by individual members or groups of band members. What they heard was both "hot" and "cool."

After half a dozen numbers Tink Mason again took the microphone and told the audience that he had just a tiny bit more history to share with them. He said it in such a way as to eke out a large "boo" from the students, with everyone laughing.

When everyone was quiet, he said that the students might be surprised to know that one of the original members of his father's band lived in their community. And they may be even more surprised when they learned that they knew this person, one of the finest performers in any of the bands of the big band era. He then said that person would play the next selection with the band, and in the typical words of introducers everywhere, he said, "Let's give a warm Oakmont High welcome to your own 'Pop Earl'."

Most of the students were surprised to see such a familiar campus figure come to the front of the band, dressed in a white dinner jacket and black formal trousers like the other players. He was smiling and was carrying his old trumpet that Jamie was so familiar with.

If the students were surprised, you might imagine Jamie was shocked to see his great-grandfather all decked out in formal attire and standing before the band that had such a rich musical history.

Then the band began to play in a style that was both from an earlier era and enjoying a modern revival. The students loved it and applauded each time Pop Earl had a solo part. At the end of the piece the students stood and cheered for both Pop and the band.

Tink then said, "We'll have Pop Earl play some more with us later."

The student reaction burst forth with groans and shouts of "More," and "Play more now."

"Wait," Tink said. "There's another part of our performance that we want to introduce now. You know that we feature music from the Swing Era when we give concerts around the country. And you know that a popular dance style of that time was swing. What we'd like to show you now is how that dance was done in its heyday. And to demonstrate swing for you, Pop Earl has agreed to perform with his favorite dance partner, his wife Em."

At this point, as the students cheered, Jamie's Ma Em came out to the front of the stage to stand beside her husband. The band began to play one of their "fast" old numbers and Jamie's great-grandparents kept up with the intricate moves of swing. They danced with the energy of their youth. They "put on a show," and at the end, "brought down the house" with students and faculty standing and applauding and whistling.

As Pop Earl and Ma Em were catching their breath, Tink thanked them for their agreeing to be part of the show and asked them if they had anything to say.

Pop Earl took the microphone and said that it was a delight to play and dance for the students of Oakmont High School; that he and his wife were so fond of the students; and that the only thing that they would like would be for their great-grandson, Jamie, to be with them on the stage.

Well, Jamie just sat there. He didn't know what to do. He was frozen.

Then the students around him began to say, "Get up!" and "Go on down there!" And his friends from other classes looked up from downstairs to try to spot him with the freshman class. Soon there were shouts of "Jamie!" "Jamie!"

And so he got up and went down the stairs and down the aisle and up the steps to the stage. He was not aware of anything as he made that long journey. He was numb. He thought he might have heard students say things like, "Way to go, Jamie," but he couldn't have sworn to that.

When he got to the stage, he still felt as if he were in another world. He barely remembered Tink shaking his hand and greeting him. He did not return to the "real world" until he went up to his great-grandmother and his great-grandfather, and they both enfolded him with hugs.

At any time before that very moment, he would have squirmed, or held back, or run off—but now, he just hugged them back.

Mom

"What does your mother want now?" asked Marsha as Bill Clem came in the front door. Marsha, due to be a grandmother but not looking it, fit, tanned, dark hair, had exasperation in her voice. She knew better, since her mother-in-law was really quite easy to relate to. Still...

"She's not well," replied her husband, not much taller than Marsha, but larger, balding, and among the legion of the UN-neat.

He looked so sad. Marsha wished she hadn't spoken so quickly, so negatively.

"Not a problem right away, but she has had a scare from her last check-up," Bill continued.

"I'm sorry," said Marsha.

"Me too—never thought she might be ill or..."

"Can we do anything?"

"Not really," Bill said, "except she's making her 'final arrangements.'"

"You mean?"

"Yes, memorial service, cemetery, all of it."

"Well," said Marsha, "it's a good idea to have your wishes down so they may be considered."

"She wants help."

"Oh?"

"Yeah, from Pete and me."

"That ought to be a big help," Marsha said, giggling.

"That's what I think, but she's serious."

"But you two haven't gotten along since..."

"Yeah, since we went for a week on Lake Orbichon with Pete and Meenie."

"That's Teenie."

"I know, but Meenie fits."

"Still, you shouldn't have said what you did about her laugh."

"And Pete shouldn't have come back so strong." said Bill.

"Anyway, how are you going to work together?"

"Well, we have our marching orders. We are to work out the memorial service with the minister. Mom even told me the only hymn she wants sung."

"What is it?"

"Amazing Grace."

"Well, it's certainly traditional. You shouldn't have any trouble."

"Yes, but you know Pete. He'll want his way, like always."

"Just meet him halfway. It'll work out," said Marsha.

Just then the phone rang.

"It's for you, Bill."

"Okay." Bill was quiet for a moment. "Oh, it's you... Yeah, she wants us to do this...No, I'm not going to do it myself. You're going to help. You're always trying to get out of...Okay, this evening. Come over...Well, I'm not going there...Okay, library, little meeting room, but you need to keep your big mouth..."

That evening, Bill waited in the library, but there was no sign of Pete. Bill was steamed.

Pete came in, finally—a taller, even bigger, but full-hair version of Bill.

"Twenty minutes late, as usual."

"Very bad traffic."

"Yeah, right. Well, let's get this over with."

"Suits me—sooner I'm out of here the better," said Pete.

They sat across the table from each other, working through what they thought their mother wanted for her service. Surprisingly good progress, until...

"'Amazing Grace,' for the hymn," said Bill.

"What?"

"You heard me."

"But..."

"But what?"

"She told me, 'How Great Thou art,'" said Pete.

"No way she said that."

"You think I'm lying?"

"Wouldn't be the first time," said Bill.

"Let's just call her," said Pete.

"I don't think we should call. Our arguing would worry her," said Bill.

"Yeah," agreed Pete.

"Why do you think she'd give each of us different hymns?" asked Bill.

"If she really did."

"Don't start that again."

"Okay, but it's still strange."

They sat silently for a few minutes, each staring at a different distant corner of the room.

"Maybe she did it on purpose," said Pete, finally.

"Whatever for?" asked Bill.

"She's pretty clever..."

"Always have been..."

"And you're pretty dense."

"You're starting up again," said Bill.

"I think she wanted us to, number one, get together on something we couldn't refuse," said Pete.

"And," light dawning, "have a problem to work out."

"That we'd have to solve."

"Right," said Bill. "I still don't think we should phone her."

"No?" said Pete.

"No, I think we should go see her."

"Yeah, let's go see her."

"Yeah, Bro, let's go see Mom."

The Old College Secret

Cameron Hershey and Aunt Minnie Devers were as different as they could be. Cameron was the new president of the College. He was Cameron P. Hershey, Ph.D. in Physics, known throughout the world for his experiments with light and lasers, and among the top educational administrators of the nation. He was married to Anne, a chemist of reputation, and they had three children who had already left home for college and work.

Aunt Minnie had prepared meals for the past three presidents of the College, going back to the time, some fifty years before, to the time of President Counts, a bachelor. She had finished the ninth grade before going to work in the college cafeteria and transferring from there to the president's home. She had offered to retire when Cameron assumed the leadership position, but he had asked her to stay on for his first year. He was aware that she knew much about who was who and what was what on the campus.

The relationship was a good one from the start as long as Aunt Minnie was allowed to do things in her own way. She would take in the schedule of meals and functions at the president's home, get the Hersheys' ideas as to their preferences, and then complete the preparations as she always had. She had contacts with persons who helped her with the cooking and serving; these persons came to the home as needed to perform the tasks Aunt Minnie assigned them.

She had been and continued to be completely trusted by the occupants of the home; conversations did not stop when she was present and doing her routine. She did not interrupt or comment on what she heard. She was like "the wallpaper on the wall," she said.

The difficulty was that she was slowing down and getting a little forgetful. This inefficiency was trying Anne's patience, for Anne liked the house to run much like a well-managed laboratory. She became more and more critical of Aunt Minnie to Cameron. The children on their visits home even suggested that Aunt Minnie be replaced with someone younger and more active.

Cameron had his hands full in managing the College. Planning for the future, doling limited funds to their best use, and coping with a mixture of strong personalities was a taxing mix of responsibilities. On top of this, he was continually finding issues from the past that provided the need for decisions for which he did not have the necessary background. He relied on some of the "old-timers" on faculty and staff for information, but with the early retirements of many of the college personnel, the information went back only a couple of decades at best.

The latest "blast from the past," as Cameron termed these surprises, had to do with experiments conducted on certain types of explosives during World War II by a chemistry professor at the College, Dr. Harvey Ruhl. His work was the subject of rumor on the campus for many years; whenever someone had suggested that Dr. Ruhl handle an extra task, it was always squelched with the admonition that "You know, he is doing that special work for the defense effort." Some on campus thought that Dr. Ruhl might have played the secret project to a greater degree than necessary.

Well, it turns out there was apparently something to the rumor. This revelation came in the form of a visit by a high-ranking member of the United States Defense Department to Dean Jim Carvellis. Dean Carvellis immediately brought the matter to Cameron. "The DOD representative says that the department is reviewing stockpiles of explosives which might be dangerous because they might eventually explode or somehow harm the environment through decomposing. They have dealt with the large stores and are now going through their records to check on smaller reserves. They found that Dr. Ruhl had reported just after World War II that he was stopping work in his laboratory with the coming of peacetime. In that lab he indicated that some four hundred pounds of explosives developed in his experiments would be stored."

"OK, Dean, then where is that lab?"

"That's just it," replied the Dean. "We don't have the slightest notion."

"Who would know?"

"Anyone who was around in those days is long since gone from the College or is dead."

"Everyone?"

"Well, there are a few retired professors and staff members still in the vicinity."

"Aha," the president uttered, finding some light in the darkness. "Can you have them contacted and invite them to my home on Friday evening to see if they can give a lead on where this load of lethal blasters might be hiding?"

"Sure, that can be done."

That evening when Jim was having dinner with Ellie and their daughter Julie, who was fourteen, he told them about the dilemma. They were as puzzled as Jim and President Hershey.

Ellie said, "I've heard my mother talk about Professor Ruhl, about when he first came to the College, and about the rumors of his work for the war effort."

"Maybe Granny would have heard something about his secret lab," suggested Julie.

Ellie agreed, "I'll ask her about that."

Later that evening Julie told her friend Rick, who lived across the street, about the dilemma. "The laboratory could not have been far from the Science Hall. Mom said that Dr. Ruhl didn't drive," Julie said.

"It wasn't in the Science Hall or someone would have discovered it by this time. How about a location off from one of the tunnels that join the campus buildings?" ventured Rick.

"I've never been in the tunnel that goes in the direction of the Science Hall. Could we take a look at it?"

"Sure," Rick agreed.

"How about if Granny goes with us? She likes to investigate things."

"Okay by me."

Granny showed up at nightfall the next evening, anxious to get started. She had suggested they wait until fewer people were on the campus to check out the tunnel. So, with flashlights in hand, they climbed into Granny's old yellow VW convertible and headed for the College grounds. She parked near the Administration Building and they went into a basement door of that building. They were soon in the old tunnel that linked the various parts of the College.

Then as they passed a door in the basement of the Administration Building, Rick inquired where the door led.

"That's to the old locker room. Years ago, there was a swimming pool in the basement here. It's since been converted to storage, but the old locker room remains."

They proceeded through the tunnel to the Science Building next door. On the way they inspected the tunnel walls for possible entrances to Dr. Ruhl's old lab. In the basement of the Science Building, they spent an hour or more looking into the rooms that went off from the tunnel.

"I give up," said Granny. If there was a secret laboratory down here in Dr. Ruhl's time, it has been closed up or is masterfully disguised. Let's go home."

The two young people agreed, and they all returned to Granny's VW and left the campus.

On Friday evening some twenty of the older retired College personnel met with the president and dean at the President's home. The president's wife, Anne, also attended. An observer would see the delight in renewing former associations, the coolness that still existed from former antagonisms, and the reminiscences of earlier times at the College. Inevitably, talk turned to the stories of the ends to which a former business manager went to preserve the assets of the College. One story that had been oft-repeated was her requiring a sorority to return the remnants of catsup and mustard used in a sorority outing and supplied by the College cafeteria.

Aunt Minnie, as usual, served refreshments with the help of her assistant, Lorna. Aunt Minnie could be heard chuckling at the stories she overheard because she had known all the subjects of the anecdotes. She was, also as usual, not terribly steady on her feet and nearly spilled the drinks and other refreshments several times. Anne, like Queen Victoria, was not amused at the lack of coordination in the old woman and whispered her displeasure to her president husband on two occasions. He, of course, noticed but ignored the serving miscues.

The president then spelled out the reason for their get-together. Most had known Dr. Ruhl by sight, but only one or two had even had a conversation with him. They all had heard of his reputed contributions to World War II explosive technology. None had any idea of where he had conducted his experimentation. After an hour or so of discussion the president thanked them for coming, and the participants thanked him and Anne for their hospitality. On the way out most said a special good-bye to Aunt Minnie. This attention to her did not "sit well" with Anne; Anne was still fuming.

After the guests had gone, Anne had retired, and the president and the dean were sharing a final drink, Aunt

Minnie, as she was clearing up, came by them and said, "I think I may know something."

"What's that, Aunt Minnie?" asked the president.

"Well, it was during the time President Counts was in office that Dr. Ruhl died. It was shortly after the end of the war. President Counts and I sometimes would talk about the College, its past and its future. He would tell me things that were on his mind—he knew that I would never repeat them.

"One day he said to me, 'Minnie'—I wasn't Aunt Minnie then—'you are one of the younger persons here and I want to share something with you. You have no doubt heard the rumors about the work of Dr. Ruhl during the war. Everything you have heard is true, including his having a secret lab on campus. U. S. Government agents called on me the other day and ordered us to seal up the laboratory since it is no longer needed. We are not to destroy any of Dr. Ruhl's notes or records because they may be needed in case of a future war when his experiments with explosives may become useful again.'"

"President Counts said that he was the only one here who knows where the lab was. Since he was getting on in years and may not be around at the time the lab might need to be re-entered again, he wanted me to be able to tell the future College leaders the location of the lab.

"He said I should keep in my memory two little bits of kids' sayings that would be the key to finding the lab. They didn't make sense to me then and don't make any sense now."

"What were they, Aunt Minnie?" asked Jim Carvellis.

"One was rub-a-dub-dub, and the other was one for the money."

"You're right, they don't make any sense," noted the president.

"But they must have been meant to mean something, at least forty-some years ago," countered the dean.

The president thanked Aunt Minnie for her puzzling contribution. After sitting for a while longer, the dean and Aunt Minnie and the president parted company promising to think further on what the two little lines meant.

The next evening Jim Carvellis was sitting with Julie and her mother and Rick on Ellie's big front porch. He told of the strange clues about the location of the lab and the need to find it and the inability of the old-timers to give any idea of its whereabouts.

After talking about various possibilities, Rick ventured, "Maybe we should run this by Granny. She knew many of the people on campus in those earlier days. Maybe those lines that Aunt Minnie quoted would make some sense to Granny."

Even though it was getting late Julie and Rick biked over to Granny's two-story with the big front porch house and found Granny finishing making jam. Several pints and smaller jars were lined up on the kitchen table. Granny offered them ice cream and cake and they didn't refuse.

Julie began telling the story of the laboratory and the storehouse of explosives. Granny had, of course, heard of this through her network of friends in the college community. She had not heard of Aunt Minnie's revelation of the three men in a tub and one for the money. Julie asked if she thought Aunt Minnie were a reliable person when it came to remembering and telling the truth.

"Well, I've known her for many years," Granny replied. "I recall a number of times when the College was going through hard times, and people were questioning the choice of presidents and deans and the wisdom of decisions. At these times Minnie has had more influence in keeping up the welfare of the College and community than people give her credit for. If she says she was told those foolish things by President Counts, then I believe her."

"But she's just a maid," countered Rick.

"Yes, those are her duties, but many people in positions like hers have a great effect on what goes on around them because of the force of their personality and their common sense."

"What do you think the little sayings mean, Granny?" asked Julie.

"Let's look at the first one," answered Granny. "Rub-a-dub-dub. What's the next line?"

"Three men in a tub," said Rick. "Maybe that's where this is leading, but it makes no more sense than the first line."

"Maybe it means more than it sounds like at first," suggested Julie. "Maybe tub means something else, such as a lake."

"Or a swimming pool!" ventured Granny. "Dr. Ruhl allowed himself one pastime—swimming in the old college pool. And he had two old swimming buddies—an art professor, Bill Evans, and the Dean of the College in those days, Clem Shickle."

"So, maybe the lines point to the pool," said Rick. "Or at least the area around the pool. But what about one for the money?"

"That doesn't make any sense to me at this time," said Granny. "Maybe if we looked where the old pool was, we can tell more about the money."

"Let's go now," voiced Rick.

"It may be best to wait until tomorrow, since it's getting so late. How about if I pick you up at ten in the morning?"

"We'll be ready," promised Julie.

As they headed for the College the next day, Granny asked, "Have you gotten any further with one for the money?"

"No. We've struck out on that," admitted Rick.

After parking and entering the old pool area in the basement of the Administration building they began to inspect the storage area that had been created from the old pool and the adjoining rooms and closets. Rick even looked closely at the solid walls for some sign of an entry way. Nothing was happening. No clue as to the meaning of the sayings that had been voiced by Aunt Minnie. They went farther afield down the tunnels that led from the Ad Building to the adjoining college halls, but they kept coming back to the pool area.

"Where did they dress for swimming?" asked Julie.

"Oh, there were small men's and women's locker rooms. In fact, we were in them a while ago," replied Granny. "Remember the two storage rooms with the lockers along the wall?"

"Let's look there again," suggested Rick. "They at least had something to do with the pool—or the tub."

They entered the storage area that Granny said was the old men's changing room and looked on the floor and ceiling and the walls.

"How about the lockers?" said Julie.

"Yeah, right," agreed Rick, "but we'll have to move some of these boxes."

After some effort they could see the old row of lockers.

"Some of them still have names on them. I wonder if the three men's names are here," Granny asked.

"Yep, here is the name 'Ruhl' on this one," said Rick. "And it's not locked."

He opened the locker. It appeared to be empty. He opened the lockers on either side. They were all empty and at first looked the same.

"Here's something," said Julie. She was looking into Professor Ruhl's locker, just above the door. A metal container had been attached to the top with small screws. "It looks as if it were there to hold something—yes, maybe his wallet and his pocket change. That's it—One for the money!"

"Sure," agreed Granny. "Is there anything in it?"

"No, it's empty."

"But we're so close to what Aunt Minnie said," noted Rick. "How about if we remove the money holder from the top of the locker?"

Rick went to Granny's car and got a screwdriver. When he returned, he began removing the metal screws. It took some effort, because they had been in the locker for many years and had rusted. When he removed the last screw, he took down the money receptacle.

"Something dropped," said Granny.

"It's a card," said Julie. She picked up the yellowed card from the floor. "It's a map!"

All three pored over the card. "Here's the Science Building and the tunnel that leads to it," noted Granny. "And here's the Administration Building and the pool."

"And there's the 'Laboratory,'" said Rick.

They went out of the locker room and followed the directions on the card toward the Science Building.

"Here's where it's supposed to be," said Granny.

"Yes, but the door is marked 'Electric Panel—Danger—Keep Out," said Rick.

"What better way to limit the number of people who would look behind this door," suggested Granny. "And Professor Ruhl would not arouse suspicion by entering, because anyone would assume his visit would have to do with his regular teaching needs."

Julie tried the door; it was locked.

Rick twisted the knob and pulled on the door. He could not open it either.

Granny suggested, "We've come about as far as we can; we shouldn't break into whatever is behind the door."

Rick said, "Let's get the dean to have a look with us."

The others agreed to this, and they headed for the Administration Building and the Office of the Dean. They found that Jim Carvellis was in and waited until he had finished meeting with an assistant dean. They told him of their suspicions about the location of the lab of Dr. Ruhl, and of their progress through the locker room to the electric equipment cabinet.

Jim congratulated them on their success so far but was skeptical about the door to which their investigation had led them. "How could a lab be in such a place?" he asked them.

Granny responded with their thought that Dr. Ruhl would not have aroused suspicion by entering that door, since his own "regular" lab would have had electric service that might have needed adjustment from time to time. She then asked Jim to get them past that door.

With an "Oh, very well," Jim had a maintenance person called to meet with them in front of the mysterious door. The door was easily opened and revealed what the door label indicated—an electric panel. The panel had a multitude of switches and connections that obviously controlled the Science Hall classrooms and its laboratories and perhaps even the needs of the Administration Building. The switches were numbered and corresponded to a drawing posted on the board.

"Not much to go on here," commented Rick as he inspected the board closely. "It's just what the sign on the door says it should be."

"But the message given to Aunt Minnie has been right on target so far," countered Julie. "It would be almost strange if this were the end of the road."

"Here's where we are on Minnie's recollections, Jim," advised Granny. "We've been through the silly rub-a-dub-dub and one for the money. So far so good, but what now?"

"Right, what next?" asked Julie. "How about two for the show," she giggled.

"And three to make ready," contributed Jim, with a laugh.

"And four to go," added Rick, adding to the mirth of all at that point.

"Well, how about it?" questioned Granny, suddenly getting serious. "We have a two here on this switchboard, and a three, and a four, and lots of other numbers indicating the circuits these switches control."

"And here below is another set of switches, labeled one through five," noted Julie. "I wonder what they are connected with."

"Let's give them a try—in fact, let's give them a try in the order two, three, four," said Rick, with only a little enthusiasm.

Jim reached down to the number two handle and flipped it. Nothing happened. He then flipped number three. No results. Looking at the others and getting go-ahead nods, he flipped number four. Nothing happened immediately—and then they heard a movement to their left. A panel from floor to ceiling on the left wall of the electrical cabinet began to move and opened widely enough to permit a person to go through. All was dark behind the opening.

"Anybody have a flashlight?" asked Granny.

"We may not need one," responded Rick. "Whoever would put a sliding door in the wall would probably also put in lights." He reached on the wall behind the door and found an old-fashioned light switch that had to be turned. He turned it and a narrow hallway lit up on the other side of the door.

"Let's see where it goes," ventured Jim.

With Jim in the lead the group followed the narrow hall as it wove its way from the electric cabinet. Jim said that from the direction they were going they must be under the hillside in back of the Science Building. In short order they reached another doorway. Jim opened the door cautiously and felt the wall for the light switch. He turned on the lights.

What they saw was a laboratory, well-equipped for the World War II era. There was none of the computer and compact instrumentation that they would expect in the modern scientific workplace. But it was evident that the work there was performed by a person with habits of care and orderliness. They walked around the room pointing to and discussing its various contents.

"Show me the explosives," called out Rick after they had checked out the room.

"Through that door, I'll bet," responded Julie.

Rick opened the door on the opposite wall from the way they had entered and switched on the light. "Here it is, all right."

It was a storeroom somewhat larger than the laboratory. Boxes of various sizes were stacked around the room. Granny said, "I'll bet this could blow us to kingdom come."

"Yes," Jim agreed, "and probably the raw materials for making the explosives are also stored here. What I am wondering is how Dr. Ruhl got the chemicals in and the end products out of here."

"Through this door," answered Julie, who had gone forward through the stacks of boxes. She pulled a lever on the door and gave it a pull. "It's stuck," she said.

Rick came over to help and together they got the old door to open. Everyone went through to the outside. They found themselves under the loading dock at the rear of the Science Building. Rick said, "It would be pretty awkward to move supplies in and out of the lab since you have to stoop down to get under the dock."

"Yes," Jim said, "but the door to the lab is invisible from the back of the building."

"And," added Granny, "it would not be unusual to see someone loading or unloading materials by the loading dock."

"We need to report to President Hershey what we have found here," said Dean Carvellis. "Will you all go with me?"

"We'd like to do that," answered Julie for the rest of the group.

"How about if we get Aunt Minnie to go with us?" suggested Rick.

"That's a good idea," agreed Granny. "She had the key to the place of the old college lab."

They went to Jim's office where he called Aunt Minnie and arranged for Campus Security to go to pick her up. He did not tell her why he was asking her to come to the president's office. He, Granny, Julie, and Rick went across the hall to the president's office and told President Hershey of their discovery. President Cameron was pleased at the success of their sleuthing and surprised that Aunt Minnie had known all these years the words that would lead to finding the laboratory.

Aunt Minnie was obviously puzzled at being called to the president's office and by the gathering she found there.

After greeting her President Hershey asked her how long she had been at the College.

"Just over fifty years."

"And you've known nearly everyone who has attended or worked at the College in that time?"

"Yes, most everyone."

President Hershey continued, "Since I have been here, I have learned how important you have been during your years here. But you have outdone yourself today." At the same time, he was thinking that he wished his wife Anne were here to see how wrong she had been in her judgment of Aunt Minnie's worth to the College. And then he went on to tell Aunt Minnie about how rub-a-dub-dub and one for the money had led to discovery of the secret lab and the storehouse of dangerous explosives.

Minnie was glad to be sitting when she learned of the solving of the old college secret. What she said was, "I am so relieved that those explosives have been found; but I'm even more relieved to know why I was asked to come here to the president's office. I didn't know what to think when Campus Security picked me up and took me for a ride."

At this she began to chuckle and was joined by all her friends in the room.

You're on Fire

"It's the latest thing," said Jim Allen, President of the Extreme National Bank, to his friend, Joe Garland, President of Right-Away Hardware, as they sat at the weekly service club meeting. They were waiting to hear the introduction of Irv "Dip" Grasso, district roads superintendent, who would be making his annual report on the main highway coming into Arch, Pennsylvania, along with his annual excuses as to why the "dip" caused by coal mine subsidence, hadn't been remedied.

"Yeah, I heard about it. I guess that was part of the price for getting Extreme to buy your Miners and Hunters Bank," said Joe.

"Oh, no, Extreme paid for the phone system as well as some other upgrades to the bank. But I guess you saw that when Right-Away took over Garland "We-Have-It Hardware?"

"Yes, and I made a pile...," began Joe.

"Not so loud about what those outsiders pay for take-overs," said Jim. "There are ears around."

"You're right about that," said Joe.

"But, like I was telling you about these phones—you call the bank and you get an operator..."

"A real person?" said Joe.

"No, no—that's the beauty of it. Don't have to pay for someone to sit there all day and take calls."

"H-m-m," reacted Joe.

"You get a list of options—directions to the bank, deposits, savings, or loans," said Jim.

"That's all?" asked Joe.

"That's all we do. But, if one line is tied up, the call goes to an Extreme answerer somewhere else. So all calls get answered; the bank employees aren't interrupted from their work."

"Sounds great," said Joe. "I can't tell you how many times a day I am up on the ladder getting some part or tool from the shelves and the phone rings, and Dad is busy or can't hear it, and I have to climb down, and then I miss the call, and then...." said Joe.

"I know, I know," said Jim. "Oh, old Dip is ready to speak—here we go again."

"Or here we don't go again—seeing as how bad the roads are."

"Right on," said Jim.

They talked every day on the phone—Minerva "Minnie" Hester and Sophia "Sophie" Palotta. Had for years.

They lived on the "Hill" overlooking Arch. Even though their homes were not far apart, steep inclines in their part of town made visiting difficult.

They always had something to say about church, members of their church ladies' group, the town young people, local drunks, and dust from the Mill that had them cleaning all the time.

"What are you doing?" asked Sophie.

"Just sitting here on the front porch snapping beans, and trying to get a breath of air," said Minnie.

"I know, if it doesn't rain soon and cool us off..."

"We do need rain—these beans are pitiful," said Minnie.

"Did you see what Laura Sanders' daughter Sue wore to church Sunday? That skirt was..." said Sophie.

"I thought it was a disgrace. I don't know why Laura lets that girl get away with..."

"And those Perkins boys," said Sophie.

"They are out of control—but, what do you expect with their father, Curt Perkins," said Minnie.

"He was a bad one from the start. He used to..." said Sophie.

"I think I see something down in the town—at the bank. It looks like smoke coming from the roof in the middle of the bank," said Minnie.

"Better call the Fire Department—the bank people might not know about the smoke," said Sophie.

"I'll hang up and do it right now."

Minnie called Rachel, the Arch town clerk. "Rachel, this is Minnie Hester, up on the Hill. Sound the alarm and get the boys out to the bank. I see smoke coming from the roof."

"It'll take a while, Minnie. Brush fire down by the part, and they're all there putting it out..."

"I wonder if they know about the smoke at the bank," said Rachel.

"You'd better call them and let them know," said Minnie.

"Good Idea."

Rachel called the bank number.

"You have reached the Extreme National Bank office in Arch, Pennsylvania. Listen to the following options as they have changed recently. If you are calling about directions to the bank, touch 1; for deposits, touch 2; for savings, touch 3; for loans touch 4; and for all other calls, touch 5.

Minnie pushed 1. "Hello, there's smoke..."

"If you are coming north on route 537, the bank..."

"I'm calling to tell you..."

"Is on the left ..."

"What? Do you know that smoke...is someone there?"

"Side of Main...."

"Oh, my," Minnie hung up and redialed.

"You have reached..."

Minnie listened to the preamble and pressed 2.

"This is Lottie Rettingole, in deposits. We at Extreme Bank are extreme in our desire to help customers. Unfortunately, I am away from my desk at present, and..." "Good grief," said Minnie and called again.

"You have reached...." Finally, Minnie hears "Touch 3."

The response is "This is Bill Schultz in savings. We're here to help you to be like the squirrels here at Extreme, storing up for the future. Sorry to miss your call, but..."

Minnie looked off into space. "I don't believe this. She hung up, redialed, and listened to the preliminaries before pushing 4.

"This is Connie Kulp in loans. We have an Extreme source of funds for your every need. I am on vacation this week. Please stay on the line for my assistant, Roger—what is your last name, Roger?—oh, yes, Roger Hudkins."

"This is Roger HUDKINS, assistant loan officer. Please leave your name..."

Minnie slammed the phone down, let out with a word that would never gain the approval of the ladies' society at church, and, with a sigh, redialed.

After the introductory instructions she hit, really hit, 5, for "all other calls."

"Hello, this is Sam."

"What?"

"This is Sam. How can I help you?"

"Are you real?" asks Minnie.

"I think so, Madam. What may I do for you?"

"Are you sure you are real?"

"Yes, I'm sure, Madam. Are you real also?"

"Of course, I'm real, and I'm calling because there is smoke coming from the roof of the bank, and..."

"What bank, Madam?"

"Why the bank in Arch, on Route 537..."

"Where is Arch, Madam?"

"In Pennsylvania."

"In the States?"

"Of course, in the United States of America," shouted Minnie.

"I'm afraid I can't help you with that, Madam."

"Why can't you?" said Minnie.

"Because I'm not in, where did you say, Pennsylvania?"

Yes, Arch...well, where in the...where are you?"

"I'm in Rangoon, Madam."

Minnie very slowly replaced the receiver and began to rock, going back to snapping her beans.

That Old Gang

Enrico Padua was never the first to arrive. Pershing "Push" Jackson was there already. He was the boss on the Outside Labor Gang—the group of workers who moved what needed to be moved and lifted what needed to be lifted in and around the paper mill. They handled fifty- and one hundred-pound-bags of chemicals, moved materials on skids, unloaded boxcars of bags, lumber, and powders in bulk, and kept the manufacturing process supplied with whatever was needed.

"Push" wasn't very pushy. He managed by saying "Today we gotta . . ." He gave directions with his eyes closed as if concentrating but at the same time centering everyone's attention on what he was ordering to be done. The eyes-closed deal also had the effect of stifling complaints from the loudest of the loud-mouths on the gang, of which there were usually a couple. The membership of the gang was ever-changing because someone was always getting into trouble or just not showing up.

Push didn't have to worry about Arnold McGregor's not showing up. Arnold was always early. The gang assembled at seven in the morning, and Arnold had been wandering about the Mill for an hour. He did that every day—no one knew why. He visited friends in various worksites, almost as if he were in charge and making rounds. Arnold had been with Push for more years than anyone knew. Both were approaching retirement age. Arnold was loyal to Push, and even though a hard worker, Arnold had earned some of the easier routine jobs that had to be performed.

Enrico had been with the gang a long time, too. In fact, he was known throughout the Mill and even the town. Not by his formal name, but by "Ricky Paddy." Young people in the town would make some point and attribute the statement to "Ricky Paddy." He had come to America in his teens and still maintained the accent of his native Italy. This accent plus his always-smiling face to the world gave him a uniqueness that caused everyone to know who he was even though much sport was made of him in this period just after the Second World War.

Ricky Paddy's vehicle was the electric skid-mover. The good news, for him, was that he did not place the bags on the skid nor did he have to help take them off. He just had to go to the place where the bags were already on the skid and move the forks of his electric cart under the skid and take it to the place where the chemicals would be used. He had been doing this for years and was well acquainted with the location and contents of the various bagged materials.

He kept hidden the fact that he could not read. He could read Italian well enough, thanks to a classical high school education in his native land before he came to this country. He just had never mastered English. Here's how he survived all these years in meeting the demands of the job that required fetching a variety of goods, making sure that they were the right goods for the job intended: He went by colors and symbols on the bags, drums, and other containers, which, luckily for him, were placed in the same locations for him to retrieve.

No one knew that he could not read. In order to keep this inability from becoming known he had through the years adopted various devices to obtain help in determining the description of new materials. Sometimes it was his eyes that were giving him trouble, sometimes he just wanted someone to "check on him" as he started to move a new type of container, and sometimes he asked a helper to run his skid mover when they were headed for a new line of bags.

He could not afford to let it be known about his lack of ability to read English. One reason was pride. He had been well-schooled in Italian and French in the old country. Having people learn that he had trouble with English was beneath his image of his own intelligence.

If Push or the other bosses knew he could not read English, they might take him off this job with the electric hand cart. He was past the point of being able to lift the heavy materials every day—he just couldn't do it anymore.

He might even lose his job in the Mill entirely. This would be a disaster, because so much of the family's well-being was riding on his shoulders. His daughter Gina was in her first year of medical school, and that was terribly expensive. His son Nicholas was in his last year of high school and planning on going to college. This would require a long-term expense.

He also did not want to let down his wife, Grace. They had met when he first came over to the States. He was a fine soccer player, the best in the region on the semi-pro teams sponsored by the various companies in the area. This soccer ability had landed him his Mill job in the first place. Grace and he had dated in spite of Grace's family's disapproval of her seeing a young man who had little to offer in the way of financial security.

Enrico and Grace persisted, however, got married and had succeeded in their marriage and raising their children. It had not been easy to make ends meet—the ends would not have met if it hadn't been for Grace's job inspecting Mill paper that was about to be shipped to customers.

Maybe not quite as important as these reasons for concern about Enrico's English reading ability was the worry that Hark Black would find out about it. Hark was the "Ugly American," even in America. He had a foul temper and a foul mouth. Even to the mildest of people he was the eternal bully. If Hark had a talent, it was a questionable one—that of stringing together offensive words. Practice makes perfect?

Then Hark would light into Arnold with matters of substance, such as Arnold's arriving at the Mill early (true) and not working hard enough (not true). Five to ten minutes of ridicule every working morning.

And no one did anything about it. Hark was tough, and so were his three brothers. It was a given that no one bothered the Black boys.

Occasionally, he went after Enrico with the usual string of bad language. And on and on. This was not something Enrico could afford to face up to with Hark, because of differences in size and Enrico's accent that would automatically lead to more mocking. So, Enrico smiled his grin and waited it out, hoping the wait would be short.

Two new guys joined the Gang in the late spring. Herschel Rohr came from back in the country where he had a small farm. He was nearly ax-handle broad at the shoulders, extremely strong from the hard farm work, but was shy and out of his element with the diverse crew. At first, he was let alone by Hark while Hark slowly gained a feel for whether Hersch would react by punishing Hark for his mouthiness. Hersch wasn't made that way—he had been used to peaceful people in peaceful surroundings. Hark, finding this out, started slowly his name-calling and insults toward Hersch, usually including a reference to "dumb farmer" and the fact that he was such a loser that he had to get a job at the Mill to make a go of it.

The other new guy was a summer employee, Ludd Darnell. College students could get jobs at the Mill and earn "good money" for tuition and other expenses for the coming school year. They filled in while the regular employees were on vacation and accomplished extra projects around the plant. Ludd was somewhat like Hersch. He was a large, strong young man who excelled in several sports. He was also quiet. The difference was that he was used to the give-and-take of town living.

The Gang had a half hour off for lunch. At this time if the weather was pleasant, they sat together outside with their "lunch buckets" and ate and rested. Even during these pleasant moments Hark could not leave well enough alone. He ran his mouth. He was not a braggart—his remarks almost always involved someone else directly, particularly the someone else that was closest by.

And he had certain times for everyone—Arnold and Enrico in the morning and now Hersch at noon. Hersch took his lunchbreak almost grudgingly. One could see that he would almost rather keep working, as he would have if he were working in one of his fields. The work was hard in the Mill but nothing like he was used to. Another reason Hersch could have done without the lunchbreak was Hark's harassment. Hersch did not know how to cope with it. When Hark swore at him, Hersch couldn't because of his upbringing, reply in kind. In fact, Hersch was so baffled by the vitriolic verbiage that he mostly didn't reply at all.

This lack of response allowed Hark to go further with very bad words. He was under the impression that the Gang was with him in his mistreatment of Hersch. It was possibly this impression that permitted Hark to begin the next stage. He would come up behind Hersch and flip his ear with a finger. He would toss water or ice on Hersch. He would flip pieces of food at his victim.

Hersch was probably of a nonresistant faith in addition to his personal bent. It showed in that in spite of his obvious strength, he endured, never replying or reacting in any physical way to Hark.

Hark was a smoker as were most of the guys on the Gang. He liked his Pall Malls, those long unfiltered cigarettes that took some fortitude to use. Naturally, after lunch the smokers had their cigarettes. About the only non-smokers were Hersch and Ludd, the temporary employee.

One day after an unusually quiet lunchtime Hark was having his smoke and was eyeing Hersch all the while. You might say it was too quiet. When the break was about over, he got up and walked by Hersch. As he did so he flipped the still-lit butt of his cigarette down the bib of Hersch's overalls, snickered, and walked on.

Hersch was not known for quick movement, but this time he did move fast. He came to his feet with a roar and began shaking the live cigarette end down through and out the leg of the overalls. He was red from effort and distress, but he just stood there, looking over at Hark.

Hark had likely assumed that his act would have been met with laughter and approval by the Gang—but this didn't happen. The gang remained quiet. They just sat there.

All of them except Ludd. Ludd slowly got to his feet and walked over to Hersch.

"Are you okay?"

"Yeah, fine."

Ludd then turned to Hark. "Hark, I've watched you since I have been here. You have used your mouth in a way that goes beyond what any of these guys should have to endure. You have especially picked on those who would be least likely to fight back. And now you have gone a big step further in harassing Hersch, who you know won't come back at you.

"Since I'm only here for a couple more weeks, I've got the least to lose by telling you this—I want you to keep your mouth shut and your hands off all of us. The work is hard enough without having your antics to be bothered with."

Hark stood there for a minute before saying anything. He surely wasn't used to anyone taking him to task. Finally, he said, "You sure you know what you're doing?"

"I'm sure."

Hark took a couple of steps toward Ludd. Ludd matched Harks steps. They were about ten feet apart. It was Hark's move. And he didn't! He just reverted to mouth, "You'd better watch yourself, college-boy. I'm not going to do anything here, but you asked for it, and you're going to get it."

They stood there looking at each other for another thirty seconds when Push said, "We've got a lot of skids to unload this afternoon—let's get back at it."

The Gang got up and went back to work.

Just before quitting time the Gang gathered in their shed and waited for the Mill whistle to blow. It was very quiet. No one seemed to want to talk.

When the whistle blew, they left the shed. While walking through the Mill yard, Enrico came up beside Ludd. Enrico didn't say anything about the noontime occurrence; what he did say was, "Think you could make it to supper tomorrow night at our house?"

Ludd was taken aback. He and Enrico had barely exchanged greetings while they had worked together. This was not unusual because neither man talked very much.

He was stopped for a moment by the invitation. Then he felt badly on the effect his hesitation might have on Enrico. He then quickly blurted, "Sure, where do you live?"

"We're on Oak Road—you know, on the way to Onego. How about six?"

"I'll be there."

As he drove along Oak Road, he was still pondering the invitation. Why? Then he began watching for Enrico's home. Oak Road wound over and around the small hills that dominated the landscape. From the house number Enrico evidently lived on the upper side of the road. The homes were poor to modest in the stretch approaching where Enrico lived. Enrico's was modest. Well-maintained. Shrubs neatly trimmed. Flowers in window-boxes and in the yard. He parked and went to the door.

His knock was answered by a woman of Enrico's age who was striking in appearance. She had light hair and blue eyes and appeared to be about the same height as Enrico. "We're glad you could come to visit and have supper with us this evening, Ludd."

"I was pleased to be asked. Thanks for having me."

"Enrico is watering in the back. Come on through and we'll join him."

As Ludd came through the door he was stunned. The living room was beautiful. Very nice furniture, beautiful wallpaper, impressive paintings. These features were set off by a luxurious tile floor that seemed to stretch through the entire house. It was a shock because of the contrast with the inconspicuous outside appearance of the house.

They walked through a similarly well-furnished dining room and kitchen to the back door. And the back yard of the house was another stunner. It was filled with flowering shrubs and plants. Stone pathways meandered through the lot. A fountain with angels provided a soothing trickling brook accompaniment. None of this was evident from the road because of the plantings on each side of the yard.

Enrico was turning off the hose and straightening up when he heard them come out the door. "Buona sera, Ludd!" he called. He came over to shake Ludd's hand. Grace excused herself after inquiring whether Ludd would have something to drink.

"Your home and back yard are magnificent," Ludd said with still a trace of surprise. He still didn't feel comfortable with calling his host Enrico and he surely wouldn't use the nickname that was used on the job, often derogatorily.

"Grace and I have worked hard to make this a pleasant place for our family."

"It's a great success. Everything is special, but the tile is so unique. How did that come about?"

As Grace rejoined them with a glass of wine for all, Enrico replied, "My family has been engaged in laying tile for generations. We were the leading craftsmen in Padua. Whenever church or government or private needs for fine tile arose, we met them. But when I came here, tile was not a big thing, so I had to get work—any work—especially after I met Grace."

They talked about the various plants in the yard, about Ludd's family, about the young people in the Padua family. Then they went into the beautiful dining room and had an excellent dinner. Grace had acquired a flair for good Italian cooking. They had veal scaloppini, spaghetti, a salad with home-made Italian dressing, and, just to have some variation, German chocolate cake for dessert.

After dinner they went once more to the large back porch of the house. Two questions were on Ludd's mind. One was, why was he here? The other was, why was such a gorgeously appointed home and rear yard masked from the public by the ordinary nature of the front of the house? Yet he hesitated to ask the second question for fear of offending his hosts, and the first question for no reason that he could fathom. He needn't have worried, at least about the first question, because Grace suggested that Enrico tell Ludd what was on his mind.

"You did a brave thing during our lunchtime, Ludd," began Enrico. "It's been a long time coming. Hark has been giving grief to us on the Gang ever since he joined it. Earlier he worked in the Mill on the paper machines, but he caused trouble on his shift, with his big mouth and his threats and sometimes a fight. He was also unreliable. So the bosses did what they usually did with guys who didn't fit in on the production end of things—they transferred him to Push."

"Why didn't they just get rid of him?" Ludd asked.

"This Mill has been here a long time, and it has become a lot like family. Generations have worked here. Seldom do they fire someone unless there is no other way out. So you get some pretty undesirable people placed here and there around the Mill. Push, for all the complaining about him, has a way of making some of these people useful."

"Tell Ludd what else you wanted to say to him," nudged Grace.

"Hark has made life difficult for me for a long time. He and a few others before him are largely responsible for the mocking of my speech and the tricks that have made my working days harder than they should have been."

"And about the house," Grace urged Enrico further.

"You see, Ludd, you get placed into a certain level in the community. My level is based upon my lack of American education and my accent in speaking. That in turn has opened only a low-level job to me. People like me, and, unfortunately, Grace and the children, are supposed to keep in our place. This means restrictions on how we talk to others who are higher up, how we act, and where we live."

Grace interrupted, "See, Ludd, we've abided by the rules in most ways. That makes it easier for Enrico at work and for our family in town. But in a couple of ways, we have refused to hold back on what we wanted. The first was helping our youngsters achieve, so that they would not have any restrictions on their future lives. And in that, fortunately, they have been successful and we have much hope for them."

"And another way you have avoided compromise is your home," suggested Ludd.

"Right," answered Enrico. "If a person in my position were to try to buy a home in the better parts of town, we would likely be stopped by deed restrictions in the area. Then, if we found a nice neighborhood without legal restrictions and bought a quality home there, I would be accused of living above my place in life. I and my family would pay a price for that in the form of worse treatment on and off the job."

"So, you've made up for it by having a pleasant home. . . ."

"Yes," Grace interrupted, "by having a modest facade and the best we could achieve with the inside and rear yard that was not in view for all to see. You'd be surprised at the number of people who have come up with this solution of having both acceptable appearance and comfort in their homes."

After thanking his hosts Ludd left that evening with a greater understanding about how his town worked. He thought he had been in an experience somewhat like a prospector who had come upon a rich vein of ore that others had passed by. The difference was that he had been invited to the site of the ore rather than having to mine for it.

Off the Shoulder

This is the rule—you sign up for half-hour blocks for computer time in the library. You try to start on the half-hour; someone will want the machine just as soon as your time is up.

A librarian on certain days offers the valuable service of introducing patrons to the Internet. This shuts down the use of certain computers for an hour while the instruction goes on. When you sign up for the block of time following the lesson, you try to start on the half-hour; someone will want the machine just as your time is up.

The trouble is, that sometimes the instruction period runs longer than an hour.

They were all retirees—the students and the users of this new device that was "simplifying" all their lives. The instructees were an attentive lot but had some difficulty grasping the rapid pace of the information and were imposs..., less adept at the hands-on feature of the teaching program. Their comments, groans, heads-back-looking-through-the-bottom-bifocal-halves squints at the instructor, and the mutterings to their keyboard neighbors would furnish the stuff for an extended piece, but are not the subject here.

The time for the lesson to be over was ten-thirty. Much had been presented and some of it learned. Satisfaction nearly rivalled frustration. Watches were being watched by the students.

Time was being monitored also by the next users who had duly signed up.

Bordeaux sat at Number 4. He was of average size, dark hair, equally patient/impatient, bright, with limited clue. He was sneaking looks at the clock on the wall far to his left.

He was ready to quit because he had absorbed enough for today and also because someone was directly in back of him, breathing heavily.

Mrs. Dancer was anxious to get to the computer to send an email to her son. She needed to remind him who was paying his tuition and his board and room and his auxiliary expenses while at the same time he was getting more than his fair share of D's. She was a little heavy, a little gray, not too tall, and had a slight breathing problem.

Bordeaux was experiencing her breathing—right on the back of his neck. He could have counted the respirations that began at the stroke of ten-thirty and did not let up. He felt he could not turn around; he felt he could not say anything to her; he felt he couldn't wait for class to end.

Mercifully, it ended. At ten-forty-two. This was twelve precious minutes into Mrs. Dancer's time. She was hyper-anxious.

Reticence was not in her nature. She had held off as long as she could, possibly out of deference to the instructor. At the exact second the class was ended, she said, "I'm waiting."

This was fairly obvious to Bordeaux. He still said nothing. The dilemma was that he still had to get the screen of his computer back to the text that was on it when he started. Because of his trying to speed up this process, his "all thumbs" default took over.

"I'm still waiting."

He almost had it. Just one more step. Whoops—missed it that time. Try again.

"You need to get off this computer so someone else can have their time on it."

He was getting somewhat steamed by this time. In spite of this heated condition, he managed to complete the required maneuver, all was as it should be on the screen.

At that second, Mrs. Dancer pulled on the back of his felt-back, secretarial-cum-computer chair, and whooom—he rolled back approximately two feet from the desk. As he came back his left knee hit the desk leg with a noticeable sound.

He was unhurt, but he kept his lack of injury to himself. Instead he grabbed his knee. And looked up—into Mrs. Dancer's eyes, which still retained much fury, little caring. She still wanted him OUT of there.

"I believe my knee is bruised."

"Oh, good grief."

"No, there really is something wrong. I feel a lump on the side," he said, rubbing his knee.

"I can't believe that you could have done any damage to yourself with that little movement."

"You may not choose to believe it, but...."

"Well, I don't."

"I don't think I can make it outside."

"You can't walk?"

"I can't put my full weight on it."

"How about if you rolled on your chair."

"That won't work. Will you help me?"

"Me?"

"Well, I could walk fine when I came in here."

"What do you want me to do?"

"Just come around here on my left side and pull me up."

She rolled her eyes and humpfed, but did as he asked. He extended up his left arm and pulled her shoulder down.

He put his arm around her shoulder. "Now, can you lift?"

She jerked up, grunting, and, staggering, lifted him to an upright position.

They started toward the library door. Halfway there, he said, "Oh, I forgot my papers and pen. They're on the computer desk."

She looked around. "It's too far to drag you all the way back there now."

"Well, just...just help me over to the circulation desk and let me lean on it."

They got over to the desk and she deposited him there. She returned to the computer area and retrieved his possessions. She returned, offering the materials to him.

"Can you just carry them along with you?" he said, again placing his arm around her shoulder.

"Let's get on with it."

They stumbled toward the door of the library. Somehow his papers became dislodged and spread over the entryway. People entering and leaving saw the debris and stood back. She maneuvered him over to the door frame and left him leaning there. She stooped and picked up the scattered papers. She wadded them up under her arm and returned to him. They assumed their former positions of helper and assisted and haltingly made their way through the door.

Outside at last. Breathing heavily, she asked, "Now, where is that car of yours?"

"Oh, my gosh, I just remembered—I rode my bike today."

"You what?"

Recovering, she said, "Can someone pick you up?"

"No one's at home."

It's the first time since his cartoon-watching days that he actually heard someone give out with a "Gr-r-r."

Back in control: "Very well, I'll get my car."

"First, I'm not sure I locked my bike."

She turns to the side and looks up, into the distance. "Where is it?"

"Over there."

They haltingly hobbled/stumbled over to the bike rack, some distance away.

"Oh, how about that. It was locked all the time."

Mrs. Dancer was perspiring profusely by this time. "Let's go."

"You know, I think I can manage to get home on my bike. My knee feels as if it is improving."

Mrs. Dancer: "If you think you can manage...."

Bordeaux quickly unlocked his bike, headed it toward the roadway, placed his left foot on the pedal, paced with his right until he picked up speed, threw his right foot over the seat onto the other pedal, and raced off.

As he zoomed along, a half block or so away, he shouted back over his shoulder, "Yes, I'm much better now."

The Shoe Exchange

My friend Jim and I were hired to be printer's devils when we were just past sixteen. Jim was more of the traditional printer's assistant in that he learned to set type, put type away in the oft-quoted upper and lower cases, and run the platen presses that were the workhorses of job printing.

Of course, we both cleaned the printing presses—we could never get the ink totally from our hands. We put away spacing that went between and around the type, swept, washed windows, and helped the printers.

I acquired an extra job of selling advertisements for the weekly newspaper, the *Herald*. In this role I visited weekly—the publishers might have said weakly—the merchants in our town. From them I sought sales of ads for their special types of merchandise and services. There were pharmacies, clothing and furniture stores, candy makers, cleaners, florists, groceries, and theaters.

Looking back, I see that it was a privileged peek at the serious conduct of business—necessary for the merchant's livelihood and important in rendering good services. I was permitted to venture behind the large two-way mirror to the inner sanctum of the druggist—always called "Doctor" then. I saw flower arrangements made and holiday candy prepared.

Shopkeepers took an interest in me and asked about my schoolwork and plans for the future. Sometimes they sold me merchandise at a reduced rate. I recall a lucky purchase of a nifty sport coat. A pharmacist gave me boxes of candy for my mother at Christmastime.

I looked forward to my weekly forays around town, anticipating success in selling and open, welcoming doors.

Except for one business. My visit there was like none of the others. It was a shoe repair shop, the busiest in town. In those days shoes were fixed—new heels and soles—not discarded when showing signs of wear. And, I'd have to say, when the guys went there for a Saturday evening shine, we, including me, were at least tolerantly received.

But it was much different when I showed up each Monday to sell my ads.

In the first place, the two brothers, working amid the various machinery, belts, and brushes, never once looked up from their work when I was there. One would be tacking on soles, another would be polishing on some whirling brush mechanism.

Secondly, they talked only with each other, never to me.

"Here he comes again."

"Yeah, what a bother. Seems like he was just here."

Me: "Hope you are both doing well today."

No reply.

Me: "I'm here again from the *Herald*. Hope you can see your way clear to continue your ad with us."

Their ad was the smallest possible—one column inch; that is, a column wide and one inch deep. In an era when, as they say, "a dollar went a long way," forking out money in advertising, even for a small ad, did not seem as necessary as it might today. So, most of the small-town businesses could not be coaxed at all into weekly advertising.

"It's not doing us any good."

"Money down a rat-hole."

Me: "Well, it's important for you to keep your name before the public, so they'll think of you when they need shoe repair."

"I wish he wouldn't come in here every week."

"It's just trouble for us."

Me: "You've got the biggest shoe repair business in town. Advertising can help you keep the business successful."

"We're too busy to have to put up with this."

"I wish he'd just leave."

Me (My weekly weakly plea): "How about, then, one more week. This ad is good for your business."

"Oh, what the heck. How about one more week?"

"Okay, but this is the last. It doesn't do us a bit of good."

Me: "You're doing the right thing. This will help your business."

"Yeah, yeah."

"Yeah, yeah."

And so, with some sense of victory I would patiently stand by while one of the brothers went to the cash register and handed me the forty-two cents required to continue their relationship with our paper for another week.

The Street Taken

"If They Could See Me Now," he sang softly as he pushed his broom along the gutter. Not far away was his large black plastic bag for the litter that dotted the curbside. Occasionally he went beyond his municipally owned jurisdiction to pick up on adjoining private property, a conscientious remnant of his days of high pay, perks, and personal satisfaction.

Yeah, he thought, maybe some of his old co-workers would like to see him now: see how far he had fallen from their, and, earlier, his view of success; see him with bib overalls and plaid shirt and baseball cap; see him older and frailer; and see him getting what he deserved for setting high standards on the job hard to attain—or be let go.

Now his "standards" applied only to dust, dirt, refuse, and remains of what others had disposed of in his bailiwick—curbside to sidewalk surrounding fifteen city blocks daily, Monday through Friday.

The company's failing had come as a shock. Savings had been used up for his late wife's long illness—and some inopportune investments. Easy go that had not followed easy come—he had worked awfully hard, awfully long, and without many intervals invested in himself.

Oh, well, push that broom, tote that black bag, block by block.

"Hello, Irv." It was Henry, sitting in his usual place on the park bench.

"Hi, Henry."

Funny, he used to be Mr. Drummond, or at least Irving. Now, it's Irv.

"What say, Irv." This came from Shelly, selling her hot dogs from her portable grill in front of the courthouse.

"Doing fine, Shelly."

On down the block, push, pull, pick up.

"Hey, Irv," called a little boy.

"Jimmy! You can't call him by his first name," this from an obvious grandfather.

"Well, you said that it's Irv."

"I know, but it's Mr...I don't know your last name, Irv."

"Drummond."

"He's Mr. Drummond, Jimmy."

"Hey, Mr. Drummond."

"Hey, Jimmy."

And so on for blocks, at his own pace, in the warm sunshine of the spring day, warm enough for a slight sweat.

At just about noon, he criss-crossed his route and stopped, as usual, at Shelly's hot dog stand.

"You okay, Shell?" he asked when there was a break between customers.

She replied, "Lots better, Irv."

Shelly had recently been divorced and had recounted her ups and downs to Irv over the past months.

Irv sat on the nearby bench, had his "two, with everything," and greeted and was greeted by the "usuals" at the stand.

When he got up, Shelly called out to him, "Okay for bowling tonight?"

"Ready, big-time," he called back as he moved on.

And, if you looked closely to see his smile, and, if you listened very carefully to catch his bright lilt, you would hear him softly singing, "If They Could See Me Now..."

The Shagnastys

Why did Elvira Shagnasty split with Henry Purloin? It was the talk of Stultzburg when scions of the two most prominent families on Quality Row in town, Rothchylde Bouvelard, announced that they were living separately. Stultzburgers had watched the storybook romance between the two youngsters unfold, contrary to the wishes of old Sy Shagnasty and Lotta Purloin, the leaders of their respective clans of suspected wrongdoers who maintained pure-as-the-driven-snow innocence.

Do not tell the United States Government, the Massachusetts State Government, and the Local Government law enforcement and prosecutorial agencies that the city homes, country homes, foreign country homes of the two families were purchased with honest money. Nervous breakdowns, sanitoria stays, and hives were the lot of members of these agencies as they detected and brought charges over the years of most of the Twentieth Century against successive generations of Shagnasty and Purloin. These heroic public servants would get *so close,* and then, poof-poof, the cases fell apart. In fact, the lead attorney in the firm that represented the two families, Winston C. Wrinkle, was known in the community as "Winnie the Poof."

This is the stage upon which Elvira and Henry stepped. No way of coming together, of course. But something happened. The fact that the private high schools in the most verdant part of New Hampshire to which Elvira and Henry had been sent were situated only seven miles apart was credited, or blamed, for bringing the two seats of power together as a cozy conglomerate. No way would these two, as middle schoolers in equally plush and private institutions in the most verdant part of Vermont, have anything to do with each other.

But in high school, more properly called prep school, or finishing school, He and She were brought together when their expensive sporty vehicles bent fenders one night on a curve in the road between Prep and Finishing. It was late, too late for them to have been out, and somehow, in their plotting to keep their tardiness from blighting further their far-from-impeccable records at Prep and Finishing, they gained a union that continued, even as old Sy and Lotta, back home, steamed.

The two young people managed to do enough work to graduate from their respective ivy-clad institutions of higher learning, which were also, oddly enough, just seven miles apart. Their internships, for which they were very well paid, were completed in the highest offices of the tallest building in Manhattan, and they, of course, continued to see each other on seaside weekends.

Knowing that they could never pull off a hometown, all-out, Stultzburg wedding, the couple joined their troth in a private ceremony in Vermont. They spent weeks working on a means of informing "The Families" of their knot-tying. They sought both expert and friendly advice. They tried trial balloons (what ifs, could it ever happens, how abouts) when they separately visited their Quality Row ancestral houses. The trial balloons were, uniformly, busts.

The best they could do, they figured, was to give up on matriarchal and patriarchal approval—that wasn't going to happen—and to combat their elders' ire by joining the assets of their generous trust funds, from which the elders had failed to provide a means of disintegration in the event that a Shagnasty and a Purloin would get together.

One would have thought that Stultzburg was the last place that they would settle down, but they came back home, bought ten acres on a hilltop just outside city limits, walled an acre or so around the somewhat fort-like home they built, and engaged with the community as much as "what they had done to their families" would permit.

The impetus behind their return was that both Elvira and Henry had been raised under the influence of their family traditions, both traditions, oddly enough, the same—that of theft. Oh, not your tiny grabbing of dollars or the occasional pieces of jewelry. Not your taking a percentage here and a percentage there. The Quality Row Shagnasty and Purloin estates were the homes of big-time, multinational, taking from national governments, multi-country plutocrats, and Dow-listed corporations. Who would have thunk it? Certainly not anyone simply viewing the serene and sedate homes that dominated Stultzburg's finest addresses.

The newly-weds both sensed the heritage of their homes and, while completing those internships and coping with their early jobs on the highest floors in Manhattan, had begun their accumulation of knowledge and early profit. They sharpened their skills but succeeded mainly by picking off individuals who had been the truly talented persons who had worked for their families in the accumulation of wealth, ill-gotten, but lots of it.

So Elvira and Henry flourished even though they were somewhat crimped in their community by the presence of families who refused to "get over it." (An early clue had been Elvira's dropping in conversation that she was getting tired of "that funny name," Purloin, of her husband and was thinking about going back to the use of her maiden name.) Therefore, it was the shock of the century when Henry left the home and moved his things to the penthouse of the Stultzburger, the hotel that dominated that center of the city. The townspeople learned of all this, but what they couldn't figure out was—why? What had happened?

It came about, as often happens, over a family matter. The couple had had two children, Percy and Portia, ideal one-boy, one-girl family. And all was serene until Percy got caught stealing M&M's from the comfort food section of the top drawer of the uber-nervous fifth grade teacher, Constance Bloat. Connie went crazy, accused Percy of many things, including stalking, and elevated the matter to a level matching the Quality Row status of Percy's grandparents, Lotta and Sy. These same grandparents, who somehow, while refusing to associate with each other, had from afar watched and watched over Percy and Portia as they grew up in the community. And, Lotta said, "I never much liked that Bloat family, anyway."

The upshot was that, after the "Top Drawer Episode" that had rocked Stultzburg had been quelled by the generous payment to Constance, more than enough for her two and a half years in the plush "rest home" in the Catskills, something happened to Henry. He decided to go straight.

"What?" his grandfather Sy was reported to have blurted.

"What?" Granma Lotta let go, spilling her usual tomato juice with something added.

It was inconceivable to the oldsters that this could have occurred to a Purloin and they could only hope against hope that it, first, was reversed, and second, did not spread. As to the first, it did not reverse—Henry stayed with his decision, based upon some teachings he had received in a trip to visit a Seer who lived on an isolated Carpathian mountaintop. Seer Roger said, "Don't steal," and Henry said, "Wow! Pretty profound." Henry came home with a change of life announcement, and that tore it.

"Get out," said Elvira.

What Elvira didn't know, which would sort of brought about a reunion if she had known, was that Henry had been stealing from Elvira's trust fund to the point that he no longer needed, nor, following Seer Roger's admonition, desired to take more from anyone else, whether family or stranger. Happy Henry atop the Stultzburger, really unhappy Elvira atop their home hill outside the city.

It was at this time that the only semblance of sympathy took hold of Grandpa Sy and Grandma Lotta. Unbeknownst to each other, they would adopt ruses to "send their cars" for Percy and Portia whenever the children were away from their parents attending private tutoring, camps, and the like. For some reason the children actually liked the old folks, and for some reason also they each proved to be immune from Grandpa and Granny's incessant efforts to teach them the virtues of serious crime.

"No matter," said Sy. "They're still sweet kids." And he and Lotta, because of their enchantment with the youngsters, began having their respective "people" meet "for the sake of the young ones" to coordinate what could be done for their grandchildren's comfort and upbringing, especially in light of the devastating developments between Elvira and Henry.

These "Assignations of My People and Your People" became personal between the grandparents one day when their really long limousines were parked nearby the school so that the children could be observed during recess. Somehow these big cars came too close to each other so that their bumpers locked, and during the time of uncoupling, the oldsters came together in the shade of a nearby paw-paw tree. Chairs were brought, as well as lemonade, and over this libation, they spoke.

Talk of the town. Talk of the town. Related by chauffeurs, lemonade purveyors, bumper mechanics, and ogling school custodians. Even without the usual embellishment, it was big. Biggest Stultzburg news since the unfortunate incident in 1973 when Constance Bloat's father, Constantine—well, let's not dig that one up again.

What was not known, however, was that this was not the first meeting between Lotta and Sy. Oh, no, they had been meeting regularly for the last thirty years. Ever since Lotta somehow thought that Sy had managed to gain control, by nefarious means, of an entire very profitable corporate subsidiary she had had her eye on for take-over. Lotta's heart swelled, and, in her temporary delirium, she passed a note to Sy through their People, stating her sincere admiration for his dastardly tactics.

Sy was smitten and they began seeing each other on the Riviera and various lavish locales. So, after the bumper interlocking, they associated in the open, with hand-holding and other appropriate demonstrations of affection. They joined their extensive operations to form the major American syndicate for skullduggery, which was still able to avoid serious law enforcement restraint.

The children visited. Elvira visited. The elders drew the line, however, at Henry. They refused to admit him back into the fold.

However, Henry ended up happy, as did the rest of the combined Shagnasty-Purloin clans. He also became a Seer, on a significant Italian promontory in the lofty Dolomites, having shaken from his sandals the dust of Stultzburg and all that of his past history there.

Troxell's Gifts

Otto left work early. Summer, and it was hot. Mercifully, the newspaper and printing plant were not as busy as in the fall and winter. The summers were more relaxed. So, let's go fishing. He climbed into his old Chev pickup. He started her and pulled out. AC was being contrary, so he turned the windows down, using the grip pliers as a crank. "Nothing wrong with this machine," he told any and all detractors of his equipment. At least, nothing that stopped all his friends who borrowed the truck for moving whatever they needed to be hauled.

Soon he had left town on the Old Sawmill Road, shady and cool, and hanging on the side of the mountain. The curves made for fun driving. He stopped at the Old Spring and filled up his Mason jar full of the coldest water, coming right out of the side of the mountain.

Going on, he came to the dirt-road turn-off that bumped up along-side Pike's Run. He followed the Run for a quarter-mile and pulled off in a space just wide enough to park. Just beyond some thick bushes was a pool in the stream that he knew about (and hoped others did not). He had discovered the cold water supported small but fun-to-catch native trout.

He opened his tackle box, baited his hook, and let the line go downstream with the current. Then, in the tradition of the best of the avid fishermen, he sat down, leaned back against a handy tree, pulled his hat down in front, and rested his eyes.

It was not hard to take—the quietly rushing stream, the gentle breeze coming down the mountain, the scent of wildflowers along the water, and the kindness of the little forest creatures who went about their hunting and gathering ever so softly.

Sleep came soon. Sleep of the contented. Sleep of the escapee from noise, movement, complications with machinery, and deadlines.

But the sleep must have been shallow because something soon caused him to stir. It wasn't exactly a noise. Everything was pretty much as it had been when he sat down. But it was—something.

He opened his eyes and looked at his fishing pole. It was secure, and no sign of a fish. Something caused him to look to his left, down-hill, and standing a couple of yards away was a man—a short man.

He could tell that the man was short because, standing a little downhill from Otto, he pretty much looked Otto directly in the eyes. The man was perfectly formed, with a head that suited the size of his body. The best way to describe him in short order would be so say, "Did you ever see the picture of a Leprechaun, dressed in green, with a small pipe in his mouth, and a scrunched-up hat on his head? Well, that's what this guy looked like."

"Where'd you come from?" Otto asked.

"Here and there."

"Who are you?"

"Troxell."

"Troxell who?"

"Just Troxell."

"What do you want, Troxell."

Troxell replied, "Just a little of your time, Otto."

"You know my name?"

"Yes."

"How?"

"I have my ways."

"What do you want with me?" asked Otto.

"I want to give you something."

Otto adopted his best suspicious look. "You do?"

"Yes."

"Why?"

"I have my reasons."

"What do you wish to give me?"

"Two wishes."

"Why would you show up here and present me with two wishes?"

"I have my reasons."

"And you can grant wishes?"

"You betcha."

"Any kind of wishes?"

"Yes."

"Why just two wishes?"

"What do you want from me? How long has it been since anyone even granted you one wish?"

Otto admitted, "Never."

"Okay, then."

"Okay."

"What's your first wish?" asked Troxell.

Otto thought intensely for several minutes. "I wish we did more business."

"Why?"

"So we could pay better wages, hire more help, and our present people wouldn't have to work such long hours."

"Not just more money for yourself?"

"What would I do with more money? I decided early in life that my only job would be to run this newspaper and do printing for our town. Extra personal funds would go to waste on me. I wouldn't know what to do with it."

"Okay," said Troxell, "done."

"What do you mean, 'done'?"

"It's been done. Your business is on a sound basis—just wait and see when you get back."

Just then Otto's phone chimed.

"Or, before you get back."

Otto answered his call. It was his assistant, Cloris. He listened intently, turning and looking at Troxell. "Well, I'll be," he said."

Otto ended his call. "We just got the big contract we've been hoping for." He thought a minute. "Are you sure you didn't know about the success of our bid?"

"What's your second wish? By the way, are you a little more of a believer now?"

"Maybe," Otto replied and looked off into space, thinking. Then he looked off into space in the other direction. Then back the first direction.

"Take your time," said Troxell quietly.

"I think I would like to have our town water system upgraded. It has high levels of bad stuff, and it's harmful for all of us, especially the very young and the senior citizens."

"You sure about this one?"

"I'm sure."

"Done."

Otto cupped his hand upon his ear and listened. "What? No call?"

"Oh, my, I would hate to think that you would have to wait until you got back to town to find out that the water system will be completely reconstructed to the level of the state of the art," groused Troxell. "Oh, my, I would hate to think that you would be so inconvenienced..."

"Okay, okay," Otto interrupted, putting his head down. "I get it. Be humble. Be grateful for my good fortune. Be thankful."

And when he looked up, Troxell was gone.

A dream. A hallucination? But the call had been real. Hadn't it? Better get back. So he got his gear together, went to the truck, and almost wrecked going down the old road, given the daze he found himself in.

At the office he got the news that the Federal-state grant for the water system had been awarded to the town—another community further up on the list had been disqualified.

Whoa, big news. But not really new news—since he'd already been told. What a day.

Otto went through the following week mumbling a little, staring into space a little, and thinking a lot. How could this—these—things happen? To him? To the town?

Maybe a little fishing was called for.

So—same fishing hole, same old handy tree to lean back on, but this time no sleeping, or even drowsiness.

Soon, Otto heard a branch move to his side, and there stood Benefactor Troxell.

Otto started to get up but was told just to remain seated.

And so they chatted a little, Otto profusely expressing his sincere gratitude and Troxell in his best "Aw, shucks, it was nothing" mode. It was a very jolly, festive occasion all around, with Troxell apparently enjoying himself as much as Otto.

In the midst of all this Troxell turned quickly to Otto. "What would you like for yourself?"

"What do you mean?"

"It's not a mind-crushing question—Is there something you would like for yourself?"

"Just for me?"

"You're beginning to grasp the concept, Otto. Something for you."

"Why in the world would you offer to do something for me?"

"I offered you two wishes, and except for raising a ridiculous question as to why there were only two and not three wishes, you immediately opted for things that would help others and not just yourself. I've been passing out favors to people for a long time, and I can't remember anyone who didn't immediately seek a personal gift."

"Well, I guess...."

"No, I mean it—you think of others; that's pretty nice. So, now it's time for number three."

"What do you mean, number three?" asked Otto.

"Something else will come your way, and, because you haven't asked for anything for yourself, this will be strictly for you," said Troxell.

"What could it be?" asked Otto to himself, looking up into the beautiful blue sky. He then turned back to Troxell; only, Troxell had disappeared...again.

"I shouldn't be surprised," said Otto, again to himself. "That guy doesn't like to stick around for idle chatter."

So Otto fished a while, caught a couple pretty native trout, and let them go.

Greatly contented he left his favorite getaway spot and proceeded through the woods. Looking ahead, he saw something bright red. Going a little farther, he saw what it was. It was a bright and shiny new truck, sitting on the spot where his old wreck had been just a short time before.

And on the steering wheel is a note, "Otto—Happy travels." And it was signed simply, "T".

Mountain Tales

Yoo-Hoo and the Sandman

Ula Stemp lived on the Mountain. The Stemps had always lived there, and she was born a Stemp and married a Stemp—Isaac, the adopted son of her Uncle Nimrod and Aunt Sarah. Their joining in wedlock was almost a miracle in that her father and Nimrod had had a falling out over a timber contract—each claiming to be entitled to a greater share of the proceeds for their efforts—when they were young men.

The feuding didn't end with Ula's dad and uncle; each generation seemed to figure out a way to have a controversy, usually, but not always, among the men. The latest was between her grandsons, Eric and Dodge, who both liked Elvira Dove. When Dodge won Elvira's hand, it had not set at all well with Eric, and they were at odds ever since.

But when Ula's—Granny Stemp—birthday arrived, no grandchild dared be missing, because, well, you know Granny. Don't make her come after you.

After Isaac's passing, Granny had for years lived alone in a small cabin high on the mountain, well above the homeplace now occupied by her daughter Cora and her husband Arn, the parents of brothers Eric and Dodge. The family had run water and electric lines up to her place, and they also made sure she had plenty of firewood. They took her to the store and to church and wherever she wanted to go.

Where she really wanted to go, ever since Dodge told her about it, was the party at the County Seat for anyone over ninety. She was ninety-four—and a half—or would be by August 15, the date of the party. This year she was sure to be the oldest and receive the corsage and the framed certificate of special recognition. She was sure because Rebecca Dove had died in December at age one hundred. The road was clear.

The family was excited, too, and were making preparations to attend. Her daughter Cora said, "Good thing it's not hunting season—no way the boys would go then." The teenagers in the family had gotten a little tired of the talk and anticipation but were always up for a trip to town. So was old cousin Claude who had saved his new pair of bib overalls for such an occasion, possibly, at age eighty-eight, thinking ahead to his own day in the sun.

Well sir, what do you think happened that could possibly upset Granny's Big Day? "What's he doing back?" asked Granny when she heard that Sanford Dove had returned from out west with his big car and was fixing up the old, abandoned Dove homestead.

The problem was that Granny and Sanford had been classmates through eighth grade in the Davis Settlement School. So it stood to reason that they were about the same age. So, it could be, just could be, that Old Sanford was older than Granny, and that meant . . . trouble on the Mountain.

If Granny was older, however, no problem. So when Sanford came by to see her one day she, very coyly, using all her wiles, moved the conversation to birthdays, even though she knew there was a danger that such talk could give Sanford the idea of entering the contest that Granny believed was hers to win. Turns out they had the same birthday. Dilemma upon dilemma. Granny did not know her time of birth. No one who would have known was still alive. And Granny had spent all her wiles. So she did not learn Sanford's time of birth, assuming he knew himself. And—she couldn't prove his time of birth was later than hers.

"Oh, why," she said, "did he have to come back now."

Anyway, even though she wasn't going to back out now, it sure took the luster off the anticipation of the Big Day when it finally arrived.

Eric picked up Granny and led the procession of cars to the County Seat. They arrived in plenty of time for the big sit-down dinner at noon. Seeing friends and enjoying the fried chicken with all the fixin's almost overcame the cloud of anxiousness that the Stemps all felt, especially Granny.

At one-thirty after dinner remnants were cleared, the festivities began with thanks to those who made the arrangements and prepared the food. Gary Smith, a sunny, chubby young man, then announced the main event. As usual he began with an arbitrary older age, seventy-five, and proceeded to go up the age scale, until he reached ninety. With more drama he dragged out ninety-one—two men and a woman; ninety-two—a man and a woman; ninety-three—a woman; ninety-four—Granny and Sanford raised their hands. The announcer went on: ninety-five, ninety-six, anyone over ninety-six? No one spoke up.

"Well," he said, "it's going to be between the Ula Stemp and Sanford Dove. Unfortunately, the committee rules call for only one winner." After learning the birthdays were the same, Gary continued, "Now, Ula, when is your time of birth?"

"I don't know," said Ula.

"Oka-a-ay," said Gary. "How about you, Sanford?"

"One-oh-five."

"Well, now, what to do?" said Gary. "I'll have to meet with the committee for a decision."

Granny was on pins and needles, the more so because Sanford, or "The Sandman" as the kids used to call him, was so calm and collected. He was over there just laughing and joking with some of the guys. Well, thought Granny, we'll just see . . . .

After a while Gary came back and announced that the committee couldn't decide between the two aged folks. The committee determined that they would ask Ula and Sanford to suggest a way out of the dilemma.

Someone in the crowd yelled out, "Why don't you shoot it out?" Much laughter.

Someone else said, "Not a bad idea—maybe a target shoot."

"Yeah, yeah," chanted the crowd, who were hunters or at least familiar with firearms, including most of the women.

"Okay," said Gary, "if the parties agree. What about it, Ula and Sanford?"

"Fine by me," said Granny. "Up to the Sandman."

"Me, too," said Sanford. "Let Yoo-Hoo, referring to Ula's childhood name, decide what weapon."

"How about the .22?" she said.

"Okay," said Sanford.

Gary, looking around for committee for approval, finally said, "That's the way we'll do it then."

Granny's family knew that she kept a .22 and was a pretty fair shot at groundhogs and the like. They knew that she was having a hard time to keep from smiling, especially knowing that Sanford had lived in the city all these years and likely had not recently been using guns.

As the contest proceeded Granny went on to win on the last shot at the target the committee had set up. In the end she was a reasonably gracious winner, more than can be said of her family, who drove around the County on the way home, blaring horns and demonstrating for their "Granny."

It was not long after the contest that Sanford paid Granny a visit and soon they were an "item" in the hill community. And, at the age of ninety-five, Yoo-Hoo and the Sandman became joined in same-age marital bliss. The ceremony took place on the top of Granny's hill with lots of family and friends as witnesses.

Not long after, Granny's nine-year-old great-grandaughter, whom the family called "Nosy Nancy," was looking through Sanford's bureau drawer. She had found a little box and brought it to Sanford who was sitting outside in a lawn chair.

"What's this?" Nancy asked.

"Oh, just an old medal."

"It says 'Expert' and 'Rifle'—hey, that means . . . ."

"Nancy, you might want to just put that back in the drawer."

"Okay, but . . . ."

"And, Honey—it's best you not show that to your Granny."

Henderson MD

Henderson, as locals describe it, an "itty-bitty" town near Accident in the mountains of the very western part of the Free State of Maryland. And Hendersonites are free—mind their own business, have a gun or two, might even know where there's a still.

It's "still" in a couple other ways in and around town. Quiet, the way they like it, except during deer season when the Baltimore and D.C. wannabe Meshach Brownings (more about him later) come in large numbers to engage in their version of hunting.

And it's "still" in one more way—still like it was eighty years ago when Virgil Oates was born. Virgil worked for the State Road all his working life, doing mowing and maintenance in the summer and plowing the prodigious snow of Western Maryland in the winter. Never missed work even when it was ice cold on icy roads. Now he does some odd jobs, especially with the summer residents of Deep Creek Lake and the winter visitors who come to ski nearby. Virgil has more than enough income to keep him in rifle ammunition, shotgun shells, chewing tobacco, and provisions for himself and Sadie.

Sadie was from a mining family in the area. They went to school together, she a class ahead, very smart, but at the same time "sensible," very important to area natives. She and Virgil lived frugally, freezer-full, and warm in their older but weather-proofed home which sat on a dozen acres overlooking but not looking down upon the town of Henderson MD.

Virgil had been a hunter all his life. Not so much for fishing, except for the first day of trout season when he hit some of the cold-water streams for the "natives." But in hunting he was both practical and in his dreams. On the practical side, he kept track of game, visiting his favorite spots before the hunting season began to determine whether there was plenty of "sign" left by the deer, bear, and turkeys to go back when it was legal. In spite of his love of his freedom he was a believer in following the rules and was even very critical of those hunters who did such improper practices as spotlighting deer, hunting out of season, and using over-the-top weapons.

On his dreaming side, Virgil had read and reread Meshach Browning's *My Forty-Four Years as a Hunter.* Browning, a revered figure in Western Maryland, had hunted the "glades" of the high country there in the first half of the nineteenth century. According to his book, in what was wilderness then Browning with his dogs hunted, trailed, and, on occasion, tackled big game to a heroic degree of effectiveness, while enduring the hardships of cold and living largely out of doors. For instance, Browning tells of waking up a hibernating bear with a candle on the end of a stick. Another time, he went into close combat, using his knife on a bear that was getting the best of his dogs.

As if this weren't enough to cause Virgil to stare at length into his fireplace on the cold winter nights, he was given a diary by a cousin of his. The diary was by another mountain hunter, Isaac Dove, and this diary recorded in the early 1900's the Dove's actual day-to-day hunting exploits as they occurred. This, in Virgil's mind, gave them great veracity and so he reread many of the passages.

In addition to hunting, it appeared that Dove liked to explore, following the old animal trails to see where they led. And they led to places unrecorded on even the maps of the day—waterfalls, caves, glens, meadows, and where certain trees, shrubs, and flowers were hidden from view.

Virgil took in all this information and inspiration from Old Meshach and from Isaac Dove and stretched his already well-established hunting habits to greater limits, to include exploring—and what better place than those parts of the high glades and adjoining mountains that had not been taken over by outsiders. So Sadie got used to his going off for several days at a time in both summer and winter. She put up with the tales of his combat with the elements, the cold, and those "contrary" game animals he sought, but she did say that she did not like the "wash day" that included his hunting outfit after his return from up to a week on the hunt.

Not that his ventures were totally unprofitable. He came back with game, of course, that provided them with food, but he also occasionally led groups of hunters to where they might find deer and wild turkeys—no guarantees, of course. He now and then went in search of ginseng—the activity was called locally "sangin'"—which in some parts of the world brought exorbitant prices.

But what he dearly loved was to mark a place in Browning's book or Dove's diary and make sure his next trip out into the woods included the spot described. With difficulty he found a two-hundred-foot waterfall that gushed with such force one could walk from side to side underneath with only minimum effects of the spray. He found the cave in which he believed Meshach had wakened the sleeping bear. He came upon the "salt lick" that enticed game day and night from their usual grazing and hunting territories.

But the spot that had somehow intrigued Isaac Dove the most was one that seemed to Virgil to be one of the most common. It was a clearing in the woods, and not a large one at that, maybe, Dove said, about a hundred fifty feet across. Virgil passed over the description the first time he read it, but he kept coming back to it and the obvious attention Dove had given it. Dove had kept visiting the place and seemed to have done an unusual amount of pondering about that spot.

Another odd thing about it was that Dove never included directions of getting to the place. So, in spite of reservations, Virgil found himself more and more intent on taking a look at this clearing. He sought every clue as to its whereabouts—where Dove had been just before and after as described in the diary, the general areas that Dove seemed to favor, where he went when he was out alone since he seemed not to want to share this location. It was not easy. It seemed as if Dove wanted to keep the place to himself, at least until he had satisfied himself about what caused this treeless sanctuary.

Whenever Virgil was hunting, he gave more attention to scouting the area for Dove's plot. He followed his instincts to go into various areas of the glades. Then he decided to mark grids on an area map and search methodically. This approach paid off finally, with the discovery of the very site that Dove had described in his diary. Even though Virgil did not show it outwardly very much, he was elated.

His elation was short-lived, however, because he was as intrigued by the spot as Dove had been and wanted to know what had kept that plot simply a clearing and not a continuation of the surrounding forest. In pursuit of the answer to this question he read the old land records at the courthouse. He consulted geologists, biologists, soil specialists, and other specialists, giving them samples of soil, hand-drawn maps of the plot and surroundings, and his best efforts to describe what he saw there. He still, for some reason, refrained from actually taking anyone there.

It was when he visited the historical section of the Public Library that he finally found something that just might lead to an answer to his quest that had been going on now for several years. He found some letters that had been written by one of the early settlers of the section of the county in which his mystery clearing was located. In one of the letters Virgil read that there was a "healing witch" in that neighborhood, and that the writer had taken a horse to that person to be cured of some problem with the horse's leg. Virgil of course knew of the tales of the work of witches, and that in these tales, witches were usually connected with evil spirits, curses, and very spooky dealings with normal people.

In spite of his initial doubt, he broadened his research into the realm of witches. He did not tell anyone of this quest for fear that they would think he was losing his reason. And, most of his study of witches confirmed the usual mythology about witches. As they say in storytelling, "He was about to give up, when...," he came upon a reference that some persons in the old days were known to be witches. These individuals, even though they might be called "witches," were considered by early settlers as a helping hand in the rendering of medical treatment. This was in areas where there were no regular physicians and when medical practice was in its early development. The healing witches, often of German heritage, relied upon natural remedies, but beyond that, the recital of Scripture while touching the affected areas of their patients. These healers treated animals as well. An example of the treatment of a horse with a lame leg would be the witch's rubbing the leg in the direction of the ground, while reciting the German equivalent of "In the name of the Father, the Son, and the Holy Ghost."*

This was interesting to Virgil, a student in the history of his county, but it hardly advanced a solution to the problem of the singular clearing that existed among a forest of trees. Until—he opened his investigation to actually inviting the various specialists onto his mystery plot. The soil officer for the area was most helpful in showing that some building had been located on the plot and that it had sometime in the past burned to the ground. Remnants of that structure were to be found upon close observation. He further found that the writer of the letters that had gotten him started on his "witch hunt" had lived nearby, at least by early settler standards.

He had explored many theories of the clearing that had been offered by friends and specialists in various scientific pursuits. They included unique geological conditions below ground, soil composition, and a variance in shade from the nearby mountain. He had come across some explanations that stretched believability such as the landing site of aliens or that the plot was a part of a pattern that gave directions for alien landings.

While Virgil thought that some of the ideas had some reasonableness to them, he tended to reject them in favor of his own conclusion. While he was a rather traditional, maybe even "hard-headed" (on occasion, according to Sadie) individual, he was drawn to the fact that the home of the healing witch had been located, to the best he could determine, upon that very clearing that had taken hold of his attention for so long. He had studied and even experienced some of the extreme hardship of early setters of that high country. He could only imagine what some trusted "medical" person would have meant to these families. He just believed, at least wanted to believe, that that plot of the healing witch's land, was in some way preserved as a tribute to the life-preserving force it represented.

**Colleagues of the author have described to him their research into the activities of healing "witches" who were relied upon for early medical treatment on the Virginia-West Virginia border of the Shenandoah Valley.*

Boy

Boy came to town, walking on the railroad tracks from the west. That was the direction from which few from the town had ever ventured.

Although the cold spell had broken, and the spring sun finally had arrived, he wore an ancient rough-knit hunting jacket, old woolen trousers, and a pair of run-down high-top leather shoes. It was later learned that he had found them in a hunting cabin where he had sought shelter.

He was rail-thin with dark, shaggy hair. He appeared to be none too clean, but, at about age fifteen, he looked otherwise like a normal kid.

It ceased being normal when Stan Farr saw him. Stan, the Oakmont High basketball coach, saw Boy as Stan was walking across the tracks on the way to town. Boy saw Stan standing before him and stopped abruptly with a very fearful look. He appeared to be thinking of a way to escape.

"How ya doin'?" Stan asked, and Boy said something in reply that Stan did not understand.

"You speak English?" Stan asked.

Some more strange words in reply.

"Hungry?" asked Stan with a hand-to-mouth motion.

The young fellow seemed to understand but was unwilling to be entirely trusting of Stan.

"C'mon," said Stan. "We can go get a burger at Mrs. Pierce's."

No response.

Stan mimicked eating, and after some patient cajoling, Boy walked with him about a block to a small eatery. "Lola Pierce's" and "Home-Cooking" signs were on the window.

The breakfast crowd had left, and Mrs. Pierce, who was kind of everyone's grandmother in age, appearance, and approachability, stood at the counter. "Who have we got here, Stanley?" she asked, using Stan's formal name. She had known his family going way back.

"My young friend here arrived in town by way of the rails from the west. And he's seriously in need of a Pierceburger.

"Better than that, I still have pancake batter. How about pancakes, sausage, and eggs?"

"That is even better—make it two orders. On me."

"We'll see about the bill later, Stanley."

While waiting to eat, Stan attempted to get some information from Boy about himself, his family, his home, anything, but nothing came through but the same foreign speech. So they just sat.

When the breakfast arrived, although the youngster was obviously well-mannered, he ate as one who had not seen real food in a while.

Mrs. Pierce noted the appearance and manners of the boy before her. She also noted Stan's puzzlement. "Need to find out what he's saying to see how he can be helped," she said.

"I thought I might ask Carley," said Stan.

"Good idea, Stanley," said Mrs. Pierce, suppressing a smile. She knew all about Carley Simmons, a hometown girl who taught languages at the nearby community college, and Stan's former girlfriend—actually, more than that at one time.

"Until you find out more, why not let the boy stay with me? I have plenty of room at home, and maybe he could help me out here," said Mrs. Pierce.

"That would be very nice, but first I want to take him to get some new clothes."

That evening Stan picked up Boy as the restaurant was closing. He looked different. While still stand-offish, he looked healthier, possibly because he had cleaned up and was getting plenty to eat. And, his new shirt, jeans, and tennis shoes made him look like a typical teenager.

They went to Carley Simmons' apartment and were greeted as though she considered everything about her visitors as entirely normal, instead of greeting an old boyfriend and a youngster of unknown origin.

After some purposefully ordinary chatting and the setting being as comfortable as possible, Carley turned to Boy and spoke to him in a variety of languages known to her. She would get some recognition when she would get into Spanish and French, but it would soon fade into puzzlement. Nevertheless, Carley didn't give up right away and pursued the possibilities until she could see that the young fellow was becoming tired and a little frustrated.

Carley adopted a rather professional look and said, "I believe it's some sort of speech connected in some way with the romance languages, such as French, Spanish, or Italian. But I have no idea what it might be."

"Maybe Latin?" said Stan. "Don't those languages come originally from Latin?"

"Yes, but the boy is obviously not dressed in a Roman toga," said Carley, probably a bit more caustically than she intended. She had, to her credit, stopped short of saying, "Dumb Jock."

Stan had to concede her point, even though he didn't necessarily like what he saw as her little bit of "attitude."

"I'm at a loss," he said. I don't know what to do."

Softening her tone, Carley said, "Of course, there is one person we could turn to."

Right away, Stan said, "Sure." He knew just who Carley meant—Miss Epworth, the retired Oakmont High Latin and English teacher. Miss Epworth had taught several generations of students, and with Mrs. Pierce, a first responder when serious issues arose in the community. "She might have a clue about the background of our young friend."

Carley agreed to call Miss Epworth, who answered on the first ring. After telling her former teacher who she was and who her mother and grandmother were and she was fully recognized, Carley told Miss Epworth about the young man who had come to town speaking something like Latin.

"That is a puzzle, Carley. Of course, I'll be glad to see you, and Stanley, and the boy. Be sure to have Stanley tie his shoes," a reference to her recollection of Stan's being typically unlaced in her classes when he was a student.

"I'll be sure to tell him, Miss Epworth," said Carley, laughing. After agreeing to meet the following afternoon, Carley hung up and broached another matter with Stan. "Can't we call him something other than Boy, at least for the time being?" she said.

"What would you suggest?"

"How about Robbie?"

"Not bad. That sounds pretty good. Well, now, Robbie and I had better get him back to Mrs. Pierce's. It's been a long day for him."

"And I'll see you tomorrow?—I mean we'll all meet at Miss Epworth's tomorrow?" she said.

"You bet," said Stan.

The next afternoon they were warmly greeted by Miss Epworth, although she made a point of looking down at Stan's shoes when he entered her home. Stan and she glanced at each other for a moment with their shared joke. Then she turned to Boy. She was obviously intrigued by the request that she meet the new arrival in town who spoke an unknown language.

Directing her comments to Stan and Carley, she said, "As you know, the only language I taught was Latin, although I did take some Spanish and French in college. I can only help to explore whether anything that might be related to my so called 'dead language' is understandable to him."

Boy, "Robbie," was sitting with the others and glancing around the room when he heard Miss Epworth come up with a series of elementary Latin phrases. He immediately looked at her with a look of some understanding.

"You may be onto something here," said Carley.

"Yes," said Miss Epworth, "Robbie has some language connected with Latin in his background." So she continued, adding longer sentences.

Robbie was saying some words back to her, but they were not registering with Miss Epworth, just as what she had been saying was missing the mark with him.

"We're getting somewhere, but I don't have the answer. Will you let me think about this for a day or so, and I'll get in touch with Stan if I come up with something," she said.

Robbie and his two benefactors left with hope for some light being cast upon Robbie's background. This might provide a key to communicating with him and planning his future.

Before parting, Stan casually asked Carley if she would like to go to the Hamburger Shack for burgers that evening, so they could talk further about Robbie. She agreed that they might profitably explore various solutions, so she said she would make herself available.

The next day Stan received a call from Miss Epworth. "I may have something that would help. Can you come by this afternoon?"

Stan readily agreed and called Carley.

When she and Stan arrived with Robbie, Miss Epworth was quick to note that her former students seemed much friendlier with each other than they had during their first visit. She put that aside without comment and went on to the matter at hand—Robbie's speech pattern.

"I have been researching the places where some vestiges of old Latin exist in the world, and have thought what is most likely," she said. "And I'd like to start with Romansh."

"Sounds as if you are speaking while smashed," said Stan.

"Don't try to be cute, Stanley," Miss Epworth said.

"Yes, don't try to be cute, Stanley," mimicked Carley.

"That will be enough from you, Miss Simmons."

"Yes, Miss Epworth."

"As I was saying, one possibility is Romansh, one of the four languages spoken in Switzerland in addition to German, French, and Spanish. About forty-five thousand persons make use of that language there."

"What did the language come from?" asked Stan.

"It is derived from Vulgar Latin; that is, the spoken language of the people, not the classical form that I taught," said Miss Epworth.

"That sounds like a good possibility," said Carley. "But why would Robbie have been here in this country, if he comes from Switzerland?"

"Good question," said Stan, "And where would we start to look?"

"I've thought about that," said Miss Epworth, "And so I contacted the Swiss Embassy. Someone there who speaks the language will call us this afternoon. In the meantime, let's have tea."

Over tea and cookies Miss Epworth and her former students talked about others who had attended the high school and the incidents they recalled from the past at the school. They were on their second cup of tea when the phone rang.

After answering and speaking briefly, Miss Epworth said, "Of course you can. He's right here."

Robbie took the phone and listened. Right away he became alert and began talking with the Swiss Embassy representative. Robbie seemed to finally become more relaxed and even giggled at something that was said. Then Robbie became very serious and was very moved, almost to tears, by what was being discussed. He handed the phone back to Miss Epworth.

She talked with the Embassy representative for a time, concluded the call, and turned to Carley and Stan. "This is what Robbie told the caller. Robbie and his mother and father were in the United States on vacation and drove to visit a Swiss community in the mountains. After leaving the community their car went off the mountain road and down an embankment. His mother and father were trapped in the car, so Robbie went for help."

"What a terrible experience for him and his family," said Stan.

"Yes, it certainly was," said Miss Epworth. "So Robbie became disoriented and came across a railroad and decided to follow tracks."

"And he ended up here in town where I found him," said Stan.

Both Carley and Miss Epworth got up and gave Robbie a hug while Stan looked on fondly.

Things moved pretty swiftly after finding Robbie's identity, although his real name they learned to be Carl. He was destined, however, to be forever called Robbie by his growing number of friends in Oakmont.

Carley found the location of the Swiss community near where Robbie's family had their accident and learned that a passing driver had discovered his mother and father. Fortunately, both of his parents were not severely injured and had only a short stay in the hospital. Carley and Stan took Robbie to see them in the hospital. They could tell that Robbie was relieved to see his folks and know first-hand that they were getting well.

Miss Epworth arranged for a reunion dinner at Mrs. Pierce's restaurant for Robbie and his family, his new Oakmont friends, and even representatives of the Swiss Embassy. At that dinner the subject came up somehow that Carl might spend at least a semester, maybe a year, at Oakmont High.

Postscript: Yes, Carley and Stan became engaged and were married. You already know some of the invited guests to their wedding ceremony. What you might not know is that in a year or so they had a little boy, whom they called—Robbie.

Hortense Quito

A rainy day. Wouldn't you know it? Hortense Quito was going to go hiking in a nearby Adirondack trail, and, while outdoorsy and strong enough for distance endurance, she didn't like to be wet. Snow, okay; ice even. But not rain.

Another thing Hortense did not like was her name. She felt terrible about this because Quitos went back generations to the Leon district of Spain. Quitos supported the very early lecturer of the ancient University of Salamanca, who when arrested in mid-sentence and imprisoned, famously returned to complete the sentence and finish the lecture. Quitos were with early explorers and adventurers on land and sea. Hortense's ancestor had been an early settler in California when it belonged to Mexico, and from that American beginning, the family spread through North and South America. Her branch members were firmly New Englanders, mostly in Connecticut.

Her great-grandfather met, was taken with, the married Hortense Gibbons, the red-haired, somewhat feisty daughter of an old Massachusetts family. Hortense became a favored family name through the years and was revered by this most recent bearer of the name. The Hortenseses she had known had been wonderful in the sense of being warm and supportive and patient with her as she was growing up, and even now.

In light of this history, she felt badly but she just didn't like her first name. What kind of nickname can you place upon Hortense? Then, as to Quito, how do you stop people from asking if you are from Ecuador? And, short of hurting members of her family who she loved, there was no way to change either name, except by changing the last name by marriage. Even in the event of marriage she had decided to keep her name.

Rain slowing down; no, it's stopped. So she decided to go to the mountain anyway, even though it was a little later than she liked to be out on the trail. Really, she should hike with someone—family and friends all said so. But that was not her style. She liked to stop and look, go faster and slow down, stay or return at her own pace and in her own time. Even good friends going along took those initiatives away, and, she thought, what is a hike with conditions attached?

Getting to the parking place at the foot of the mountain she decided on a trail of medium length, considering that it was now after three. She was actually familiar with the trail but still took along a flashlight and windbreaker in her backpack.

She headed up the mountain, taking in all the sights that would be missed by many, but which she had come to learn over the years from other hikers and people who knew the mountains. She looked down at the stand of tall oaks that had never been harvested—"grand" was the word she came up with to describe them. Looking to the ground she knew to gently lift the leaves of a certain plant to find the brilliant little red berries beneath. When she neared the top, she began to see the shrub from which she had taken leaves to make a tea to be applied as a treatment for poison ivy. Lots of things to learn on the mountain.

The trail wandered along the crest for a quarter mile, and then turned to form an alternate way back to where she had started. She considered it wise to move a bit more quickly because this route, while very beautiful, also came close to some overlooks that fell steeply into the hollows below. Moving downhill faster was not a major effort, but she still had to be aware of roots and rocks on the path, as well as being mindful that she was in a territory that belonged to wild animals.

So she stayed alert to her surroundings as she moved along. Reaching the point where the path came within a few yards of the highest drop-off into the valley below, she thought she heard an animal sound. At first, she thought, maybe a bobcat. Or maybe even an irate squirrel. Or perhaps a bear cub.

But it was coming from beyond the edge where the flat turf ended. Perhaps a cliff-dwelling bird. Worth a peek—but a careful peek. She advanced to the edge and looked down. She could not see anything, but ventured a "Hello-o-o." Then she listened and heard a rather clear "Hel-l-p," from below. Another "Hello." Another "Help," louder and more piercing this time.

"Who are you," she hollered.

"I'm Bobby." She could tell he was a boy, probably pre-teen.

"Are you okay?"

"Well—no," came a youthful, exasperated reply.

"I mean, are you hurt?"

"No. I just got too close the edge and the ground gave way and I thought I was going to fall all the way, and..." Bobby's voice became shakier and was perhaps giving away to some signs of panic.

"Listen to me, Bobby. I have to ask you a couple questions, and I want you to answer me clearly. Can you do that?"

"Okay."

"First, are you in a place where you won't fall anymore?"

"Yes, I hit on a little place that caught my fall," said Bobby.

"Second, do you have on warm clothing?"

"Yeah, my mom made me put on a heavy shirt and long pants before we went out on the trail this morning, but then I went way ahead of them, and maybe turned on another trail, and..."

"Bobby, we'll go into all that later. Now we have to get you back up here," Hortense said, with a firmness of voice that she had to maintain for the boy, but at the same time belied some uncertainty as to how the heck she was going to pull it off.

"Okay, thanks," said Bobby.

Carefully moving forward and looking down she now could see the grassy ledge where he had fallen, even though she could not see the boy.

What to do now was the question. The first thing she did was yell "Help" as loudly as she could in all directions; she could surely need the help. But with dusk not far off it was unlikely that other hikers were still on the trails. Then she looked around. She recalled that she had passed long grapevines hanging from trees as she had descended the mountain. She ran as fast as she could back to where the vines were, but they extended far up into the trees, and she had no way of getting them.

Tramping around in that area she came across an old vine that had come loose from above. Pretty old, and maybe not long enough. But she had no other choice she could think of, and the light was fading already.

"You still there?" she said as she got back to the edge.

"No, I left and went home," said Bobby.

"Very funny—now listen up, Bobby. I'm going to..."

"What's up?" came a question from back at the path.

Hortense turned to see a tall, lanky Park Ranger in familiar khaki uniform and broad-brimmed hat coming toward her.

Hortense said, "We've got a problem here. A boy, Bobby, on a ledge some distance down, and I've been trying to figure out how to get him up before it gets too dark."

"I heard that a boy had gotten separated from his family, so I offered to check this trail. He made it a pretty good way. By the way, I'm Pete."

"What's going on up there?" came an anxious question from down below.

"We've got some help, Bobby. Just hold on. We'll get you," said Hortense. Turning to Pete, "But how? All I have is this old vine, and it may not hold, and..."

"I guess it's all we have, but maybe we can find another and weave them together," said Pete, "but before that I'll call to the other Rangers to let them know Bobby has been found." After moving a bit up and down the path he found a place for his phone to work and made his call.

Soon he came back and said, "The family is much relieved, but they are searching far down on the other side of the mountain. I told them to bring climbing gear, but for now we'll just have to make do with what we have here. I did find another length of vine. We can only hope it will hold one of us to go down," he said.

"What?"

"Well, the boy may be in shock or not be able to handle the climb."

"Oh."

"And—just one more thing, given the condition of these vines, I would be way too heavy to do the job."

"You—you don't look too heavy to me."

"Afraid so—think you can do it?" said Pete.

Hortense looked around, and said, "Guess I'm the only one here. Wish I were big and fat."

"You certainly aren't that, and..."

From below, "I'm getting kinda cold down here."

"Okay, Bobby, I'm Pete, and we're on our way," said Pete.

"We?" weakly questioned Hortense.

Ignoring this, Pete began to intertwine the vines, and Hortense helped from the other end.

Pete said, "About the only helpful thing I have with me is a length of twine, and we need that to make a loop in the end of the vines—just hope they will be long enough to get to our boy."

"And strong enough," said Hortense.

"Yes, of course—that, too." After securing the looped end, Pete tied the other end of their rescue "rope" to the closest strong tree trunk.

"We're ready to go," he said.

"We again."

"Listen, I wish I could..."

"I know—I'm going to do it. I'm just a bit..."

"Nervous?"

"More than that—but let's go."

After testing the loop as well as possible Hortense sat at the edge of the drop-off, and said, "Well, here goes nothing."

"I wouldn't exactly say that," said Pete, not taking his eyes off her as he moved back along the vines toward the tree. "I'll use the tree to help ease you down. Now, whenever you're ready."

"I guess now," Hortense said, and moved slowly down from her safe perch.

"How's it going?" Pete called.

"Wonderful—lovely view—wish you were here," came the reply.

"Getting close?"

"Pretty soon."

"Is it gonna reach?"

"It'll just have to reach."

"Good luck."

In a few moments, "I made it, Pete—and Bobby here is a fine, brave young man."

"He is that," yelled Pete. "Is he ready to come up?"

"Let us talk a little down here, and I think we'll be ready soon."

After a few minutes—"I'm ready, Pete," came Bobby's voice, more confidently than Pete had expected.

Pete began to pull the vines slowly and steadily and after what seemed a long time to him, and probably longer to Bobby, the boy's head emerged in view. "Bobby, hold very still while I secure the vines to this tree and I'll help you up over the edge."

"Okay," came a shaky voice that indicated for the first time what a trying time this had been to the little boy. When Pete boosted him onto firm ground, Bobby gave him a huge hug, and Pete, full of relief, hugged back.

"Here, put this jacket around you, Bobby, and also here's a candy bar. Guess you like candy?"

"I love candy. Thanks. But, what about the lady?"

"Think we ought to get her?"

"I really do. She's been great, and…oh, you're kidding."

"You catch on fast. Now, let's check our equipment. We've got to go over these vines to see if they are strong enough to hold her—she's much heavier than you."

"Yeah, but we'd better not tell her that," said Bobby, showing wisdom beyond his years.

Pete and Bobby inspected the entire length of the vines. Each found a place that was weakened when Bobby was pulled up. They each shook their heads at discovering this.

Pete delivered the news. "Hey, nice lady."

"Yes?"

"Are you okay? Are you safe?"

"Not enjoying this much, but I'm very safe here."

"Well, hate to have to tell you, but we found weak spots in the vines. They won't do the job in getting you up. We'll have to wait on more help with better gear."

"Oh, my. It's getting dark."

"They should be here soon with good equipment and even lights. Are you cold?"

"I've been warmer."

"Let her have the jacket," said Bobby.

"You sure?"

"Yeah," and together they let the jacket down to Hortense.

After what seemed a long time, especially to Hortense, the rescue party came with full rescue equipment. Soon Hortense too was up on sound ground, complete with a triple tearful hug with Bobby and Pete. Relieved parents hugged Bobby the moment they saw him.

As the family and the rescue team were moving along the path, Pete turned to Hortense and said, "I don't even know your name."

Oh, boy, thought Hortense. Oh, well. "It's Hortense."

Pete took a step back, almost stumbling.

"It's not that bad," she said.

"No—it's not that. That's my Granny's name, and we all love my Granny."

For some reason it seemed the most natural thing for the two rescuers to find themselves holding hands as they headed down the trail.

Biddy Haymaker

Part I.

Biddy Haymaker was rotund, a woman of average height, red hair, remarkably beautiful countenance, and a body that just kept on growing. Biddy was the president of the oldest silver mining company in the country. It was not the largest, but through Biddy's leadership, following in the shoes of her "Pop," it was profitable.

Pop had been Buddy Haymaker, who came from a farm family as his last name would indicate. But Buddy took off from his Indiana farm, went west, and joined with a partner in reworking an old silver mine. The yields from that mine and others just kept growing.

When "Pop" died, Biddy took over not only her father's mining ventures but also the family Colorado ranch. The ranch was in a broad valley, within sight of snowy mountain peaks. She raised Hereford cattle, sheep, goats, llamas, belted pigs, and Rhode Island Red chickens.

She was as welcoming to fellow humans as she was to the animals. No stranger was ever turned away without something that met their needs, ranging from a handout to a job to a prodigious hug. "Camel" Rogers, her manager and constant second in command was a broken record of "Biddy, you can't take in more strays—animals, workers, table guests, and overnighters."

Biddy's reply was, "Well, Camel (real name Campbell, but with a face that suited his nickname better), are we broke?"

"No, we're doing okay."

"Well, then...." (End of conversation.)

Biddy seemed to be always on the job, with the mine, with the company, with the ranch, or just coping with and enjoying all her varied acquaintances and those depending upon her. Her one diversion was motoring in her big old Lincoln up into the mountains. Usually, she took a carload or even a caravan of cars, pick-ups, or whatever happened to follow. And she always had her cook prepare enough grub for all for all day.

Tales of these treks were spread throughout her part of Colorado. "There they go," neighbors would say, counting the vehicles from one to what seemed to be the agreed-upon high of fourteen.

Once in a while, Biddy took off alone for an overnight or two. Her kitchen staff knew that she took along more food than she could consume in her stay. Everyone in contact with her held back from inquiring as to her destination, but it was a very hot item of conjecture. All sorts of theories abounded, but no one, not even Camel, knew where she would go. No clues were forthcoming as to what or where. There was a letter some time ago that Camel had seen from a "Joshua Bender."

Then on one cold November night, Biddy called her cook to prepare provisions for several days. She called to Camel to gas up a four-wheel-drive vehicle. And, bundled up, turning down Camel's offer to come along, she took off.

Part II.

The suspicion of Biddy's trips finally began to eat Camel alive. He decided to follow Biddy in an unfamiliar car to see just where she was headed. After a winding two-hour drive through the snowy mountains and valleys, Biddy's vehicle came to a stop at a small inn just off the side of the highway.

Biddy pulled into the gravel lot and began grabbing her bags, peeking over her shoulder to ensure no one was watching. She then headed into Apartment 6. Camel discreetly parked his car in an empty lot across the street, watching

Biddy closely from the driver's side window. Camel quickly realized Biddy was not alone.

The dim lighting in the room cast a silhouette of a tall, hunched man. Camel staked out all night, waiting to see who Biddy was visiting. After a long, chilly winter night, the sun began to rise over the horizon, melting the frost that coated Camel's windshield. Camel noticed Biddy exiting the apartment in between the streams of melted ice on his window. Wiping the frost off the window and rubbing his tired eyes, Camel watched Biddy get into her car. When Biddy pulled away, Camel raced out of his car and quietly went to the window hoping to catch a glimpse of the other person in the room.

He could see just through a tiny sliver between the curtains. He got a glimpse of what seemed to be the back of an older man. Camel was eagerly waiting for the mysterious man to show his face, and then, suddenly, "Camel, what are you doing here?" asked Biddy. She seemed frantic and confused.

Camel scrambled to put words together. He nervously responded, "I wanted to make sure you were safe on these icy roads."

Part III.

Biddy replied, "Camel, let me take this breakfast into my friend inside; then you and I can go to the dining room and get some breakfast, and I can tell you everything you need to know. Then we will come back here and you can meet my friend."

As they entered the dining room, the owners, Bev and Jim, greeted them. Biddy made introductions and said to them, "Today I will be eating and talking with my right-hand man, the manager of all that I own. Tomorrow we'll resume our usual breakfast together."

After Biddy and Camel had finished their breakfast and were lingering over their second cup of coffee, she began her explanation. "Years ago, when my Pop passed away and I assumed control of the silver mines, a man by the name of Joshua Bender did for my father what you do for me. We fell in love and were engaged to be married when he was in a terrible accident in the mine. He was supervising the placement of support timbers and was holding one when it gave way. A large beam and loose rock from the ceiling of the mine fell on him. It displaced his shoulder and upper arm so badly that they couldn't be repaired properly. As you will see when you meet him, his back is hunched."

Camel said sympathetically, "I'm so sorry, what happened then?"

"Although I pleaded with him, he refused to marry," said Biddy. "He said he didn't want to tie me down to a cripple."

"I felt the least I could do was find him a place to live where kind people could look after him, and it wouldn't be too far so I could visit," said Biddy.

"And those other times when you had that caravan of cars follow you, with enough food for an army?" asked Camel.

"Well, Bev and Jim have taken such care with Josh I didn't want to burden them with meal preparations when I visit, nor when all that 'caravan,' as you called it, followed me. That caravan was retired employees and their families that Josh had supervised at the mines. They wanted to keep in touch and they came from long distances to visit him. And all the food Cook prepared was in microwaveable containers," said Biddy.

"I wish you would've told me all this long ago," commented Camel.

"I'm sorry, too, but you could've asked. Let's go to Josh's apartment. He has two bedrooms and after you meet him you may want to rest in my bedroom after being in your car all night."

As they walked to Apartment 6, Camel said, "You're a remarkable woman, Biddy Haymaker."

Up on the House Top

She was eighty, and she had lived all her life in a small house on the road that ran along the top of the mountain. She was small, quick in her movements, and as others described her, "still bright as a silver dollar." Her name was Ida Mae, named for her two grandmothers. She wore feed sack dresses and wore her iron gray hair in a bun. She wore serviceable shoes, an old canvas coat, and fretted little about her appearance.

She had married early, to Ernest, but he had died cutting timber, before he was thirty. Their one child, Millie, had passed away at age three with an unknown fever.

So she adopted everyone on the mountaintop, good and bad, amiable and crusty, old and young. Her soup kettle was always on, and the ladle favored anyone who was sick or just needed cheer.

"What are you doing there?" shouted Martha, her nearby neighbor. Martha couldn't understand why everyone made such a fuss over Ida Mae. They had gone to the one-room school together, competing in spelling, arithmetic, and, later, Ernest. Seemed as though Ida Mae always won, and Martha lost.

But when you're "on the mountain," it's good to have someone near. So Martha didn't much let on, and the two old ladies actually got along pretty well.

But Martha was nosy. And she was critical, especially of Ida Mae. Lucky that Ida Mae could shrug it off—most times.

"Just throwing on a little hay," she said, standing next to her ancient Dodge pick-up.

"Where you taking it?" asked Martha, guessing it was another of Ida Mae's "do goods."

"Oh, up to the shed."

"But your calves are here in the barn."

"I know that."

"But there's nothing in that old hill pasture now."

"Oh, yes, there is, and winter's coming on," replied Ida Mae as she quickly got behind the wheel of the Dodge and started it up with a blast of smoke and considerable engine noise.

She drove back by the barn and through the little stream fed by the nearby never-failing spring. She stopped to open the gate to the pasture. Pulling the old truck into lower gear she proceeded up through the meadow that Ernest had cleared of timber so long ago.

She stopped near the top of the grade beside the old shed that was now nothing more than a leaky roof and sides with a number of boards missing. She had helped Ernest build it when they ran more cattle and needed an extra place for feeding and storage.

Now the shed just sat there, door long gone, weathered, and not fit for much.

But, as Ida Mae had said, winter was coming on and for some years now it seemed that deer, and sometimes other animals had found their way to the shed for shelter and food during the blowing and snowy cold.

The hay she brought would disappear, and Ida Mae would bring more.

"Really doesn't make sense," she said to herself. "They're wild animals. They know how to look out for themselves. They don't need me breaking my back throwing in hay for them. Oh, well, I've done it for so long—and maybe just a scoop or two of calf feed."

Looking around, she was still caught up in the beauty of the continuous view of the mountains that went on and on like waves in the sea. She smiled at the pleasure the view gave her—how could you not smile.

As she stood there, she felt the first cool winds of winter come in, causing her to shiver, and think about all she had to do to prepare for the coming hard season. After a second shiver she climbed into her truck and went home.

Ida Mae did not know she was being watched. Three pairs of eyes looked out from the overgrowth that bordered the meadow. Old Deer couldn't see so well, but his nose was on alert, and he was quick to sense movement. But he knew it was Ida Mae. She had provided winter feed for generations of his family.

Also, Fred Fox and "Bunny" Rabbit knew what Ida Mae had always done, preserving the old shed when anyone else might have torn it down, and bringing up food—Ida Mae would likely bring some carrots and other food at the first sign of snow.

"Fine lady," said Fox, the most eloquent of the group. But he was also the wordiest. They dare not let him get started, so both Deer and Rabbit quickly gave their agreement.

"She's been doing that since that old truck was new, since the headlamps still shone, since..."

"Oh, boy," thought Rabbit, just got to change the subject. "What about, 'scuse me, Fox, if we did something for her for a change?"

"Not bad," said Deer, keeping Fox quiet and joining in Rabbit's proposal at the same time.

"Super," said Fox. "She's done so much. She's come up here when she had to wade in deep snow, carrying..."

"But what could we do for her?" asked Deer.

"Let's think," said Rabbit.

"Yes, let's just think, and plan, and..."

"How about we all think quietly?" said Deer.

"Oh, very well," said a very stifled Fox.

After a few minutes, Rabbit said, "I've got it. How about if we give that old truck a paint job?"

Deer and Fox slowly turned to Rabbit. "How, Rabbit, do you propose that we...Oh, well, thanks for trying." Both

Deer and Fox knew that while Rabbit had a good heart, he didn't have the quickest mind in the forest.

Fox then spoke up, and before Deer and Rabbit could again hold him back, suggested, "How about we fix the roof on her old house? I know it's been leaking, and with winter coming on..."

"Pretty good," said Rabbit. "But how do we fix a roof?"

"We don't," said Deer, "by ourselves. But we get help. She feeds the birds, too, in winter. They would help—by flying new shingles up to the roof. I even know where there's a pile of split shingles."

"Who pounds the nails in, and if someone does, wouldn't that ever-so-slightly spoil the surprise," asked Rabbit, suddenly operating at the top of his game.

"Won't use nails," said Fox. "Smarty-Pants Owl has discovered a new glue-like stuff by mixing pine tar and some other things. It will hold those shingles just fine. Just need a glue pot and some patience."

"Now we need a meeting, all the birds and other animals," said Deer.

"Even that stinkin' Squirrel?" asked Rabbit, referring to his archenemy.

"Got to have Squirrel. He's pretty good on roofs," said Deer.

"Oh, very well," said Rabbit.

"Must move fast," said Fox. "Winter's coming soon—cold winds, snow, some sleet..."

"Let's go, then," said Deer and Rabbit together.

So the days before the first snow were spent planning, preparing, and then repairing the numerous leaks in the old cabin roof. Even Ben Bear, a little sleepy before retiring for the winter, helped. It was a little hard to keep him from making noise as he worked—he wasn't the daintiest of the animals.

Finally, and quietly, the roof job was completed. Deer, Fox, and Rabbit assembled all the workers in a meeting behind the barn. Deer started the meeting with, "Wake up, Ben Bear."

Seeing all were alert he introduced Fox, who very eloquently told everyone they had done a splendid job, without making even a sound that would let Ida Mae know what was happening. "And it could have been different—we could have made a lot of noise, and..."

"Sure wouldn't want a lot of noise," said Rabbit.

"No—no noise," said Deer.

"Don't need noise," said Bear.

"Okay, okay," said Fox, "but we still did a great job."

And all the animals agreed.

Next day, an early winter rain hit the mountain. Ida Mae was standing on her porch looking at the rain when she noticed that Martha was out, too."

"You know, Martha," she yelled over to her neighbor, "there's not a drop of rain coming through this old roof. I can't understand it."

And just a little way off some very happy animals said nothing—not even Fox. They all just smiled to each other.

The Night Visitors

The people in town really shouldn't call him "Mad Dog" Wayne. Wayne Boscombe had a fair fight with Mark Loren. It was just that Mark hit the floor in an awkward way—a way that caused his untimely death at age twenty, same as Wayne.

These two had never been real friends but had tolerated each other in sports and in their small high school class. The were both good athletes and caused other teams to fear the always-smaller Oakmont.

Wayne was blond and more muscular than Mark, but Mark was bigger and stronger.

What caused their fight was a trivial matter, really. Mark had been drinking even before he entered the local watering hole, the Rendezvous. And he was loud, too, as he spoke on his cell phone. Too loud for the proprietor, Eddie, and when Eddie told Mark to tone it down, Mark reacted by shoving Eddie. Wayne got in front of Eddie. Mark took a swing at Wayne, and it was then that Wayne's not-even-real-hard punch decked Mark. And Mark didn't get up.

So why did Wayne run? Well, this was the second fight he had had recently—the first resulting in a warning from the chief of police.

Then there was Wayne's family. His older brothers and even a rather large, loud sister, Mireld, had reputations of being belligerent, drinking, and even some petty theft.

So Wayne's first inclination—to run—was the one he went with. He headed up on the mountain where he was very familiar and very comfortable—good thing it was spring and not the harsh winter season up there.

And Wayne stayed gone, in spite of police and even friends who searched extensively. And he remained away, even through the next spring and the spring after that.

"Wonder where he is?" asked Irv Cortland, editor of the Oakmont Herald, just after opening the office on a beautiful May morning. Irv was dark, solid in body and temperament—but with a ready twinkle eye and ability to see both the funny and sad parts of any situation.

"Could be anywhere—he knows every bit of the mountain," answered Rusty Canter, the long-time printer at the *Herald*. Rusty's old-time handlebar mustache told it all about his outlook on life and his dim view of the present age.

"And the mountain is big," said Lettie Green, reporter for the paper and fiction writer in her spare time. She had red hair and pink complexion and was known to give her opinion readily. Some said she often "spoke too soon."

The mountain was a kind of anomaly, rising sharply behind Oakmont, but starkly alone, since no other mountains surrounded it. It was treed most of the way up, but bald on the top where extensive pasture supported cattle that were summered there.

In spite of the beauty of the setting, things were not good in Oakmont, having seen the closing of the glass plant and two or three other businesses that had employed hundreds of people in the town. Some had left to find work elsewhere, but the Recession had made the prospects of a job anywhere pretty dim.

And then the Recession hit, and the town was suffering, many people living on unemployment benefits, food stamps, and welfare payments. The suffering showed not only in the severe drop in the economy, but also in the outlook of the people. They had gone from fully employed, with few cares and full of fun, to the dismal views of those with little sustenance and even less hope.

Of course, in many things the exception proves the rule; those residents of "Quality Row," major business owners, inheritors of family money, and professionals, seemed to be "doing all right." Really still doing all right was Mabel Crosby, a descendant of one of the town's founding fathers. She lived in the largest of the big houses on Quality Row.

Mabel was the last of the real wealth that had intentionally or unintentionally ruled the town for generations—and she reputedly had great wealth, coming initially from large, early stock purchases by her grandfather, which now amounted to significant holding in present-day behemoth corporations.

Unfortunately, Mabel was not liked in town. She socialized with persons similarly well-off from other places, spent little from her huge purse in Oakmont, and was unfriendly in the casual meetings with townspeople in church, store, or on the street.

Some said that she had a disappointment in love in early life, which led to her lack of warmth and friendliness. Her bitterness showed up even in her choice of style of dress and hair style favored by a generation long gone and her retention of her old Packard automobile for conveyance. Her driver, Harold Hanson, was about the only person in town she spoke to on a day-to-day basis.

As Mabel remained in her big old home, the population dwindled; but not all the young men who left were heard from in their new jobs or even while receiving unemployment insurance benefits elsewhere. They were just gone. The explanation often was, "Well, you know how those young guys are—you can't count on their writing." Or, "They'll let us know when they've found something."

Then help began to appear for the least fortunate of the citizens of Oakmont—at night. Footsteps would be heard on the porches of those who had been hardest hit and were most down-and-out. Upon opening the door, the resident would find a package—not a large bundle, as might indicate foodstuffs or clothing or other essentials. No, it was invariably a small package containing something even more essential—money. Enough money to tide the household over the rocky period they were going through.

It happened again and again. Some people began to stay awake at night in anticipation of good fortune coming their way. Those who had received their money boon watched their not-much-better-off neighbor's doors.

Daily, at the *Herald*, the topic for discussion over and over was the good fortune of the townspeople who received aid by messengers from some unknown benefactor or benefactors. "Who could it be?" became the question of the day, week, month, year.

Conjecture even became tiresome, and a little frustrating.

"Let's go up on the mountain," said Lettie, just after the winter thaw when Spring was certain in the town and probable at higher elevations.

"There still might be some snow on the old road. Could be rough," replied Irv.

"I know, but something tells me we need to take a look around up there," said Lettie.

The next Saturday morning the two journalists piled into Lettie's old VW bug and took off up the winding dirt road that hung on the side of the hill. That road would deliver them to the top after a continuous climb filled with switchbacks. The view was wonderful, if you didn't stop to consider the sheer drop off to the right. One false move and one could be a long time in space before hitting the railroad tracks and the river far below.

And the snow in the shaded portions of the road caused the bug to momentarily spin its wheels, but fortunately it would catch and go on.

Near the top, Irv had an "I wonder" moment. He knew just what Lettie had been thinking in heading up the mountain, and it wasn't the three-state view. He knew she felt that Wayne was holed up somewhere up there, and, because she and Irv had grown up roaming that mountain, they had a fair chance of finding some sign of him.

Others had searched over the years Wayne had been gone but had found nothing. Their searches had nearly all covered the mountaintop. This made sense, since it was the most habitable; in fact, remnants of old homesteads still dotted the higher elevations where the land flattened out in a manner more suitable for farming.

Irv's wonder had to do with that part of the mountain below the road. Not all of it, because most of the way up the side of the road just dropped off in the form of a cliff.

However, toward the top, even the land to the right as they drove along was only tilted, not up-and-down.

Lettie, perhaps by way of repaying Irv for accompanying her in the increasing cold and even some fog, went along with his suggestion that they pull over and at least take a "little look" down over the slope.

Now, why was it that they found the trail? Did Lettie sense something down there or was it just a lucky find? Because not twenty feet off the old road they came upon a well-used lane where vehicles had passed not long before. After re-inspecting the roadside vegetation, they found that the entrance to that lane had been cleverly concealed by someone who did not want it found.

They followed the ruts that had been pressed into the leafy undergrowth and descended gradually among a long-standing growth of large oaks and other trees. They heard a bleeping clatter ahead and found a pond full of frogs; the frogs ceased their loud noises when the visitors came near.

About a hundred yards ahead smoke was rising from among the trees. Because of the narrowness of the little valley the smoke would be difficult to discover from any distance away.

As Irv and Lettie approached the smoke plume they heard voices, laughing, and an occasional holler. Irv suspected it was a group of hunters and whispered this to Lettie.

"Maybe so," replied Lettie, but not with great confidence.

"Well, who, then?"

"We'll just have to see," she answered.

And see they did and not without surprise, for there in the clearing seated around a campfire were Wayne and some of their other friends who had been missing in Oakmont.

"And look who else is there," said Irv, in a low voice.

"Yes, Harold Hanson, Miss Mabel's driver, and there's her big old car over beside that cabin," said Lettie.

It was not the only vehicle; several cars and pick-ups were in evidence. And there were actually two cabins, well-constructed and suited to the wooded area that concealed them from being seen from the outside.

"Should we..." Irv started to ask, when Lettie marched into the midst of the camp scene with a "Hi, guys."

"Hello, Lettie. Hello, Irv. What are you two doing here?" asked Wayne.

"We just took a ride up the mountain, and here we are," said Irv.

"Guess you found me—us," continued Wayne.

"Guess we did," said Lettie.

"It's like this..." started Todd Turner, standing now to face the visitors.

"I'll tell them," interrupted Wayne, and he proceeded to reveal the history of his leaving Oakmont after being accused of the injury to Mark; the others' joining him one by one; and their gradually acclimating themselves to their mountain retreat.

"But what's Harold doing here?" asked Lettie.

"That's a little more complicated," said Wayne.

"Does it have anything to do with Robin Hood?" asked Irv.

"You might say so, in a way," replied Wayne.

"In what way?" asked Lettie.

"We do give away things, to people who need them."

"In what way is it not like Robin Hood?" Lettie pursued.

"We don't steal."

"Well, then, how...?" asked Irv.

"I think I know," interrupted Lettie. "Somehow you have gotten Miss Mabel to help finance your giving."

"Busted," said Wayne, smiling.

"How did you do that? She's always been so tight with her money," said Irv.

"She came to us—or, at least, Harold came to us—with a message from Miss Mabel."

"Harold?" Lettie directed her attention to Miss Mabel's driver.

"What Wayne says is true," said Harold, a gangly, hair-slicked-down, kind of throw-back to a couple of generations in the past. "Miss Mabel saw herself getting older with no heirs and started thinking about how she had always treated people in the town so badly. She just decided to try to help during these hard times."

"I've heard that she wasn't always so withdrawn and stingy, but that something in her past made her that way—maybe a man she was in love with," said Lettie.

"Well, for whatever reason, she has given us money to buy things for Oakmont people who are in need, with the condition that it is not to be known where the funds come from," explained Wayne. "I couldn't do it all by myself, so some of these guys came to help. We've actually been having a pretty good time of it."

"Yeah," agreed a one of the young men who had been listening to the conversation. "There hasn't been a lot of work in town, and this donating has given us a pretty good feeling."

"What now?" asked Harold, looking at Irv and then at Lettie.

"Yeah," said Wayne. "This way of life and giving to people who have hit hard times depends on us quietly going about our work. I say—quietly."

"We know what you mean," said Lettie.

"And we know what the gifts have meant to the town," added Irv. "I think you can count on Lettie and me keeping quiet about this."

"But you run a newspaper," questioned Wayne.

"I'm sure we'll get a great story that's fit to print—one of these days," said Irv.

"I wonder if anyone would believe us anyway," said Lettie. "Robin Hood, in this day and age?"

I'll Take the High Road

Of all the kids who had gone to Oakmont High, Bill Sargent was considered to be probably the brightest. Before he arrived his two older sisters had attained about all the honors the school could bestow, and they had gone on to University to attain more. But Bill surpassed them in promise. And, he was generally well-liked, except by his teachers when he occasionally argued some point with them and he was often proved to be right.

He was plenty big and moved well, but he had little interest in his school's sports teams, to the dismay, and with some, displeasure, because, as many said, he was a natural. Six-foot, lean, dark hair, a natural smile, he got along well with both his peers and those older than he. Girls were interested in him, but his interests centered upon the out-of-doors and the draw of the mountain that rose behind his home.

Sometimes he took along his rifle to claim game that crossed his path, and sometimes he kept a fish or two that had found his hook, but mostly he liked to cover the many trails that covered the mountain. An old boyfriend of one of his sisters had the same attraction to the open spaces and had taught Bill to identify plants and trees, as well as the lore surrounding them. For instance, Bill learned of a shrub the leaves of which, when boiled down, made a tea capable of treating poison ivy rash. He knew where the last remaining stand of "native"—never been cut—timber was, in a deep ravine in the far reach of "his" mountain.

Any number of girls would have hiked the mountain with him, but he would go out with a couple of his buddies to fish, or to meet his pal, Pete, on top, in order to shoot targets or just explore. Even more often he headed out alone, with sandwich and canteen, and pushed himself to cover more of the almost endless extent of the mountain and its slopes.

All this was not predictive of his future. In high school and college his path was the same as that of his mother and his sisters—research. The difference was that their interests were centered in chemistry and physics, and his focus was always toward biology. And, as he went further up the education ladder, he delved further in the smallest components of nature: cells and smaller entities.

But for now, he was still in high school, still hitting the mountain every chance he could, and observing the snow falling with the expectation of some depth. That meant only one thing in the days before the development of the ski slopes—sledding. Now, when one thinks of sled-riding they see a neighborhood run that is over in a minute or two.

However, Bill and his friends lived at the foot of the mountain, and more especially, an unpaved mountain road went up that mountain, clinging to the mountainside as the road curved around its natural contours. Not a vertical drop over road edge, but close to it. No guard rails. A "passin' place" here and there; otherwise, someone has to back up. But the good news was that few cars and trucks took that route when it snowed, for obvious reasons. The better news was often that the last vehicle to travel the route was a big truck with dual wheels that made for just the right width for a sled to gain speed down the mountain and be fairly certain of not going over the edge.

And the run was a good one—could be quarter-, half-, or full-mile, or go on up higher another mile. A good run on a crisp moonlit night with a slight glaze on the track.

Someone had built a fire near the bottom of the run. It was rumored that some of the older fellows were going to bring out the "Big Eastern," the legendary long sled that several guys came down the mountain on in a sitting-up position.

Bill and a number of his friends—boys and girls—headed up, greatly anticipating a long run. Lots of laughing, teasing, and bragging. When they had gone a little over a half mile, they heard a shout, "Get out of the way!" Someone had started higher up and was speeding down. What a pain. Everyone had to jump to the side and everyone did pretty well—except Bill. Bill could hike forever, but he could not be called graceful by any means. So he was late and the rider had to swerve into a snowbank to avoid him. The guy just lay there on his sled, and slowly got up, obviously stewing.

"What are you—deaf?" was the question. And the questioner was not a guy, but a girl. And she was steamed. "You don't know enough to get out of the way? You can't even jump sideways?"

Bill was smart, but not particularly good at coming up with a good reply, especially when the cause of the verbal onslaught was a really aggravated woman. So he made some lame utterance, and the girl got up shaking her head, grabbed her sled and slammed down on the track to continue her run.

Naturally, Bill's friends laughed at his misery from the ire of the sledder. They decided that they did not know who she was—she was not a student in their school. Someone suggested that she probably lived "on the mountain."

"Mountain people" were little understood by those "in town" even though the residents up the grade had inhabited their small farms and homes for generations. One reason for the lack of information was that the young people attended a small neighborhood grade school and middle and high schools that lay in the direction away from the town. Except for occasional shopping or attendance at town events they were seldom seen. Indeed, the mountain people had been used to being self-sufficient to the extent that they had a lesser need for goods and services than most people.

Bill had, of course, in the course of his mountain travels, come upon and had a certain appreciation for the hardiness of the individuals he met. So, when he saw the young woman who had chastised him begin her trek back up the long road home or for another run, he did not hesitate to go up to her. He did this even knowing he would have to face the inevitable comments from his friends.

"Sorry I got in your way," he said.

"Guess you're a little slow."

"You got me there," he said.

"But, it's okay—I mouthed off a little too much."

"No worries. Uh, everybody's going to Jim's house for hot chocolate—want to come along?"

"I shouldn't..."

"Why not?" he asked.

"I don't know anyone, and..."

Bill knew what she was going to say—that she came from a different place, from which one was not always readily accepted. But his reply was, "Well, you know me. We've met twice now, once up there and once down here. By the way, I'm Bill."

"I'm Bonnie, and, well, I guess it will be all right," she said.

So they showed up at Jim's house, and tossed their coats and ski caps on a pile. It was then that Bill saw how pretty the girl he had just met was. Wow, he thought, as he introduced her to his pals from school.

His friends all said hello in a friendly fashion, but Bill could sense that some were withholding judgment, not willing to give full acceptance. And this attitude only increased in the following weeks when it became clear that Bill and Bonnie were dating and they occasionally came to town for Bill's school events. Bill knew that she probably did dress and act a bit differently, but he saw the whole person and he liked what he saw.

Also, when he went to see Bonnie in her home, he learned to know her much better and to appreciate how independent she was, how she could hunt and fish and enjoy the land in a way that many in town did not. He was welcomed into her family and enjoyed their hearty meals, their way of being able to fix anything, and their tales of time spent coping with and enjoying nature.

Bill and Bonnie were an "item" through high school and began college, Bill in biological sciences and Bonnie, just as bright and maybe brighter, in botany with an interest also in scientific instrumentation. They both put to good use the scholarship assistance they received.

Her academic successes matched his, and when they came to Oakmont, there was no longer the whispering that had occurred earlier—well, maybe a little. And, Bill was welcomed by all in the mountain community, in part because he readily admitted that he didn't have their skills but he was willing to learn. Of course, after their eventual marriage, the arrival of two girls and a boy only enhanced their fitting in and on the mountain as well as in town.

Because their interests were so close, when they completed their academic degrees, they became a research team. They studied and made significant progress in the medical uses of plant life. Their successes led them to their own laboratory at a Los Angeles university.

They built a beautiful home, where else but on the top of a canyon to the east of Los Angeles, and enjoyed a good life of home and work, with all the time they could spare with their family out of doors.

In their home they built a beautiful, large fireplace that became the center of their household. And, on each side of that fireplace could be found an older, slightly out of date, sled.

Amelia

Amelia was a flight attendant on a large international airline. A dark-haired young woman, she was very good at her job, possessing the level of authority needed for her responsibilities. Her workdays were hectic as she managed the large number of passengers in her domain, with all their demands, differences, and eccentricities.

The pilots on her flights very much respected her ability to capably control all that went on behind them on the plane, but they still delighted in calling her by the name they had given her—Earhart. Probably that was inevitable. She didn't mind; she actually enjoyed the attention, since it was given in a friendly manner.

She was confident in her abilities and had a right to be. She was smart, good at math and solving problems. She played the violin, a good athlete, and, following a favorite uncle, had become a pilot, skilled to the instrument level. She could have done many things, but she had always wanted to be helpful and the job in the air seemed to be a perfect fit, for now.

Her regular run was Kennedy to Munich. She liked both ends—the life in New York City, with all the places to go and see, and the restaurants and the theater. At the Munich destination, she liked to explore the city and the smaller towns and villages and was especially fond of going out into the forests and mountains in all the seasons of the year.

Because she liked skiing, her favorite season was winter. On her days off and vacation time she visited a number of the great ski venues. She had skied from childhood in Maryland, but had become so much more accomplished as the mountain challenges grew.

Her "ski buddy" for many of these mini vacations had been Emily, an attendant on a competing airline. They constantly gave digs about the inferiority of the other system, but both she and Emily were professionals in their positions. Emily was a bit shyer, somewhat less adventurous, but at the same time was dependable when Amelia suggested some new place to go. She was good company, a big advantage from Amelia's point of view.

It was February and their latest plan was to go a bit farther than usual, into the ski areas of the Dolomite Mountains. A pilot friend of Emily's had suggested a lodge inside the Italian border. The region had changed hands in past wars, with the result that the staff was German-speaking as was the nearby area.

They rented a car at the Munich International Airport and set out for their lodge, a little over four hours away. They were prepared for slow going in some places because of the severe mountain weather. It was lucky they had started in the morning because the roads in some places were icy with patches of blown snow. The deeper snow was good news, however, to anyone who anticipated the well-covered slopes.

They found the lodge located part way up on the side of a high mountain. The view was stunning, with snow covering the normally rocky terrain of the Dolomites. They could see that it would be a treat to visit there in the summer as well as winter, when the mountain breezes in the café area next to the hotel would likely be very popular.

They went in to meet the proprietors and signed for their rooms, arranging for breakfasts, but leaving dinner to be determined, depending upon the length of their days on the slopes. Their rooms were bright and comfortable and very welcome after the tension of the long drive.

After breakfast the next morning they suited up and made their way to the chair lifts. Amelia chose the more difficult run while Emily took an easier course until she could add a bit to her confidence level. They agreed to meet for some lunch later and so set off for the mountain.

They caught sight of each other once during the morning when their runs came close together but otherwise faced their individual challenges. Amelia's was the slowness of her chairlift, as she was ever anxious to get back on the downhill. Emily's, on the other hand, was getting off the lift, especially if the snow and ice had mounded at that point. Good morning for both, however, and after a brief lunch, they headed back for a long afternoon.

Dinner back at the lodge was welcome as was an evening by the fire. It was not a long evening, however, because the weariness of the day set in and bedtime came early.

The morning was bright and held promise of another great day. Emily claimed some soreness and said that she might go only to lunchtime. As they lingered over coffee, she asked Amelia if she had seen the house that was perched on the side of the mountain within view of the ski lodge.

Amelia said, "Yes, it's up there all by itself. I wonder if it's vacant or if someone lives there. It's a little forbidding."

"I thought the same thing. Great view. Wonder if they ski," said Emily.

"Let's inquire," said Amelia, who got up and headed with Emily to the desk, behind which was an elderly attendant whom they knew as Fritz.

"Fritz, what do you know about the house that we see toward the top of the mountain? It doesn't look as if it is part of the resort property."

"No, no, it is very separate. No one goes there."

"Why not?" asked Amelia.

"In the first place, it is surrounded by tall fencing. People have reported strange activities there for many years, even large trucks coming and going," Fritz said.

"Odd," said Emily.

"Yes. It is owned by an older English gentleman who had been very plain to anyone who goes there that he doesn't want them about. It is said that he was managing director of an international company, what you Americans would call a CEO, I believe."

"Thank you, Fritz," said Emily, and back at the table, "I wonder why the Englishman keeps to himself."

"Yes," said Amelia, "a strange person."

"In a strange home."

"Let's go there," said Amelia. "We will be taking the afternoon off, and we could drive up and…"

"Whoa, there—we don't know anything about him. For all we know he may even be dangerous."

"Well, I plan to give it a try. I want to know more—at least what the house looks like up close."

"If you go, I guess I'll go along," said Emily.

After a long morning on the slopes and a late lunch they once again approached Fritz for directions.

"Nein, nein," he said. "You don't know enough about the people there and what they might do. You mustn't."

After the women showed their determination, however, Fritz told them of the route that would take them to their destination. By the time they got near the house the sun had come closer to setting on the horizon. It was very windy, as mountains can be, and cold.

The first thing they encountered was the high steel fence that Fritz had told them about. But the gate was wide open. Why have an imposing fence and not have the gate secured?

The rather large house was chalet-style, of dark wood and a long porch along the front. The entrance was to the side of a small carpark. It seemed that the only light was in the front room off the porch.

"Well, we've seen it—now let's go," said Emily.

"Very interesting. Such a nice place. A place to be enjoyed. I wonder if such a person really enjoys it."

"Maybe yes—maybe no. Anyway, it's none of our business. Let's be off," said Emily.

"I'm going to knock on the door," said Amelia.

"Are you crazy?"

"Maybe—but I'm going to anyway," and she got out of the car and headed to the door. Emily, very reluctantly, followed.

Amelia, appearing braver than she felt, walked to the chalet door, Emily almost beside her. Hesitating, then knocking, wondering what to expect.

She didn't expect who answered the door. It was a conservatively dressed older man with a gracious smile. Pleasantly, he said, "Hello. Are you lost?"

"No," Amelia said. "We are staying at the lodge," and pointed in its direction. We saw your interesting home and decided to ride up here."

"Pleased that you did," he said. "I'm John Seeger. You are welcome to come in."

Hesitant, but perhaps lured by his welcome, the women entered and followed the man to the impressive great room of the chalet. There he motioned them toward a fire pit for the great stone fireplace. The room featured wooden walls and rafters and hefty, comfortable furniture. Wall lighting and table lamps gave the room a warm glow.

"But," said Emily, whose courage was increasing, "this was supposed to be a very unwelcome place."

"I know the stories they tell, and those stories have been largely true—but things have changed recently."

"Changed?" said Amelia.

"Yes, but we can go into all that in a little while. But first, how about some hot cider and sandwiches? I was just going to prepare something for Anthony and me."

"Anthony?" Amelia said.

"Yes," said John. "He's my son. He is with my old firm but has been helping me here. He'll be in soon."

"A sandwich sounds wonderful," said Emily, feeling acutely the hours since lunch.

She and Amelia walked around the large great room while Mr. Seeger could be heard making his preparations in the adjoining kitchen. The last rays of the sun were dimly glowing in the west over the endless succession of the Dolomites.

"Hello. I didn't know we had company."

The women turned and saw a young man standing there.

"I'm Anthony," he said, extending his hand. Anthony favored his father, although taller.

Amelia and Emily introduced themselves and made apologies for dropping in uninvited and unannounced.

"Not to worry," said Anthony. "It's been a long time since this house has had visitors and it is a welcome change. I must make myself presentable for Father's version of dinner. I hope he has made you welcome."

"Oh, yes," said Emily. "He has been very kind."

"I'll be back soon—make yourself at home," said Anthony.

The women sat by the fire for a time until both father and son reappeared, the father carrying the container of hot cider and Anthony bearing a tray of ham sandwiches. All then sat in the various chairs surrounding the fireplace, each telling of their past and what they were engaged in at present.

John was most interesting in his longing to return to tend his roses at his English cottage in the Cotswolds. He made it sound very inviting when he described the views of the fields, hedges, and distant hills.

All during this pleasant time of introductions and some laughter, Amelia was still wondering about the purpose of this place—with its fencing, strange activities, and, especially, what had changed so that it was open, even welcoming, now.

After dessert of a delicious pudding, John said, "Well, I guess it's time to tell you a few things about this place. I know you have been wondering."

"Yes," said Emily, "we have been rather curious."

"Well—" began John.

"Dad, maybe we could give them the condensed version, and then they can ask questions."

"Yes," said John. "I've been known to get carried away in my story-telling," to which Anthony nodded in agreement.

"Well," John continued, "you probably know that during the Second World War many valuable, some priceless, paintings and other pieces of art were seized from homes and museums for the benefit of the Third Reich. When this became evident, various groups came together to preserve as many of these treasures as they could. My grandfather was a member of one of these groups, calling themselves "The Preservation Society."

"This group, made up of persons from several nations, of course engaged in various other activities that were known to the public," said Anthony. "This made it easier to conduct their collecting of the valuables they wished to preserve from wartime loss."

"And they did very well, but you can see the need to find places to hide the large number of acquisitions. No building could house and preserve all the items, and besides, it was necessary to have an environment of controlled humidity and the like," said John.

"So they hit on some sort of cave atmosphere, which led them to here," said Anthony.

"Here?" asked Amelia.

"Yes, but maybe we could show you rather than tell you," said John.

The hosts then got up and motioned to invite Amelia, intrigued, and Emily, slightly uneasy, to follow them as they went through the long hall to the back of the house. There they came upon a large door that seemed to enter into the mountain itself.

Although the door appeared very heavy it opened easily for Anthony. Inside was very dark and they could feel a cold draft on their faces from deep within. John turned to an electric panel and switched on bright lighting in the tunnel.

"What is this?" asked Emily.

"You've probably heard of, or maybe visited, the Salzburg area of Austria?" asked Anthony.

"Yes, *Sound of Music* and the music festival," said Amelia.

"And," said Anthony, "salt mines. The area is known for its mountains of salt," said Anthony.

"But," said John, "an industrial group explored for salt in the Dolomites and they attempted one mine—and you are entering it."

"Here?" said Amelia.

"This is it—let's go back a way," said John.

"Is it safe?" asked Emily.

"Yes, as far as we will go," said John, and they proceeded through the cold tunnel until they came to a vast room carved in the mountain. They could not even see the extent of the room in the darkness. "Salt was mined by continuous flooding with water and forming a solution with the salt. That solution was then dried and the salt that remained was prepared for various uses."

"This mine was not a long-term successful venture, going down only a couple of levels of flooding and extraction," said John. "You can see the next level here," approaching a rather large hole in the "floor" of salt. "And you can see how the workmen could go from level to level in the mine."

The women could see two wide boards slanting on their edges down to the next level.

Anthony said, "They would slide on their backsides down the boards holding on to a rope on each side to stop their slides when they had reached the bottom. Kind of fun, really. Also fun is to go a couple levels down to a lake formed by the flooding. Very eerie to row across the lake when all the lights are turned off."

"I'll bet," said Amelia, shivering.

"I imagine you are getting awfully uncomfortable by now in this chilly underground—but these were the conditions for best preserving works of art—and the various niches on this level once stored an abundance of the works of the great masters. Let's get back now to where it's warm," said John.

"You see," continued John after all had returned to the fireside, "even though the mining venture was not productive, the collection and storage operation managed to save countless treasures. I wish you could have seen them, all bound and kept safe during and after the war."

"After the war?" asked Emily.

"Yes," said Anthony. "An even bigger job was locating the proper owners after the extreme disruption of wartime. Some had been killed or died in the war, some were missing, and, even after ownership was determined, heirs had to be located and notified. It took years."

"Sounds like a large effort," said Amelia.

"And it just ended. You just missed the truck carrying the last shipment down the mountain for distribution to some likely very grateful people," said Anthony.

"So—now you are open for visitors?" said Amelia.

"Yes, it is a welcome change to all these years of secrecy, wondering whether someone might steal these masterpieces," said John.

"Or if some deterioration might be taking place, I suppose," said Emily.

"Yes," said Anthony, "I am the fourth generation with at least some of this responsibility, and now..."

Amelia could see the visible signs of relief in both men, and it seemed appropriate when John proposed a champagne toast in celebration of the day.

The women asked father and son to join them for dinner at their hotel the next evening. This began a firm friendship between England and "the Colonies," as Anthony called the States.

So it did not seem strange at all when Anthony found business reasons for visiting Amelia from time to time, nor when they finally married and lived in London part of the time and as often as they could in the beautiful Cotswolds. They were visited there and in London from time to time by Emily and husband Eric, and—indicating that Emily was no longer so reticent or hesitant—their four children.

And, from time to time, the families vacationed in the beautiful Dolomites and visited the former mine of treasures there.

The Little Red Coat

It was not much of a farm. In fact, it was called Notalotta Farm. But it had been a favorite place of youngsters from elementary school age on up to learn to ride horses. The original teacher was Miss Loretta, a former circus trick rider, who was also "good with kids." She bought this small run-down acreage some forty years before, mainly for the very substantial barn. She added on to the barn as she acquired an ever-greater number of horses.

When Miss Loretta retired, Miss Sharon, a young horsewoman, took over. Ruddy of complexion from being out in all sorts of weather, not particularly careful in dress, and not afraid of the hard work of caring for horses, she somehow passed on to her students the love of horses and the desire to ride well.

The person who gave the farm its name, after looking it over for the first time, was still there. George, a stocky Black man, of uncertain age but certainly over seventy, was still tending both horses and kids. Although, like Miss Sharon, "no nonsense" in the way the animals should be looked after and treated, he was revered to the extent that even past students often came back to see him.

Even though the young riders liked both Sharon and George, it was hard to understand why they would endure the conditions for riding at the Farm. In the first place, they had to saddle their own horses, and brush and feed them afterwards. The students would ride no matter in all sorts of weather—cold, rain, snow, wind—didn't matter, they still rode. And, except for the ring by the barn and the jumps in a nearby meadow, the land was nothing but ravines, rising up and going down, sometimes muddy, always rocky. Often, at least one parent in a family would not be able to watch, especially their smaller children, riding off on those large horses.

But Miss Sharon and her assistants taught safety in the saddle every day—you might even say they were strict with their charges, but the kids kept coming back for more. And parents came to accept that Notalotta, not much to look at, a place for their children to grow in confidence and responsibility.

Because of the large number of youngsters, one thing that really "bugged" George was the number of items that were left behind after the lessons. He said he would "throw it all away." They knew he wouldn't, and although they listened to everything about riding, they still left stuff. So he finally came up with the idea of a line of pegs to hang lost items of clothing and a number of cubbies for everything else. Now and then, students would be marched over to pick up what they had left.

After one such effort at clearing out the pegs and cubbies, little remained of any value, except for a little red coat. It was not new; in fact, it was a style of some years earlier. But it was still a good warm jacket. After asking about the coat for several weeks Miss Sharon looked at it closely and saw a rather worn nametag stitched into the coat—Roberta Gilbert.

"Yeah, that's Bobby Gilbert," said George. "She came here for lessons. But that was over twenty years ago, and I think she now lives way over in Carrville."

"How would this jacket just show up now?" asked Teddy, one of the assistants.

"Search me," said George. "But I remember she had an aunt, Mrs. Reilly, who used to bring Bobby sometimes. I'll give her a call."

Later that week George said to Sharon, "I talked to Mrs. Reilly. She couldn't figure out how Bobby's jacket could show up here. She did tell me that Bobby had not been well; that she was losing the strength in her muscles."

"That's too bad," said Sharon. "She had evidently been a very active person."

A few days later George said that he had gotten a call from Roberta Gilbert. She said she couldn't tell more about the jacket she had as a child. She had also said that she was distressed that she was no longer able to ride. Her doctors had said no to any such vigorous and maybe dangerous exercise.

"Wish we could get Bobby up on a horse again," George said.

"Well, we've seen how people with disabilities have been able to enjoy riding again if the proper care is taken," said Sharon.

"That's right. Maybe I'll call Tommy Bradshaw. He may have an idea."

"Who's that?" asked Sharon.

"Tommy used to ride here—even worked cleaning out the stalls for a time. Then he went to college and then to medical school. He's a fancy doctor now in Atlanta. He might have an idea."

After getting the number of Dr. Thomas P. Bradshaw, George called and asked if Tommy Bradshaw was there. He was passed from receptionist to assistant to office manager, who asked, "Who is this?"

"Just tell him George is calling from Notalotta."

"Oh, my. Is this some kind of funny business?" she asked.

"Just tell him, please."

Soon Dr. Bradshaw was on the phone. "George, I'm so glad to hear from you. Sorry about the delay. How are things at Notalotta?"

"Going about the same as usual, Tommy, but I have a problem I'd like to ask you about." And George went on to tell about Bobby Gilbert and her medical condition and her wishing she could ride.

"I knew Bobby well. We rode together. Maybe I can do something. Can you get me the name of one of her doctors?"

George got the information to the doctor and not long after, Dr. Tommy Bradshaw called George. "George, I've talked with Bobby's doctor and agreed to take responsibility for getting Bobby to the farm and to try to get her riding again."

"Knew you could do it, if anybody could, Tommy."

Everyone at Notalotta was pretty excited when, a few weeks later, Roberta Gilbert and Dr. Thomas P. Bradshaw showed up, wearing their riding outfits. Sharon had selected the steadiest horse, Nell, for her, and the big bay, Arthur, for him.

"Guess we have to saddle them," said Bobby.

"Yes, you do," said George, but this time he helped put her saddle on.

"We must pull the girth tight," Bobby said.

"You learned well," said Sharon. She then, with Tommy's help assisted Bobby onto Nell. After getting settled, they proceeded slowly to the ring.

The pleasure that could be seen in Bobby's face was matched by the satisfaction felt by Dr. Tommy and the Notalotta crew, especially George.

After the ride Sharon provided some sandwiches and sodas to treat the visitors. They were all sitting around outside the barn, when a young girl, about eight years old, showed up.

She stood there, with her hands on her hips, and said, "Can anyone tell me where my red jacket is? My Mom got it for me from Goodwill, and I've lost it."

A Shocking Incident

Jamie Farmer was not a farmer—he was an electrician. He had gone to trade school for his training. He could have gone to college. He was plenty smart—good enough grades, but he wanted to learn a skill like his father, Ike, a machinist.

Jamie had passed through his apprenticeship with ease, a quick learner of the practical side of the trade. With another young electrician, Gloria, they started First Rate Electric Service.

Luckily, they started during a boom time for new houses so jobs came quickly. They could, and probably should, have employed others to help, but they had decided to make it a two-person operation.

They managed to keep their relationship professional while still having lots of laughs at the errors they made starting out, quirky customers, and life in general. They were seeing other people, Jamie was dating Joan and Gloria was engaged to Bud. They didn't double date much—day to day on the job was plenty of contact.

Jamie was a wiry lad and usually did the crawling in tight spaces while Gloria, fuller of figure, prepared and directed. She often said that she was not happy with the prospect, while working in a dusty, dark space, of a spider "sitting down beside her."

Usually they worked on new construction, with easier access and quicker finishing of the job. Occasionally, they got the challenge of rewiring, which took more time, more crawling, and more contorting to get the rewiring put in.

Sid Koontz made a living, a good living, buying up old houses and refurbishing them for a turnaround profit. He had a good eye for a property that needed just enough work to make it desirable at a marketable price. He began hiring Jamie and Gloria for all his work.

Most of the homes were less than fifty years old; now and then, however, Sid called on First Rate to take on wiring that was from their great-grandparents' era.

Such was the big old farmhouse, sitting on rather large acreage. The home had been last updated in wiring in the late 1940's, but it had been a sketchy job, and so Jamie and Gloria were starting pretty much from scratch.

Gloria laid out the electrical plans after Sid showed them the improvements he would be making. Some of the work would have to be planned on the go because of the old thick walls and really old timbers.

They set aside two weeks for the job but quickly revised their schedule because of one obstacle after another. An interesting discovery was the presence of a log structure that the farmhouse had been built around. The log house went back in time to the early settlers. The log cabin originally had a dirt floor, but a wide pine board floor had been installed.

A more interesting find in the basement of the farmhouse followed.

"Hey, Gloria."

"What?" she replied from just above.

"There's extra wire down here."

"Extra?"

"Yeah," he said, "and not the same kind. It is expensive cable and even an extra electric box to support it."

"Probably goes to the barn," she said.

"No, it goes the other way."

"But," she said, "That is the way to the fields. Why would wiring be needed in that direction?"

"Search me," said Jamie.

Later, when ready to call it a day, Gloria said, "You doing anything right away?"

"No plans," said Jamie.

"I've been wondering about that cable you found. Let's check it out."

They went outside to the foundation wall. Jamie said, "The wire would come out about here."

With a spade he began digging a little trench beside the house. He found the wire in short order. They began walking in the same direction as the wire had emerged from the house. About seventy-five feet from the house, they came on the wire again. It had been exposed by erosion of the covering soil.

"It's going in a straight line," said Gloria. "Should we check on it every hundred feet or so?"

"Yep, good plan," said Jamie.

They were successful at the next one hundred and also at two hundred, but it was taking some time to determine a positive location, so it was getting late. They agreed to check further tomorrow.

After making good progress in the house the next day, they again went out along the same route. They found the wire at three hundred but not at four hundred feet.

"It wouldn't come this far and just end," said Jamie.

"No, but finding it gets a little trickier."

They began making holes along the probable path and were rewarded in about forty feet.

"It splits," said Gloria.

"Sure does," said Jamie.

They were standing at the beginning edges of a large hay field.

"Well, we've seen where it's come from, but where are the two wires going?"

"And why," said Gloria.

The next morning Gloria said to Jamie, "I talked with Bud about that cable and how it split. He said he'd stop by to help us after work."

Jamie said, "We can use the help. I talked with my mom last night. She grew up near here and said the Hiltzes who lived on this farm were considered strange by their neighbors."

"How strange?"

"Well, they pretty much stayed to themselves. Even the children didn't mix much with others at school. Then, in the 1960's, they just up and left."

Several evenings of digging and trial and error revealed the ultimate direction of the wires. They turned and followed both edges of the hay field. Periodically there was a buried rusting wiring box where something had been years ago attached.

Before all the unearthing had been done, the digging crew had reached the conclusion that the wires supported lighting for an airfield. Further questioning of nearby residents revealed some rumors of nighttime lights, but as to what years the lights occurred were even more obscure.

So, sitting around at a double date at the couples' favorite pizza parlor, the subject came up again about the probable airfield with no answers in sight. "Too long ago," said Bud. "But I think it had to do with the Second World War. And, you know the Hiltz family, who lived on the farm early on, were known to speak with a foreign accent. I think they were spies."

"Well, we did have several military posts nearby and some defense plants—very good place for a spy operation," said Jamie.

"Or," said Joan, "even an entry point for other spies to come into this country."

"They were up to something," said Gloria. "Maybe we'll never find out."

It appeared that Gloria was right about the lack of closure on the strange happenings at the Hiltz place, until, quite by accident, they learned more. The truth was, as often happens, not what was anticipated—not by a long shot.

It happened this way. Sid Koontz, who had employed First Rate, had been told by the electricians what they had found regarding the wandering wiring. While looking at a piece of property in the next county, he came across the Hiltz name as adjoining landowners. In checking land records, he found the family had acquired their property soon after disappearing from their former farm with the supposed airfield.

Over a Saturday brunch at Bud and Gloria's, now married, Sid briefed the two couples on what he had found. After taking in this new information, the question was, should anything be done?

"Let it go," said Jamie. "It's too long ago."

"And we're not completely sure about what happened. All we have is some old wires and a big hayfield," said Gloria.

"But," said Sid, "What if what we think the Hiltzes were doing was wrong?"

"They were going against our country," said Joan. "My grandfather was wounded in the War, and, at the same time, these people were..."

"The thing is, we just need to know more," said Gloria.

"And how do we find out more?" asked Sid.

A reasonable question, to which no one had an answer. Not long after, however, a coincidence occurred that moved the mystery along. Sid was looking into buying another piece of property for renovation. The house was in a community some distance from where he usually invested. The adjoining property owner was a Hiltz. And, in pacing off the boundaries of the yard of his possible purchase, Sid met that neighbor.

"You thinking of buying here?" asked Mr. Hiltz.

"Yep, if the appraisal checks out."

"It seems to be a sound house."

"Yes, it appears so."

They continued to talk, and Sid thought, what the heck, and he asked what was on his mind. He wanted to know whether Mr. Hiltz was a member of the airfield farm family. What Sid learned then was the story he related to the electrician couples when they got together on his return.

"He really knew what had occurred during the War on that hayfield landing site?" asked Gloria.

"Yes, but we got it all wrong—and I mean, *all* wrong," said Sid.

"You mean, they were not the bad guys?" said Bud.

"Bingo—and then some. It was like this..." Sid told what he had learned. "The airfield was used after—not during, World War II."

"After?" Jamie said. "That's crazy."

"Wait a minute—not so crazy. The Hiltzes were members of a group of pacifist farmers who settled in our county and nearby before the War. They were nonresistant and opposed to the war they saw coming in Germany."

"That still doesn't explain...." said Joan.

"Here's what happened after the War," said Sid. "Germany was destitute and dependent on America and others for aid. The Hiltzes and others got together the products of their farm and gardens and what they could afford to send to their families and friends left in Germany. The Hiltz farm was the collecting point, and they wired their field so they could fly out at night."

"Why at night?" asked Gloria.

"There were still anti-Nazi feelings in the community that extended even to those opposed to war," said Sid.

"Did you tell the man you met how we had gotten it all wrong?" said Jamie.

"Yes, and he said they had faced that suspicion when they left—but they were confident they had done the right thing."

"And, it's too late now to make amends," said Joan.

After a moment of silence, Bud said, "Maybe not. Maybe we could have the family, and their friends, come over and...."

"And," said Jamie, "We could have a get-together at their old farm...."

"And we could have neighbors come over to meet on a friendly basis—at last."

"Jamie and I could see if we can use the old electric cable to connect some lighting for the occasion," said Gloria.

"It is kind of a re-connection, after all these years," said Sid.

"After all these years," echoed Jamie.

Uncle Jimmy's Last Run

Dedicated to the many Railroaders in our family, listed at the end of this story.*

"Uncle Jimmy" Sherman climbed on the double diesel for a night-time run. This was an unusual event in two ways: It was his last turn having spent forty-three years, man and boy, as he said on the railroad, as a fireman and an engineer. He was now at the top of the list in seniority on the division which led to the second thing that was unusual: for some years he never had to work at night, only in the daylight.

James Nathaniel Sherman was born for the railroad. His father and uncles had held various jobs on the same division as conductors, boss of the wreck train, yard supervisor, and, of course, engineer, going back to the day when it was all steam. In fact, some of the older ones marveled that they had made the shift to diesel and had even fought the new engines when they had come onto the line.

Uncle Jimmy's physical make-up—a little heavy for the pull up into the cab of the engine—may have made it difficult for him to be an engineer, but once he got into his seat, having made his check of the engine, he was in his intended realm. He was as one with the mechanism of the metal beast. He also knew the territory, having traveled the entire division, yards and all, for his entire career. He knew every bridge, every slow-down that was in his orders, every dangerous spot where there had been a wreck dating back to his father's day on the road.

It was because of this competency and knowledge that he had been selected for this run; in fact, he would be in control of the only engine running in the division tonight. That would be pretty eerie in itself, but the rest of the situation was even more unusual.

Hurricane Samantha had hit the east coast of Florida with level 4 force and had aimed straight at Miami. The results were not as bad as New Orleans, but Samantha was not only strong but she was also wide—so wide that she struck with a vengeance in not only Miami but also the towns north and south of Miami. As a result, the coastline and to the west were leveled by the great power of the storm. Both mobile and conventional homes, stores, schools, and all types of buildings suffered severe damage. The high tide that had come in with the storm added to the devastation and, in addition, took out bridges and tore up roads.

Utilities suffered extreme loss. Electricity was out in a swath seventy miles wide, except for power created by generators. Especially the older and weaker residents suffered from the lack of air conditioning along the hot weather coast. Standard telephone and cable television services were disrupted.

But it was the harm to the water systems of the towns in the Miami area that had Uncle Jimmy preparing for his last run. Since water was an essential service, emergency crews were hard at work restoring the buildings, piping, and holding tanks. Work was progressing at a rapid pace, but the chemicals essential in water purification were running low—and the plants serving a large population used a lot of chemicals.

The supply of these essential chemicals was located some one hundred fifty miles up the coast of Florida. It was crucial that they be delivered right away to the Miami area. Trucks might be used but essential bridges were not passable, roads had not yet been repaired, and the traffic control systems were down because of the disruption in electricity.

Fortunately, by some stroke of luck, the rail tracks and the railroad bridges had survived the storm—at least as far as a quick inspection by the emergency road crew could determine as they traveled in their rail-adapted vehicle. In their report they said it was important to recognize that the system was apparently safe for light-weight usage, but they could not guarantee what would happen when a heavy locomotive passed over the rails.

Another problem for rail travel was that just as the highway traffic signals were out, so were the crossing gates and signals, since they were also dependent upon electric power. This was not an insignificant problem, because people were driving in large numbers, especially around their immediate areas, in spite of emergency management officials' pleas that they remain home for the time being. The vehicle drivers were driving over the crossings with little caution, assuming that no trains would be moving.

Despite these well-known danger factors, town officers called upon the railroad to consider making a run to deliver purification supplies to their water systems. Most of these plants were not far from the rail lines, and so the materials could be dropped off at certain central points for redistribution by truck.

Before closing the door on a project they considered unlikely to succeed, the railroad division superintendent and staff wanted to talk with someone who knew the line into Miami—so they called in Uncle Jimmy. The officials explained the need for the water supplies and reviewed the report of the inspection crew.

Uncle Jimmy knew that the crossing signals were out in the Miami area. He asked, "How many crossings are unguarded?" He was not prepared for the answer.

"One hundred twenty-eight."

"Whew," was all he could say, before indicating that he was willing to try—provided some conditions were met. He said that he wanted to go at night when there would be less traffic. At each crossing someone would have to stand guard and stop traffic when he went through. Sidings would have to be identified so that he could drop off a freight car at each distribution site—and make sure that the switches were suited for manual movement.

Two other demands: First, he wanted Engines 1817 and 2183 for the run. He and his father before him were convinced that engines—steam or diesel—have something like personalities, more reliable or less reliable; and for this he knew he needed the best. His second requirement was that Dru fire for him.

Actually, no one "fired" anymore, the way that they used to when the steam engines required feeding of wood in the early days and then coal. Uncle Jimmy's father, also named James, used to tell of his earlier job firing and running engines on the Cranberry and Seventeen-Mile grades on the B&O in the mountains of Western Maryland and Eastern West Virginia. The fireman was almost never allowed to rest on the way up the mountain, especially if the engines were pulling fully loaded cars. The elder Sherman told of other exploits and dangers as a steam engineer, such as getting ready to descend the treacherous Seventeen Mile Grade and discovering that the brake pressure was low. The rail officials were familiar with Dru. They knew that she had a regular turn on the division and had worked on the engines for two years. They did not know that her full name was Drusilla, which she considered a little formal, and to counteract which may have been partially responsible for her being a tomboy as a youngster and working jobs that ordinarily were held by men during and after college. And she was Uncle Jimmy's granddaughter. Uncle Jimmy was aware that she "knew her stuff" around the trains and knew that she would be adaptable in an emergency. In addition to Dru, a veteran conductor and two other rail employees had been chosen for the run because of their familiarity with the tracks in the division and with the switches.

The time of the trip was the next night. The boxcars were being loaded at the water chemical distribution center. The plan was to get to the first of the unprotected crossings at eleven when automobile traffic would be reduced.

Two watchmen with portable lights were being assigned to each crossing. The watchmen were recruited from railroad personnel and local law enforcement. They would be briefed on the schedule of the train going south and kept apprised of the approximate time of return. A communication center was established in the railroad division office with connections to the engine, the drop-off sites, and the watchmen.

Dru picked up Uncle Jimmy, Grandpa to her, at his house. Granny had packed lunch buckets, containing enough, Uncle Jimmy said, for the train crew and most of the watchmen along the tracks.

When the railroaders had left, Granny called her daughter, Carol, Dru's mother, and both agreed that the trip appeared to be rather routine. But, as Granny said, "You never know."

Uncle Jimmy went over their engines carefully, knowing that they would be beyond assistance once they reached the hurricane devastation area. Two passengers joined them in the engine. Tom was included in the trip because he was a civil engineer with expertise particularly regarding bridges. He was just a few years out of the university but gave the appearance of competence and care with detail that had caused the older rail staff to place much confidence in him. He was taller than average with sandy hair and a quick-to-laugh personality.

Ray, the other man, was older and both gray and balding. From his weathered look he had obviously spent much time out of doors in his work with the maintenance of way workers who kept the rails and roadbed secure for movement of the trains.

The engines proceeded to the materials warehouse and were hooked up with the loaded freight cars. They arrived at the first signs of hurricane damage at ten o'clock and occupied their time for the next hour rechecking the train and going over their plans for the night.

At eleven Uncle Jimmy pulled out. Even though they could see the effects of the winds some lights were still on and crossing gates and signals were still operating. This, however, lasted only for a few miles.

Then the lights went out—literally. Street illumination was gone. Houses were dark. They could see where the train crews had sawed and removed the downed trees from the railroad right of way. Car lights and homes served by generators were the only things that could be seen away from the tracks.

Soon they came to the first unlit crossing. Uncle Jimmy's first thought was to slow down to be sure that the crossing was manned and therefore safe. But he had his orders. If they were to reach the drop-off points on schedule, they had to keep moving on. He did hang onto the whistle somewhat longer than he was used to doing.

"One down," Dru said. And the passengers agreed. Of course, they would have agreed with almost anything she said. They were aware of what an attractive young woman she was.

"Yeah," said Uncle Jimmy. "Tom, will you make sure that our phones are connected to the communications center?"

Tom dialed his cell phone, said a few words, and gave a thumbs up to Uncle Jimmy.

Despite his unease the old engineer had to admit, as they passed crossing after crossing lit on each side by the watchmen's lights, that the trip was going smoothly.

The lights along the way, while not extremely bright, were numerous and varied. Some of the watchmen had lanterns, mostly Coleman-type, but occasionally an old-fashioned kerosene. The pattern of the swinging lanterns was noticeable and brought back memories of earlier days to Uncle Jimmy. Other watchmen used flashlights, typically heavy-duty. These were flashed directly at the train after the sentinels made sure that approaching highway traffic had been warned. Once in a while an obviously older watchman made some of the traditional signals used in the past by railroaders. Uncle Jimmy gave an extra toot of the whistle to these persons—while against railroad rules, who was around to challenge the train whistle?

Occasionally a car or two would be stopped at a crossing, the drivers often outside waving or in their cars flashing their brights at the train as it passed. Uncle Jimmy dimmed his engine light in recognition.

Evidently the word had gotten around that a train would be passing through—not big news to residents living near the railroad. But it was certainly under different circumstances than normal. So, with not much to occupy people without electricity they lined some of the crossings or stood in their backyards and flashed lights and waved. Some even cheered as the train went by. Dru was especially moved by the recognition, since her experience on trains had been routine and often monotonous.

In fact, she and the other occupants of the cab were enthralled at the beauty of the varied lighting in the otherwise pitch-dark night. It was an experience to take in, enjoy, and hopefully remember at a later day.

Dru's concern that some crossings might be unmanned proved to be unfounded. The organization of the watchmen had been well-done, and after a while the train crew just kept rolling. One of the two hitches in the journey was a switch that gave Ray some trouble at the first point where they dropped off two of the boxcars.

The other possible problem was not even noticed by any of the individuals in the cab except for Uncle Jimmy. They were going over a long bridge just north of Miami in an area especially hard-hit by the hurricane. In the middle of the bridge Uncle Jimmy noticed a slight sway, not too much but an indication of some damage. He noted the location for special attention on the trip back north.

They backed their cars into the assigned unloading sidings and pulled out quickly to be on their way to the end of the run. Conveniently a turn-around was located near the last drop-off siding so that they did not have to return running backwards.

They took little time in turning around and were soon on their way north. All were relieved to have "delivered the goods" without incident.

When Uncle Jimmy reached the long bridge where he had sensed possible damage by Samantha, he slowed down to a crawl. Dru and the others knew something was not just right by the drop in speed and by Uncle Jimmy's intent demeanor. He eased the engines along by feel as much as by intention, relying upon his years on the road to determine where proceeding was sufficiently safe. The bridge seemed endless. How could the river be so wide? Where exactly was the maximum damage? Would the bridge hold the weight of the two heavy engines?

After what seemed an eternity the lights of the engine picked up the far embankment, and in a moment they were on solid land again.

The crossings going back home were similar in appearance—watchmen were still at their posts and they waved to the engine crew as they passed by. Few cars were waiting and the former by-standers were evidently home in their beds.

Uncle Jimmy and Dru and the two passengers were very tired as they approached the terminus of their trip. The tension of anticipation had been working on them, and they were glad to be pulling in, just as dawn was breaking in the east.

Several rail officials and public emergency officers greeted them as they came in and listened as Uncle Jimmy reported on the successful delivery. They congratulated the entire crew on their night's work and completion of their important mission.

The crew acknowledged their praise and not long after the visitors left. Ray said good-bye and left for home. While Uncle Jimmy shut down the engines, Tom lingered long enough to ask Dru if he might see her in the future. She said that she'd like that.

Dru drove Uncle Jimmy home in the early daylight. Naturally, Granny was waiting up as she had so often done in the years that Uncle Jimmy had railroaded. She had biscuits and eggs and sausage for their breakfast as Dru knew she would.

As the three sat around the table with the last of their coffee Granny asked her husband, "How was it?"

"Oh, you know, same as always."

**The Railroaders in our daughters' and grandchildrens' family are Diane's father, Rex Chilcote, grandfather Charles Chilcoat, and uncles Charles Chilcoat and James Leatherman; and Paul's father and mother, Kemper Cline, Sr., and Irene Cline, Kemper's brother, Warren Cline; Irene's brothers Callie, William, and Perry Neff, brother-in-law Thomas Kelly, and uncles Joe and Jim Grimes.*

Stories for Children

The Old Ice Cream Shop

One day Beth and her brother Matt went to the Old Ice Cream Shop to get cones. Beth was nine and Matt was six.

They noticed the counter to the rear of the shop. The clerk told them that Mrs. Hudson sold old-fashioned homemade ice cream there.

When they went to Mrs. Hudson's counter, she wasn't there. Matt saw that there was another room farther back.

"Maybe Mrs. Hudson is back there," he said, as he went behind the counter.

"You'd better not go there," said Beth.

"I won't hurt anything," said Matt as he went behind the curtain that hid the back room.

"Wow!" he said.

"What?" asked Beth.

"Come and look," he answered.

The first thing they saw was the balloons covering the ceiling—red, blue, green…every color. In the center of the large room was a pile of toys—big as a huge fire truck.

The children could see toys for girls—dolls, games, dress-up kits, and more. Matt couldn't believe the stack of balls, space ships, bikes, and more than he could ever ask Santa to bring.

Around the room were a series of booths. The children started to explore, and they found that the booths, with their bright colored umbrellas and walls, were actually workshops. And the people working were very busy.

"What are you doing?" Matt asked the first person he saw. That person might have been an elf. He might have been a little person, about as tall as Matt.

"We're making sprinkles," he said.

"Sprinkles?" asked Beth, puzzled.

"Yes, you don't think all those sprinkles Mrs. Hudson uses come out of the sky, do you?"

"No, I guess not," said Beth, looking at all the colors and sizes that the elves—or little people—were making.

In the next booth were the balloon-blowers. Their booth was very large because so many balloons take up a lot of space. The children saw all colors of balloons, and at one end were the balloons for special times—Happy Birthday, Happy New Year, Happy Valentine's Day, and more.

At another booth were the doll-makers. When Beth began to ask a question, one of the older workers said, "We don't have time to stop right now—we have a big order for a children's home. Come back next week, and we'll show you how we make all kinds of dolls."

"Okay," said Beth. "I'd like that."

Going on, Matt and Beth made short visits to the shops for making bikes, little kitchens, doll houses, and more. They also went into the gym where all the footballs, basketballs, all kinds of balls, were being tested.

The game room had walls to keep in the "bing-bing-bing" and the other sounds of games being tried out for the first time.

At each place the workers seemed happy to see them and asked them to come back again. Beth and Matt said they hoped that they could.

Pretty soon, when they got around to where they began, they heard a woman's voice saying, "I'm sure they are nearby. I'll just look back of this curtain."

It was Mrs. Hudson, smiling as she said, "Children, your mother is here."

Their mom was glad to see them. She said, as all moms do, "I hope they weren't too much bother."

"Not at all—we hope they will come back soon," said Mrs. Hudson.

"We?" asked their Mother.

"I mean 'I,' of course. You know what I mean, don't you, Beth and Matt?" said Mrs. Hudson.

"Yes, we know," said Beth, and she, Matt, and Mrs. Hudson all smiled at their little secret—what was behind the curtain of The Old Ice Cream Shop.

Cyril

Cyril was six and in his first day of school.

The students gathered in a ring on the floor around the chair of their teacher, Mrs. Nance.

As they waited for Mrs. Nance to take her seat, Tommy whispered to a boy beside him, "What's your name?"

"Cyril," he said.

"Cereal?" said Tommy.

"No…" Cyril started to correct Tommy.

"His name is Cereal," Tommy told Sandra, next to him.

"Cereal?" said Sandra and told Lon, who was next, about Cereal's name.

"You mean—like Captain Crunch?" said Lon.

"What?" asked Betty, who was next in the circle.

"That boy there is a captain," said Lon.

"Like in the Army?" said Betty.

"Who's in the Army?" asked Jimmy who was next to Betty.

"Can't be Cereal—he's too young. Maybe it's Mrs. Nance," said Betty.

"Think we ought to salute?" asked Jimmy.

"I guess we should," said Betty.

"Everybody get up," shouted Jimmy.

And the class stood, and as Mrs. Nance approached the circle, the whole class turned toward her—and saluted. And Mrs. Nance smartly returned the salute.

What you have just read is, of course, the children's story; but as is often the case, there is more, a tale for us older children—

What the youngsters did not know was that Mrs. Nance, way before she began to teach at Oakmont Grade School, was an officer in the United States Army. She still possessed some of the discipline for which she had been known by her troops; or more especially the discipline that she expected from her troops. Oh, my, you mean to say that that pleasant, motherly, helpful teacher was once the nemesis of any slothful soldier? You betcha.

The principal at the Oakmont Grade School was Egbert Humbert IV, the last of a long line of educators, his father, grandfather, great-grandfather before him. Egbert differed from the elder Humberts, in that, while they were benevolent 'Berts, Egbert turned out to be a tyrant. He was not a large person, and, to make up for this, developed a booming voice, which he delighted in using on little kids and tremulous teachers alike.

"What must we do?" asked perpetually nervous Nellie (yes) Frontenbush. Her only act of rebellion was, upon Egbert's order that all the staff be clean-shaven, refusing to remove her moustache. Several of these professional educators were gathered, in their usual cowering condition, in the teachers' lounge, the only sanctuary from you-know-who in the whole building.

Maude McDermott, a towering, rather large-boned woman who had been at the school since it had opened, and had taught several of the present teachers, including Mrs. Nance, who was a thrice-blessed grandmother, boomed, "I don't know, but all I want now is a cigarette," which always spurred Prudence Pendleton to say, "You know, Maude, you really oughtn't (only English-speaking person who still clung to oughtn't) smoke," to which Maude would say to her, as she had for the past forty years, "Yeah, it's gonna stunt my growth."

"This is getting us nowhere, and we seem to never get anywhere with Humbug." That secret name had been the only means which the good teachers of Oakmont had come up with to get back at the source of their misery.

"I did hear something the other day," said Ms. Pendleton, when all became quiet. "About Mr. Humbert."

A chorus of "What? What?"

"He was in the Army."

"Ours?" asked Miss Maude, as she was known to all within or even shouting range of the schoolhouse.

"Yes, at least I think so," said Prudence.

"Illustrious career, I suppose," said Mr. Sirk, art and phys ed.

"Not so much, I gather," continued Prudence. "In for three years and came out as a PFC."

"Is that good?" asked Maude, whose point of reference was the First World War.

"Not so hot," said Mr. Sirk, whose first initial was, unfortunately, B.

"Hmm," said Mrs. Nance, suddenly sitting up straighter, throwing out her chest a little further, and looking off to the distance, but saying no more.

In fact, Mrs. Nance, AKA Col. "Mad Monica" Nance to her troops, said only a word or two until the next day at the monthly teachers' meeting in the auditorium. Humbug was conducting the meeting in his autocratic fashion as usual, leaving little room for disagreement or even others' speaking, when Mrs. Nance rose from her seat.

"Point of order," she said.

"Yes, yes, what is it Ms. Nance?"

"I've been on this faculty for twenty-seven years."

"Yes, yes, get to the point."

"And," she said, "I've never spoken in faculty meeting up to this time."

Maude whispered to Prudence, "And she used to talk in class all the time—couldn't get her to shut up."

Mr. Humbert said, "Interesting, Mrs. Nance, but what of it?"

"I finally have something to say." Until that time her fellow teachers had wondered why she had worn a long coat to the meeting in the warm auditorium.

She suddenly removed her coat, revealing Full Bird Colonel "Mad Monica" Nance, in uniform, standing tall. Her next words were long-remembered in the halls and the environs of Oakmont Grade School.

"Get down and give me five, Private!"

At which point Principal, Private Egbert Humbert, before he had time to think, dropped to the prone position and began giving, as ordered, a series of five push-ups.

During this activity, which proved to be rather strenuous to Humbug, the faculty rose as a single body and quietly left the hall.

Minus Four

Jimmy was a very nice little boy. He had dark curly hair, was about average height for third grade, and got along in school very well.

Until—that one day, that is. All was going well in Mrs. Tompkins' class that morning, then to the cafeteria for a lunch he especially liked.

Then it happened, after lunch in a review of numbers. He was good at numbers, but for some reason made the mistake when it was his turn, when Mrs. Tompkins said, "Jimmy, what is seven minus four?" This exercise was so very easy for him, and also for most of the class. But before he thought, he said, "Two."

No one said anything for a minute, and Mrs. Tompkins said, "Jimmy, I believe you might not have heard...."—when the class began to laugh.

Roger, who wasn't always very nice, especially to Jimmy, said, "That was an easy one," and continued laughing.

"Everyone makes a mistake now and then," said Mrs. Tompkins, but someone, maybe that smarty, Carolyn, started saying, "Minus, minus,..."

The class then began to say, "Minus," until Mrs. Tompkins gave them "that look" (you know the one), and it soon became very quiet. "Let's go on," she said, and the other students answered the problems with few mistakes.

No one had noticed that Shirley had not joined in the laughter. Shirley and Jimmy often walked to school together as they lived near each other. And, she didn't join in when the students continued after school and in days afterward to say "Minus," or "Minus Four" when they came near Jimmy.

The name-calling bothered Jimmy a lot for a time, but as the days passed, he would just smile. As he told Shirley, "I'll just not let it worry me too much."

The Christmas holidays came and went and about the only youngster who still gave Jimmy a hard time was Roger. So going to school wasn't so bad anymore.

Then came the day in the spring when Mrs. Tompkins' class was working on spelling. It was ol' Roger's turn and the word was "barely." Roger was, to give him credit, a good speller, but on this day, before he thought, he blurted out, "b-e-a-r-l-y."

Well, the class started to laugh, and, with Carolyn leading them, began making snarling noises like a bear. Again, Mrs. Tompkins called for a halt to the animal noises, but for days after that Roger had to listen to growling from his classmates.

But what no one seemed to notice was that Jimmy and Shirley didn't join in on giving him a hard time. So—now there were two students who kept silent.

And—maybe the next time someone made a mistake, it would be three, and next time more, and the time after that—well, you do the math.

Buddy L with His Trunk Turned Down

Everyone knows how a lucky elephant charm should look. Well, first, of course, it's got to look like an elephant. Then, it's got to be small—small enough to attach to a bracelet, or—keep in a secret place. But mainly, the elephant's trunk has to, absolutely has to, be raised into the air. That's what makes it a *lucky* elephant charm.

But what do you do with an elephant charm with its trunk pointed down? Well, not much. What's it good for? No one really wants it.

This was the exact problem for Buddy L, the little elephant charm whose trunk pointed toward the ground. Not Buddy L's fault—that's just how he was made.

One day, while Violet, his owner, was sorting through her jewelry case, she came upon Buddy L. She looked him over, wondering what to do with him. She had a choice. On the one hand, she could have kept him safe and out of sight, even if she wouldn't show him in public.

But no, she was not the type of person who knew loyalty, or kindness. She was not a very nice person. But, even knowing this about her, you will be surprised at her next action—she threw Buddy L out of her open bedroom window onto the sidewalk below.

"Ouch." You might imagine how much that hurt—in two ways. One, long way to drop and land on hard concrete. Two, hurt feelings toward Violet, a person Buddy L had attempted to serve for a long time with as much good luck as he could come up with.

So Buddy L lay there on the edge of the walk while kids, young people, old people passed by. Buddy L could not yell very loudly, so no one heard him pleading with the passers-by, not to step on him with their big feet.

Late afternoon came and Buddy L feared he would have to spend the night on the cold cement. A light rain began.

"Oh, swell," thought Buddy L. "What a life I now have."

Then, perhaps because he became visible in the last rays of the setting sun, someone stopped, bent down, and picked him up. This person, a middle-aged man, looked him over real good, and bang, tossed him down again, saying, "Humph, turned-down trunk," and walked on.

More pain and more bad feelings for Buddy L. "Oh, my," he thought.

But his worry didn't last long because someone had seen him being tossed down—and right away picked him up. It was James, a young boy out walking his little dog. Good thing the dog didn't see Buddy L and pick him up in his mouth. But the dog was watching a cute little poodle across the street.

In fact, James' dog was very interested in the poodle, so much so that he pulled his strap loose from James' hand and began to run across the street. And it was a busy street with lots of cars and trucks going by.

Big problem for James. His dog was young and wasn't well-trained yet, so James feared his little dog might get lost.

So James did what he shouldn't have done—he prepared to cross the busy street.

And he almost did—but Buddy L was still in his hand. Buddy L made as much of a move as any elephant charm—lucky or not—could ever be expected to make. It wasn't much, even Buddy L admitted that afterwards, but somehow it was enough.

When James reached the curb with his eyes only on his disappearing little dog, something—Buddy L?—made him stop, just in time. For a big car was almost upon him, and even though the driver tried to stop, it would not have been in time to keep from hitting James.

After the driver moved on by, and James was safely across the street—at the proper crossing—James looked down at Buddy L and smiled.

From that time on Buddy L and James were always together. James would take Buddy L out of his wallet and tell people how he thought Buddy L had saved his life—a real lucky elephant charm.

Now I know what you're thinking—if the writer of this tale were any kind of proper storyteller, it would be recorded that, somehow and in some way, Buddy L's trunk would now, ever since James' near-accident, be turned up, rather than down, similar to all the "lucky" elephant charms you've ever heard of.

But let James finish the story in his own way: "You see, a person or an animal charm—or even an elephant charm—doesn't have to look a certain way to help others. They can appear just as they are and be special. I wouldn't trade Buddy L for a dozen so-called lucky elephant charms with their trunks up in the air."

And Buddy L also considered himself to be an elephant charm who was very lucky.

Cupid's Big Day

The trouble began when Cupid got up on Valentine's Day. The problem was with his bow. Its string had broken and old Giuseppe, who fixes bows as well as shoes, was on vacation with Pinocchio and so could not get the bow fixed in time for Cupid.

So even though Cupid got up really early on February 14, he couldn't greet all the people who were in love because what good was Cupid without his bow?

When he finally started his rounds at ten o'clock, he heard a small voice saying, "Now you just stop right there, Mister."

"Are you talking to me, little man?"

"Do you see anyone else around?" replied a small man dressed in green—a Leprechaun.

"I should have said, what right have you to stop me?" said Cupid.

"The Queen told me to find you."

"Oh, my, the Queen."

"Yes, 'Oh, my, the Queen.'" You see, Cupid knew that the "Queen" was the Queen of the Fairies, and he also knew that the Queen was in charge of both Valentine's Day and St. Patrick's Day.

He went on, "And she said that since you were late in doing your job, you cannot be in charge of your big day. I'm in charge of today, as well as March 17." And with that, he disappeared.

Cupid said, "What shall I do. What shall I do? I must serve all those today who are in love." He considered his dilemma for a moment and decided that he needed more time. So right then he stopped all the clocks in the world. Time stood still.

He thought and thought, but was not getting anywhere at all.

"What's wrong?" came a voice.

Cupid turned to see Glenda the Good Witch sitting nearby.

"I've made a mess of things on my big day," Cupid said, and explained what had happened.

"That is a mess," Glenda agreed. "Hmmm."

"Why are you hmmm-ing?"

"I was just trying to think of some way you could still perform your duties today."

"Oh, please, think," said Cupid.

"Well, I'm having lunch with the Queen of the Fairies today. I'll talk to her about your 'mess.'"

"I'd be ever so grateful," said Cupid.

Just then the Leprechaun reappeared, saying, "And I'd be kind of mad."

"This is no day to be mad," said Glenda.

"You tell him," said Cupid, glaring at the Leprechaun.

"Let's stop this arguing until I return," said the Good Witch, and both Cupid and the little man agreed.

After what seemed a long time, at least to Cupid, Glenda returned, and said, "Start the clocks. Here's your bow, all strung. Start flying."

"You mean it?" said Cupid, and without a further word he started the world's clocks and flew off to do his Valentine's Day duties.

"I'm a bit curious," said the Leprechaun. "How did you get the Queen of the Fairies to agree to this?" One could see that he was not pleased with this decision of the Queen.

"Well, when we talked seriously about what had happened, the Queen suspected that someone was behind this whole thing. She made a couple of phone calls and found that it was the Evil Witch. Do you know anything about this, Leprechaun?"

"Maybe."

"Did the Evil Witch talk with you?"

"Maybe."

"You can 'maybe' all you want, little man, but the Queen of the Fairies has not only permitted Cupid to go to work today, but also that you . . . ."

"Me?"

"Yes, you—are grounded for St. Patrick's Day."

"Oh, my! Oh, my! How will all those great parties go on? How can there be those great parades? And, no 'Wearin' of the Green?'"

"Oh, those celebrations will go on. It's just that this year you won't be part of it."

The Leprechaun thought for a moment. "Then—who's in charge of St. Patrick's Day?" He was thinking—as if anyone could take my place.

"Would you believe—the Great Pumpkin."

"What? . . . What? . . . What?"

"And, Glenda went on, "the Queen of the Fairies told me to tell you one more thing."

"What now?"

"You know how, first there's Valentine's Day . . . ."

"Yes?"

"Then, there's St Patrick's Day . . . ."

"Yes, yes."

"Then there's . . . ."

"Yes, go on . . . ."

"APRIL FOOL!"

"Relax, Leprechaun—you are still in charge of the Wearin' of the Green!"

The Annals of Medicine

A Compilation of Seminal Articles

Introduction

When leading physicians get together and discuss the most influential medical journals, the talk inevitably turns to *The Annals of Medicine.* Whether their need is to be shown a new life-saving procedure, a better way to serve patients, or a means of surviving their office and nursing staffs, they go to the *Annals* first.

In the early days of medicine there was no such dependable up-to-date reference. Of course, the old Latin and German publications were useful to those who had mastered those languages, but it is well known that physicians are scientists, not scholars of the irrelevant, so that their educational scientific focus precluded serious language study. One early printed matter proved useful and very nearly derailed the start-up of the *Annals.* This, of course, was the *Leech Review;* however, this revered source went out of existence with the demise of its founder and principal contributor, Irving Leech. So serious is the determination to keep the *Annals* as *primo medico* that the editorial board has obtained a court order requiring any other by the same name to be called the *Faux-Annals.*

The beloved founder of the *Annals,* the Eminent Psychiatrist, Ina Trance, perceived a serious need for a journal that would transcend all areas of medicine. Little did he know that the medical disciplines would subdivide and subdivide some more, to the extent that very serious practitioners and researchers are spending their waking hours with the left ear or the *medius digitus.* His publication has served these subfields while at the same time provided doctors with the "big picture."

Because of the diversity and quality the articles that have appeared over the years in this honored journal, the selection process was necessarily very rigorous. This process was headed up by Celestial Quimby, inventor of the Quimby Bladder. Dr. Quimby persevered for years in her work because although it is well known, the Quimby Bladder is not found in all people. She has shown the same perseverance in the present editorial task of selecting only the top articles for this compilation.

Here then are the definitive analyses of the medical specialties selected for the first volume of compilations of *The Annals of Medicine*. No doubt, professional and public sentiment will demand that all fields of medicine receive a similar treatment.

Orthopedic Surgeons: The Beginning

Medical specialties often start in Europe. Such was the case of Orthopedic Surgeons.

In the little town of Uber Wrot in Bavaria was the butcher shop of Ernst and Otto Schlepp. They had inherited the business from their Vater, Johann, and were known far and wide for their cutlets.

Ernst and Otto's only problem was that they disagreed about the precise procedure for cutlet creation. Ernst was big on the Hapsburg Diagonal, while Otto favored the old favorite of the Holy Roman Empire (HRE), the straight across and down.

When they were fussing, they retreated to their own individual cutting blocks. Fortunately, they remained kind to their loyal clientele during spats, and it was often difficult to tell that they were on the outs.

They were orphaned at age forty and forty-two, respectively, but they had a little sister Gertrude, who looked after them. She cooked, cleaned, and generally managed their home; however, the first call on her time was for lifting things. For Gertrude was also their big—big—sister. And in Uber Wrot and the surrounding countryside the citizenry depended upon Gertrude to lift their wagons out of ditches, hold their porches up for placing new supports, and righting fallen trees.

But, enough about the boys' Little Schwester, although she will play a significant role in the first days of Orthopedic practice. The moving force in the creation of this specialty was fate.

Who knew that a horse fly would bite the lead horse of Karl Offenbach's prize pair of Percherons (serious writing here, folks), and thus cause them to bolt down the main road into town. All went well, albeit quickly, until the runaway team came into contact with Manfred Friedrichson, who was crossing the town's main street after a serious Schnapps session at the local watering hole.

Manfred was feeling no pain—at least until the moment that the horses, and the hay wagon they were pulling, hit him. Manfred was a big—big—man; in fact, he was often suggested as a prime candidate, the only candidate of suitable size, to be a match for Gertrude.

Manfred went down, seriously hurt, precisely in front of the butcher shop. He remained conscious, but moaned and groaned while rubbing his left hip. It seemed that the other bruises and cuts were minimal compared with the damage done to that hip.

"Get Herr Doktor Schopenhauerdorff!" commanded Wilhelm Schutz, the principal and only representative of the Polizei in Uber Wrot.

"Have you vergessen, Willi, der Doctor ist in Schlaffen," observed Frau Lukas, never missing an opportunity to deliver bad news. (Please note that Schlaffen was a nearby town from which the von (later van) Winkles emigrated.)

"Go to Schlaffen, then," cried Willi, to anyone who would help, in the crowd that was forming.

"Help me now," yelped Manfred.

"Ja, ja, he needs help now," opined Frau Lukas, never missing an opportunity to pose an apparently unsolvable dilemma.

The boys, Ernst and Otto, were out on the porch of their shop by this time, and in the first words spoken by either to the other that day, Otto observed, "His hip bone is protruding, Ernst."

"Yes, and a large hip bone it is," said Ernst, voicing not only concern but admiration. He continued, "Little Herr Doktor Ess (the fond name of the townsfolk for the doctor) would have a difficult time putting that back into place. We might even find it difficult."

"What are you talking about, Ernst? Dat ist the typical give-up-before-you-start attitude of a Hapsburg Diagonal-er."

"Oh, ja, would you recommend the coward's way of the HRE across and down-er?"

"You boys have got to help," said Brunhilde Ludwig, known to be sweet on both of the butchers, such good catches in the community, but she was unable to choose between them.

"Oh ja, try," chanted the gathered crowd, closing in on the boys, and leaving Willi unattended.

Manfred screamed, "Someone help. I don't care who."

The boys approached him in their usual business-like manner and assessed the situation, a little push here, and a little pull there, Manfred continuing to yell in agony.

"Get him in the shop," said Ernst, while Otto ran ahead and placed their two cutting blocks together. (Medical history buffs will undoubtedly be quick to note that this was the creation of the first Orthopedic Operating Theater, or as some would say, Theatre.)

Manfred was placed on a large—large—makeshift stretcher and carried to the butcher-blocks, on which he was gently, but not gently enough to suit him, laid.

"Someone hold him," commanded Otto.

"None of us can do it; he's too massive," countered Frau Lukas, never missing an opportunity to indicate lack of ability when ability was called for.

"Okay, then—this is a job for Gertrude," said Ernst.

"They're bringing in Gertrude." This was on the lips of every person who was jammed into the butcher shop. (They could have sold tickets at this point.)

Gertrude was off that day from any lifting work and was humming a little tune in the kitchen of the Schlepp home, located behind the shop.

Her happy humming was interrupted by Lotte Heft, her good friend. "The boys need you, now," said Lotte.

"I'm making strudel," said Gertrude, "and I can't leave it."

"It's Manfred—he's hurt."

Gertrude's head jerked around at the mention of Manfred. She left her strudel and raced to the shop.

"Good, Gertrude's here, said Ernst. "We need you to hold him down, if you can."

"If I can?" responded his easily miffed sister. "Didn't I lift the corner of our house when you boys needed to repair the foundation?"

"Ja, ja," admitted the boys together, sheepishly.

"Und didn't I do a barn-raising single-handedly?"

"Ja, ja."

"So—let's get on with it," she said, as she grabbed around Manfred's upper body, at the same time looking deeply into his eyes, which were rather bulging at this time. (Medical history buffs will be quick to note that Gertrude Schlepp thus became the first Orthopedic Nurse in the history of that Noble Caring Profession.)

As a result of Willi's being held firmly—and at the same time, tenderly—in a stationary position, the boys could go to work and snap that old hip bone back into place. The Uber Wrot population still recalls the dramatic resounding pop as the joint was restored to its proper condition.

Not much more to tell. Manfred married Gertrude and the couple had seven large—large—children. Ernst married Brunhilde and moved to a home on the outskirts of town. She is said to have chosen him over Otto as a result of being somehow mesmerized by the sound of the Hapsburg Diagonal. And Otto, strangely attracted to Frau Lukas, who lost her husband, Herr Lukas, in that unfortunate incident with the three-pronged pitchfork, married her to his eternal regret.

The Uber Wrot citizens, in appreciation of the efforts of the Schlepps, erected signs on the entrances to the town giving credit where credit was due. Ernst and Otto thus became the first in a long, distinguished line of Uber Wrot Orthopedic Surgeons.

Dermatology: The Annals of Medicine

Introduction: In an effort to raise the level of understanding of the various medical specialties, the Editorial Board of *The Annals of Medicine* utilizes differing descriptive approaches. What follows is the Annual Meeting format with its understanding that these practitioners are here to get Continuing Medical Education credits—and a great weekend at the expense of Pharma.

Setting: Annual meeting of the Dermatological Guild, the Association of Five-Star Dermatologists. Members of the Guild are watching a video.

Video:

Dr. Derm: Bob, it would have been much better if you would have come to see me before the left side of your face fell off.

Bob: Well, you and I play golf every Thursday afternoon, Dr. Derm, and I would have thought...

Dr. Derm: Bob, you can't expect us professionals, with so much on our minds, and out for a little relaxation, to notice...

Bob: Yes, but...

Dr. Derm: Tut, Tut—It's too late for finger pointing—by the way, they're not there.

Bob: What aren't there?

Dr. Derm: Your fingers.

Bob: That's why you have to get the ball out of the cup for me, Dr. Derm. I can't...

Dr. Derm: Bob, you can't expect us professionals....

Bob: By the way, Dr. Derm, when are you going to allow me to call you by your first name? We've been playing golf every week for nineteen years, and...

Dr. Derm: There you go again, Bob. You don't seem to understand how it is with us professionals.

Bob: But…

(End of video)

Dr. Derm addresses his colleagues: Fellow practitioners of the Crown Prince of Medical Practices—the hallowed specialty of Dermatology. I'm so pleased to appear before you today and very honored to give the annual Homer P. Squamus lecture on issues at the forefront of our sainted work.

Many of you are old enough to remember when Homer roamed the halls of Dermatology. Can't say enough of his mentoring skills, especially his finesse with the old nitrogen bottle. Oh, yes, there was that unfortunate incident when Dr. Homer got that defective bottle and blew off Margaret Ballou's left ear—but, hey, once in a forty-year practice...Not too shabby a record.

Now, about the short video I just showed you involving my former golf partner, Bob. That episode in my office shows how very unreasonable patients can be.

Here is the rest of the story. What Bob did not mention, and you will, like I, think him very ungrateful when you learn that I had worked diligently over a three-year period to save the right side of his face. And, get this, he wouldn't have lost his right ear if he hadn't refused to use the 300-power Lock and Loaded Sunscreen which I prescribed for him. But, no, he had to…

But I digress… The second and more important issue that emerges from the video with Bob is his refusal to be properly respectful in addressing physicians of our calling. Now, you can go around being palsy-walsy with the GPs and the Internal Med people, and who really cares about the Orthos—they don't send anyone our way—unless a patient has gotten a severe sunburn of an arm bone or a leg bone.

[Wait for laugh] In short, I'll not have Bob call me by my first name—I don't care if his foot falls… Oh, my, I probably shouldn't have said that; patients will sue you over the least little thing these days.

Oh, well, these are just some of the trials that you and I go through daily in service to the Crown Prince of Practices—Dermatology.

The Early Days of Gastroenterology

Setting: Medical School Class

Professor of Gastroenterology: Class, this film will show an actual depiction of one of the early important events in the history of our chosen specialty.

[Lights dim. Film rolls.]

On screen: "Medical History: How It Went Down—and Up"

Setting: Headquarters of the Gastroenterology Association Specialists (GAS)

Doctors, complete with white smocks and stethoscopes, sitting around on comfortable couches and chairs.

Time: Early days of Gastroenterology.

President of GAS: I've just gotten some bad news.

Vice President: What's that, Lionel?

Pres.: Johns Hopkins University has just discovered a sure-fire way to determine the health of the esophagus and colon by using a teeny-tiny pill that goes through the system and comes out blue if there is a problem.

Secretary of GAS: Why, how do we make any money if it's all over so quick—we've been dragging out the process by testing samples over a six-month period.

Board Member, BM: Yes, that means at least eight or nine appointments—big bucks. And light work.

President: Sh-h-h. BM, you know better than to bring up crass stuff like that.

Vice President: Old BM's right, you know. Big revenue to be lost, all because of those eggheads at Hopkins.

Secretary: Let's just not do it.

BM: What?

Secretary: We're the Gastro...I can never pronounce that.

Vice President: I know what you mean, Gassy. We're the experts.

Gassy: Don't call me Gassy—but that's the point. If we don't approve this new pill...

President: ...it'll never get off the ground...

Vice President: ...and it's back to lots of office visits and big bucks.

BM Number 2: But can't we do something that will find out what's going on down there?

President: BM#2, why don't you use the technical language? You know research shows that using the big words enhances billings by a factor of three.

Vice President: Still, he has a point—we need to come up with something to counter the blue pill.

Secretary: Let's call Vergil.

BM: Yes, Vergil is really smart.

Vice President: He'll come up with something.

President: But you know Vergil had his medical license taken away. String of questionable research projects, you know.

BM#2: Details, details. We need help. Call him.

President: Is he out of jail?

Vice President: Yes, last week.

President: [Dials phone] Vergil? This is Lionel. You know, Lionel, with GAS. That's right. How are you? The Board is sitting around discussing the blue pill. You've heard of it? Good. We want to get your take on it. What can we do? [Listens] What? You say you've been working on the problem already. You say you've come up with a solution? [Lionel listens for a time.] You want to what? You want to run a tube down the throat with a light?

BM: How in the world?

President: Sh-h-h. No, not you, Vergil. BM here is overreacting, as usual. And what else? [Listens]

President: You also want to enter the other end with a tube and a light?

Secretary: Same tube?

President: Same tube, Vergil? Oh, I guess that would be carrying economy a little too far. Well, thanks for your ideas. We'll get back to you. Oh, you won't be going anywhere? I see—you're still under house arrest. See you, Vergil. [Puts down phone.]

Vice President: Well, that's just fine. That's really just fine. Vergil has let us down this time.

BM#2: His plan sounds good to me. Big bu...Oops—can't say that.

Secretary: What's wrong with Vergil's idea, Mr. Smarty-Pants Vice President?

Vice President: It's just this: How do we enter our domain with those cute little tubes?

BM: We just knock out the patients and shove the tubes down—and up.

Vice President: No, I mean—JURISDICTION.

President: Oh, good grief. I forgot about JURISDICTION.

Sergeant at Arms: [Silent until now, but the one relied upon for legal and other aggravating issues] He means "up there."

BM#2: Up and down?

Sergeant at Arms: Yes—up there is governed by the ENT people.

Secretary: And they're still a little testy because the Eye specialists dumped them for not being smart enough.

Vice President: They'll never give permission to run that tube through their territory.

Sergeant at Arms: And that's not all—that's just the up there. There's also the...down there.

President: Oh, good grief. We'll never get permission... By the way, who has JURISDICTION down there?

[All sit silent, each looking out into space, pondering… Film ends.]

Professor: And that, class, was the first of our historic films. Next week, we'll show the battle with the ENTs—actually only the Ts. The Es and the Ns…Well, I won't spoil the drama by giving the story away. Class dismissed!

Surgery: Eminence Personified (Annals)

A Case Study

Seated comfortably beside the pool of his luxurious mansion, the noted Surgeon, E. Pluribus Large, was handed a phone by his faithful butler, Dubious. "Thank you, er, er..." said the great Doctor.

"Dubious, sir. I'm Dubious. I've been with you for thirty-one years."

"Of course, of course. That will be all for now, Du...—What did you say your name is?"

"Yes? (The Doctor answering the phone.) What is it? I'm very busy here, trying to relax at home... Oh, this is the hospital, eh? You have a very difficult case? Involving an earlobe, you say? Why are you calling me? Why not call that fake, Dr. Abner C. Lose? You called him last week for that follicle case—and he has such a poor record with follicles. Well, never mind. Let's get to the issue here. The main thing is—will you send a car? I can't just show up driving myself. People will be watching when they see this is big—involving ear...You say the car is on the way? Is it the big black BMW? I like that one. Good, good. Now, have nurse Autoclave standing by—oh, she's there already? Good, good."

Arriving at the front entrance of the hospital Surgeon Large emerged majestically from the big black BMW and gave a brief wave of the hand to the large group of his fans waiting there. Not a large wave; that would be too self-serving. Large knew well how to maintain his big-time celebrity status.

Upon arriving at the operating theatre he greeted Nurse Autoclave. "Are we all ready, Guinevere?"

"Ready," replied Nurse Guinevere.

These two professionals made up a storied pair in medical circles. They had worked on innumerable important cases over the years, but undoubtedly earlobes were the rock-solid basis for their sterling reputation.

Inquiring minds might wonder why the notable Large shares the spotlight with his nurse. It is only rumor, but there was the unfortunate incident regarding emergency surgery on the exemplary lobe belonging to the star pro football player, Leon Grunt. Leon's left lobe had become detached in the Big Game, and Dr. Large and his team had been called in. Somehow the lobe became mixed into the lasagna take-out that Dr. Large had picked up on the way to the hospital for his post-op snack. Clearing the surgery except for his faithful nurse, he had been forced to require Grunt's right lobe to perform stellar duty on both sides of the star's ear. Nurse Autoclave somehow convinced Grunt that his ears had always been in her words "that short," and never to mention the matter again. Further rumor had it that the Nurse seemed to have been able to raise her lifestyle considerably, at about the same time of the "Grunt lost and found."

The present patient was a woman, Myrtle Schlub, age 63, who l had been throwing darts in her neighborhood pub, the Indelicate Pelican, named for a very tall, thin man who, after losing his false teeth while engaged in a hot dog eating contest—he had just passed 34—began screaming nasty words at the contest sponsors. Nasty words, it must be remembered, have no place in a nice pub.

But I digress...No matter how it happened, it was an earlobe challenge, especially since Myrtle showed up on the gurney with her left ear still pinned, or more accurately, darted, to the target game board.

"Hm, big job, Chief," muttered Nurse Autoclave. "But we've had worse."

"What do you mean, 'we?'...oh, yes" seeing her eyebrows raise, obviously recalling some documents that had been passed between them on the Grunt occasion.

The eminent surgeon went to work with his assortment of specialized scalpels, along with an elaborate set of pliers, a Phillips screwdriver, and a small grappling hook. (Actually, the grappling hook proved unnecessary in the end.)

After a lengthy Gargantuan operation and a significant post-op and rehabilitation period, the patient recovered, which was predictable, since Dr. Large had a rather impressive 57 per cent success rate in his specialty, which surgeons everywhere agree is among the most dangerous to patients.

The careful reader will have noted immediately that this case study meets the usual careful exposition found throughout *The Annals of Medicine*. What is not so obvious is the points of instruction that this case holds for the neophyte earlobe surgeon. These points include the following:

Eliminate all nurses from the operating room, as their integrity, truthfulness, and professionalism have no place in a surgical setting.

Often the scalpel alone is not enough to do the job in complex operations. The story would take too long to tell, but in an early case, the jacking up of a 1963 Ford Bronco was a necessary part of the protocol.

Lastly, consider whether the really first-class surgeon, especially when part of a revered specialty, such as earlobes, or even follicles, would really want to show up in a BMW. Why not a Maserati, a Lamborghini, a...?

Dentistry: Colonial Times to Today

Crenshaw, the Dentist

Publisher's Note: Avid *Annals* enthusiasts will recall that the author indicated that the Medieval Times would be explored after the Greek and Roman Periods. It is a pattern with this author that he finds it, now as in the past, difficult to focus in any serious way, so that we have not been able to continue with the much-anticipated exploration of the medieval period; but, what are you going to do? We must be grateful that Cline has experienced sufficient periods of clarity to produce even the following.

Crenshaw decided to become a Dentist. The revelation came to him in an instant, while, of all things, he was serving his first weeks in Army basic training. And, he made his decision on, of all places, the drill field.

This medical career path was a natural path for Crenshaw because he descended from generations of that profession. Perhaps the first in his lineage was the ancestor who served in one of General Washington's forts in western Virginia during the French and Indian War. In fact, one of the most significant massacres of that War involved the settlers from the fort offered Crenshaw's services to an Indian Chief, Short Fuse, who was disturbed by an ache in his molar. It is to be presumed that the earlier Crenshaw did not perform the required service with appropriate deftness because Short Fuse brought in his braves and carried off all the fort's occupants to Ohio to be, as the Chief said, "dealt with" at leisure there. Old Crenshaw was battered and left for dead. He survived, however, and giggled every time he related the story, without referring to the botched dental treatment. He would say that it was a close call as to whether to be beaten and left for dead—or, go to Ohio.

Giggling was a Crenshaw characteristic through the years. A Revolutionary-era ancestor giggled with delight at the fine sets of wooden teeth he turned out in his woodworking shop. Dentistry was, he said, "what he had to fall back on," if the chestnut blight spread to other species of trees.

In the Civil War Era, a Crenshaw Dentist distinguished himself at Appomattox, all be it in a somewhat negative way. Confederate General Robert E. Lee was ready to present his sword in defeat to Union General Ulysses S. Grant when his, Lee's, upper set of false teeth popped out of his mouth and fell to the ground, upon which General Grant accidentally stepped on said plate, breaking it into multiple pieces. General Lee then threatened to "call the whole thing off," until General Grant offered him his spare set, which, as history records the event, fit admirably well. You may have anticipated the fact that Grant's spare set, which saved the day, was the work of a giggling Crenshaw.

The mention of the word "history" above calls to mind that many readers of the *Annals* have marveled over the uncanny ability of this author to utilize historical technique in spite of the fact that the author was trained in the law, not history. Of course, that legal training has been brought somewhat into question by a daughter, an attorney, who, in anticipation of having people visit her home for the evening, said, "Dad, don't say anything legal—you embarrass me." So much for the charm of frankness in children. Editor daughter similarly questions, for reasons quite puzzling to the numerous devotees of the *Annals*. Said daughter (Lawyers think the use of "said" has a certain charm to it.) has, on occasion, upon reading her father's written word, placed, starting at the top of a page and extending to the very bottom, a large question mark. Alas, jealousy in the young is a pitiable quality.

We move on to World War I, in which, in the trenches of France, it occurred to Grandfather Crenshaw that the gas might come in handy professionally—not *that* WWI gas, of course, but some perhaps aromatic aeration that would place the patient at complete ease. The rest is history. When Johnny Crenshaw came marching home, he went directly to his friend, Osgood Pipette, Chemist, and the two collaborated to create the first gas used in Modern Dentistry. The gas these two original thinkers came up with failed, unfortunately, to pass the sniff test, because the subject who was given their formula was wont to strike out, with force, against the person administering said gas, causing some near-death experiences.

His son, father of the latest scion of the family, picked up the mantle of the dental lineage and had no difficulty until his service to our troops in Europe in WWII. The Allies were winning until Father Crenshaw had a succession of extractions in one day somewhere near the front lines. The moans and sometimes screams alerted the German soldiers. When enemy soldiers approached to investigate, they started, as a spark starts a fire, a counterattack that has gone down in history as The Battle of the Bulge. Father Crenshaw was punished by banning him from further extraction for the duration of the War, which, to him was a serious penalty because he dearly loved to be giggling while pulling teeth.

In spite of these minor military setbacks, Grandfather and Father Crenshaw were credits to their profession. Of course, it was somewhat distracting that the infernal giggling was concomitant with every success. The present-day Dr. Crenshaw took no notice of this family quirk while perpetuating said quirk loud and often. But it is Dentistry, not hyper-behavior that demands our attention here. Behavior issues will be treated in our usual analytical fashion in the *Annals* chapter on Psychiatry, the capstone section of this monumental, according to the critics, historical work.

This brings us to consider the current Dr. Crenshaw—never known to have a first name, only Doctor—is a legend in his own time for his numerous exploits and adventures in all things concerning the lower face. In spite of all the trials—literally—of his ancestors, he has proven a super-hero to his fellow DMDs and DDSs everywhere. He has filled and pulled on Land, at Sea, under Sea, in Battle, and even in Space. The single blot on this exemplary record came when he added another dimension to his practice—that of Virtual Space. It turns out that no amount of denial could counter the harm to his practice that was done by his giggling efforts on patients who weren't there.

The Laugh-Booth

Dear Dr. Z:

Thank you so very much for your inquiry regarding the most significant product of the Medical Equipage Corporation—the Laugh-Booth. This product was in development for nineteen years, during which time we were able to arrive at the unique and useful product that is revolutionizing the Physician Office of Today. In order to fully apprise you of all the virtues and value of the Booth, I am sending herewith our answers to the most-asked questions about our finest creation.

What is the Purpose of the Laugh-Booth? Well, Doctor, you know when you have a patient in the examining room and they are describing their "condition" to you, and you find their description uproariously funny, and you want to laugh, and you can barely hold it in, but you do, and you think you are going to bust, but you are able to barely make it out of the examining room door, what then? Where to go to relieve the combustion of humor that has overtaken you, and still maintain the professional demeanor and decorum that has been the hallmark of your practice? To the Laugh-Booth!

What is the Laugh-Booth? The Laugh-Booth is a fully sound-proofed phone-booth size cloister for, when the door is securely closed, letting out with however outrageous guffaw that you need to expend in order to relieve yourself of the patient-induced dilemma related to that poor person's description of symptoms that have caused them to come to see you for relief.

What was the Final Link that Permitted the Corporation to Create the Perfect Laugh-Booth? After toiling over plans, blueprints, and designs for ten years, the Corporate Engineers were sitting around one day and Cecil

Thwate, Lead Mechanical Engineer, asked, "Whatever happened to those phone booths that we made our phone calls in?" Ray Picker immediately decried Cecil's ending his question with a preposition. Homer "Cool" Settler said, "I haven't seen any of those around lately. Wonder what they did with all of them?" And there you have it, the Historical Moment when the germ of the idea was formed that led to the development of the Laugh-Booth. You see, Doctor, it was a mere nine years later until this Crack Team put together the Crying Need and the Solution, which was to utilize old phone booths as the shell for the Laugh-Booth.

How come you can reach the Higher Decibels of Hilarity in the Laugh-Booth and still not be heard? Good question, Doc. You see, it's in the insulation. We have gone to great expense to find the most effective sound-deadening materials and have combined them into the strongest yet thinnest possible lining for the Booth, while still leaving room for you to pound on the Substantial Walls during High Peaks of Outburst and have no danger of breaking the booth a part or being heard by Office Staff—who are always looking for the slightest provocation to render idiotic the very person who...But I digress.

Any Testimonials? Over the years we have heard from hundreds of MDs, ODs, DOs, DDSs, and such, who have raved about the Life-Saving Function that the Laugh-Booth performs in their practices. Here's just one, picked at Random: "Dear Laugh-Booth Corporation, The other day I, carefully noting that "Office Staff" had extended the Little Stick outside Examining Room 34 (my signal to go in), entered 34 and found Ms. X, a rotund fifty-six-year-old woman. She was in what the advanced medical books call a "Bad Way." Did I fail to indicate that my specialty is Gastroenterology? She then proceeded to give what the diagnosticians call a Vivid Description of her symptoms. Well sir,

I made it through those symptoms by the hardest, excused myself, left 34, and ran to the Laugh-Booth, where I had an Ultimate Let-Go. I can safely say that on that day, your product, that Good Old Laugh-Booth, saved my practice, my office, my home, my big old boat, my kids' overly expensive matriculations…you get the idea. Gratefully, L.O., MD.

Need we say more? I think you get the picture now, Doctor, regarding the usefulness of this Essential Product. Physicians and Dentists tell us that they would not, nay, could not continue to practice their professions without the Laugh-Booth. We hope to hear from you soon so that you, too, may be able to enter your Examining Rooms with the confidence that you can sublimely handle any Symptomatic Description that may be laid upon you.

Yours very seriously,
I.M. Lame, President and CEO

A Skit

Between You, Me, and the Lamp Post

A Musical Revue

(Inspired by a production in Lyme Regis, England, in June 2001)

Setting: In a park at dusk with a bench and a very old lamp post.

Actors: Helen, who is a mature woman, and a hidden man, who speaks for the lamp post.

(Alternative staging might be accomplished by substituting actors of opposite sex and different age. It may also be done in a second version with song and dance, perhaps through supplementary spotlighting elsewhere on stage. It may also be shortened with the omission of selected songs.)

Helen: (Walking wearily along; shouts ahead) Go on to the fireworks. I'm going to sit and watch them from here. (Sits on park bench.) Whew! (Leans back on bench contentedly and looks about. Begins to hum a tune.)

Lamp post: Tuckered out?

Helen: (Looks about)

Lamp post: I said, 'Tuckered out?'

Helen: (Looks up and around)

Lamp post: You might as well look at me—I'm the one who is talking.

Helen: (Apprehensively) What?

Lamp post: It may not seem possible to you, but I am talking to you.

Helen: Why?

Lamp post: Because I can, I guess.

Helen: Do you do this often?

L: No, only now and then. Last time was in '98.

H: Which '98?

L: It's not as bad as that—it was in 1998. Don't be frightened. I can talk, but I can't move.

H: Are you sure?

L: Have you ever seen a lamp post move on its own?

H: No, but I've never heard one talk on its own, either.

L: I guess it seems strange to you, but not to me. I've been doing it for so long. I used to have gas, you know.

H: Beg pardon?

L: I mean, my light was by gas, before I was electrified.

H: You have been around a long time.

L: Like I said. By the way, what was the tune you were humming?

H: I'll Get By.

L: I always liked that one.

H: You know songs?

L: Sure. I've heard them all, from concerts in the park, radios playing, people singing and whistling—and humming.

H: I guess you sing, too.

L: I don't like to brag, but...

H: All right, all right.

L: Actually, I remember songs going back to the other ‘98—1898.

H: You do?

L: Sure.

H: My grandmother especially liked, After the Ball Is Over.

L: Me, too. But it’s pretty sad.

H: Yes, since the girl’s boyfriend thinks her brother is her new beau.

L: Guess you’ve never been in that situation?

H: Once, something like that. How about you—no, I guess not.

L: No. Could you sing it for me?

H: What?

L: After the Ball

H: Here?

L: Well, I can’t very well leave where I am. Come on.

H: (Gets up and looks around. Sings After the Ball.)

AFTER THE BALL

L: Very nice.

H: (Starts to walk away.)

L: Where are you going?

H: This is a little ridiculous—singing out here with no one around.

L: What am I, chopped liver?

H: (Sitting back down) I’m sorry. I wasn’t thinking. After all, there is a talking light post here.

L: That’s better. How about World War I?

H: What about World War I?

L: Know any songs?

H: Certainly, Over There, Pack Up Your Troubles in Your Old Kit Bag, lots more.

L: I liked one just after that—Yankee Doodle Dandy.

H: You sing it.

L: I'm shy.

H: I'll say. You're shy about a lot of things.

L: What a thing to say.

H: I'm sorry. Why don't you sing this one?

L: As I said, I'm shy. You do it.

H: Oh, very well. (Sings Yankee Doodle Dandy.)

YANKEE DOODLE DANDY

L: I feel like saluting.

H: Sure, right.

L: Know any other old ones.

H: My mother used to sing Alice Blue Gown.

L: That was quite a hit. Sing it.

H: Oh, all right. This is kind of fun. (Sings Alice Blue Gown.)

ALICE BLUE GOWN

H: And then there's another one she used to sing, I'll Take You Home Again, Kathleen.

L: Good one.

H: (Sings.)

I'LL TAKE YOU HOME AGAIN, KATHLEEN

L: How about your dad? Did he sing?

H: Only when he was shaving—Way Down Upon the Suwanee River.

L: Stephen Foster. I especially like another one of his, Beautiful Dreamer.

H: Me, too. I just might sing that.

L: Be my guest.

H: (Sings.)

BEAUTIFUL DREAMER

L: How about a hymn?

H: You're kidding.

L: No, I mean it. There have been lots of sunrise services and vespers here over the years. And some of the hymns are beautiful.

H: Like which one, in particular?

L: You choose.

H: You want me to sing a hymn? Here? Now?

L: Why not?

H: Then, if someone comes by, I should take up a collection.

L: Don't be a smart aleck.

H: Oh, all right. (Sings.)

IN THE GARDEN

L: I liked that.

H: (Looking to the sky) The fireworks are magnificent.

L: Yep, I've seen some good ones over the years.

H: Too bad there's not a song for lamp posts.

L: But there is.

H: Don't be silly.

L: I'm not being silly. Have you heard of The Old Lamp Lighter?

H: Of course. I just forgot. (Sings.)

THE OLD LAMP LIGHTER

L: You almost have me in tears.

H: Oh, sure.

L: But we got ahead of ourselves with the lamp lighter song.

H: How so?

L: We missed World War II.

H: And those are some of the best songs.

L: True, but also they can make for sad memories.

H: Yes, I lost an uncle in the South Pacific, and a young man from our neighborhood was killed in Germany.

L: What were your favorites?

H: Of course, Kate Smith singing God Bless America sort of got us through the war. And her theme song was When the Moon Comes over the Mountain.

L: And I remember the songs that got up our courage and resolve for the long war effort.

H: Like what?

L: Like Comin' in on a Wing and a Prayer. How about The White Cliffs of Dover—can you sing that for me?

H: I didn't know this was a private concert.

L: Well, you know, it's a long time between my talking with anyone.

H: (Sarcastically) Yes, I can imagine.

L: Please.

H: Very well. (Sings The White Cliffs of Dover.)

THE WHITE CLIFFS OF DOVER

L: Nice. Thanks.

H: Don't mention it. There are also those songs that remind us of the separation of people during the War.

L: Like I'll Get By.

H: And I'll Be Seeing You. I think I'll sing that for myself. But you can listen.

L: I pretty much have to listen.

H: Yes, I guess you are not going anywhere.

L: Are you mocking me?

H: No way—it's too much fun reminiscing with you.

L: Sing.

H: Okay. (Sings I'll Be Seeing You.)

I'LL BE SEEING YOU

L: Weren't there some crazy songs around the time of the War?

H: You mean like Mairzy Doats?

L: Just like that.

H: Will you join me?

L: What would it look like if someone came by and heard me singing?

H: About the same if someone came by and heard you talking. I've got it—How about if you say the words for the meaning of Mairzy Doats?

L: Can't do it.

H: C'mon. You owe me.

L: Oh, very well.

H and L collaborate on Mairzy Doats.

MAIRZY DOATS

H: That was fun.

L: It really was.

H: It looks as if the fireworks have ended. My family will be coming back soon.

L: I hate to see this end. Yes, it's been a real sentimental journey.

H: Is that a hint?

L: You have time—and promise you'll come back.

H: I promise (Sings Sentimental Journey.)

SENTIMENTAL JOURNEY

H: Calls to family approaching. (Family unseen) Weren't the fireworks spectacular? What did you say? What did I do while I was waiting? Oh, I can't tell you. That's between me and the lamp post.

(Curtain)

Poem and Children's Story
by Diane C. Cline

Autumn

Autumn leaves are falling
Plants and flowers dying
Autumn chores are calling
Whispering trees are sighing

Golden and red leaves softly turning
To a color of dullest brown
And we see sad hearts yearning
Watching the leaves fall down.

Many people love the golden Autumn hue
For Autumn is a brilliant time of year
We know it pleases him and her and you.
Yes, we all can't wait till Autumn is near.

Cami's Little Creatures

Once upon a time there was a little girl named Cami. She was three years old.

Now Cami lived in Florida near a Swamp and she made friends near there.

There was Al the Alligator, Sally the Snake, Molly Mosquito, and Freddy Fly.

One day Cami said to her mother, "I think I'll go down to the Swamp and visit my little friends."

Her mother said, "I'll pack you a lunch and you can share it."

So Cami took her little lunch pail and went out into the bright sunshine, down a grassy slope to the Swamp.

Al the Alligator was snoozing beside the swamp in the sunlight. Cami went over to him and said, "Hi, Al, I brought some lunch to share with you."

"Oh, Hi, Cami" said Al sleepily. "I'm too sleepy to eat right now. Rest a bit, then I'll join you."

While Cami was stooping over talking to Al there was a "buzz buzz buzz" around her ear then a little prick on her earlobe. "Oh, Molly, that wasn't very nice," she said.

"I'm sorry, Cami," said Molly, "but I couldn't resist, how're you doin', otherwise?"

"Pretty good," said Cami, "but I can't get Al awake to eat lunch with me. Would you care to have some lunch?"

"No thanks," said Molly, "I just had some."

Cami heard a different kind of buzz, then it was quiet, but she could feel something walking on her forehead, down her cheek, now on the tip of her nose. She put her fingertip to her nose and Old Freddy the Fly said, "Hi Cami, how's tricks?" She lowered Freddy from her nose on the side of her finger then looked at him.

"Freddy, have you had lunch yet?"

"No, but I'd rather wait 'til you're through then I'll get the crumbs," Freddy said. Sally the Snake came slithering up from the edge of the swampy pool.

"Oh, Cami! I'm so glad you're here, everybody's so lazy today and there's no one to talk to. Let's go over to that nice flat rock and have a nice little lunch."

So Sally and Cami went over to the rock and spread out a nice lunch of peanut butter sandwiches, milk, and apples.

It wasn't too long until Al, Molly, and Freddy joined them, and they chattered away happily.

After they had eaten their sandwiches, drunk their milk and almost finished their apples, they heard someone calling. "Cami, come home for your nap."

Cami stood up, brushed the crumbs from her dress and said, "It's time for your naps, too." She bent down and picked up her stuffed alligator and snake, little plastic fly and mosquito, and started up the steps to her room.

Credits

All stories written for our Family and Friends

Stories of the City

"He Was Just Sittin' There" ©2021 by Paul C. Cline, edited by Diane C. Cline

"Papa's Place" ©2017 by Paul C. Cline, edited by Diane C. Cline

"Silver and Tin" ©2014 by Paul C. Cline, for Diane

"Win or Lose" ©2010 by Paul C. Cline, edited by Diane C. Cline

"The House on Eighth Avenue" ©2020 by Paul C. Cline, edited by Diane C. Cline

"Where Have I Seen This Before?" ©2020 by Paul C. Cline, edited by Diane C. Cline

"Percy—99" ©2002 by Paul C. Cline, edited by Diane C. Cline

"The Lincoln Project" ©2022 by Paul C. Cline, edited by Diane C. Cline, for the Village on the Isle Writers' Group

"The Millian Dollar Doll" ©2010 by Paul C. Cline, edited by Diane C. Cline

"Macadamia" ©2022 by Paul C. Cline, edited by Diane C. Cline, from a suggestion by Michael Rex and Christina Chilcote

"The City Zoo" ©2022 by Paul C. Cline, edited by Diane C. Cline

"The Horse Up a Wall" ©2022 by Paul C. Cline, edited by Diane C. Cline

"Go, Wally, Go" ©2023 by Paul C. Cline, edited by Diane C. Cline

"Time Out" ©2009 by Paul C. Cline, edited by Diane C. Cline

"Rules: Senior Softball League" ©2016 by Paul C. Cline, edited by Diane C. Cline

"Enjoy Your Prunes—Be a Regular Person" ©2022 by Paul C. Cline, editing spurned by Diane C. Cline

Military Stories

"The Sarge" ©2011 by Paul C. Cline, edited by Diane C. Cline

"Not a Walk in the Park" ©2009 by Paul C. Cline, edited by Diane C. Cline

"Figure Head" ©2015 by Paul C. Cline, edited by Diane C. Cline

"'Old Folk' Tales" ©2002 by Paul C. Cline, edited by Diane C. Cline

Small Town Stories

"Ikey Crump and the Middlebury Fair" ©2021 by Paul C. Cline, edited by Diane C. Cline

"Uncle Jim's Treasure" ©2003 by Paul C. Cline, edited by Diane C. Cline

"Daisy, Daisy" ©2023 by Paul C. Cline, edited by Diane C. Cline

"Pray for the Race" ©2022 by Paul C. Cline, edited by Diane C. Cline

"The Snowman" ©2022 by Paul C. Cline, edited by Diane C. Cline, in response to "Trust" for the VOTI Writers' Group

"Great Grandfather" ©2001 by Paul C. Cline, edited by Diane C. Cline

"Mom" ©2010 by Paul C. Cline, edited by Diane C. Cline

"The Old College Secret" ©2000 by Paul C. Cline, and edited by Diane C. Cline

"You're on Fire" ©2019 by Paul C. Cline, edited by Diane C. Cline

"That Old Gang" ©2000, Paul C. Cline, edited by Diane C. Cline

"Off the Shoulder" ©2003 by Paul C. Cline, edited by Diane C. Cline

"The Shoe Exchange" ©2011 by Paul C. Cline, edited by Diane C. Cline

"The Street Taken" ©2011 by Paul C. Cline, edited by Diane C. Cline

"The Shagnastys" ©2022 by Paul C. Cline, edited by Diane C. Cline

"Troxell's Gifts" ©2012 by Paul C. Cline, edited by Diane C. Cline

Mountain Tales

"Yoo-Hoo and the Sandman" ©2022 by Paul C. Cline, edited by Diane C. Cline

"Henderson MD" ©2022 by Paul C. Cline, edited by Diane C. Cline

"Boy" ©2021 by Paul C. Cline, edited by Diane C. Cline

"Hortense Quito" ©2022 by Paul C. Cline, edited by Diane C. Cline, from a name suggested by our daughter, Camille N. Cline

"Biddy Haymaker Part I" ©2022, by Paul C. Cline, edited by Diane C. Cline; "Biddy Haymaker Part II" ©2022, by Tyler J. Coulton and Ashley R. Hodges; "Biddy Haymaker Part III" ©2022, by Diane C. Cline

"Up on the House Top" ©2018 by Paul C. Cline, edited by Diane C. Cline

"The Night Visitors" ©2010 by Paul C. Cline, edited by Diane C. Cline

"I'll Take the High Road" ©2020 by Paul C. Cline, edited by Diane C. Cline

"Amelia" ©2022 by Paul C. Cline, edited by Diane C. Cline, from names suggested by our daughter, Alice C. Morris

"The Little Red Coat" ©2022 by Paul C. Cline, edited by Diane C. Cline

"A Shocking Incident" ©2021 by Paul C. Cline, edited by Diane C. Cline

"Uncle Jimmy's Last Run" ©2006 by Paul C. Cline, edited by Diane C. Cline

Stories for Children

"The Old Ice Cream Shop" ©2021 by Paul C. Cline, edited by Diane C. Cline, for our Great-Grandchildren

"Cyril" ©2021 by Paul C. Cline, edited by Diane C. Cline

"Minus Four" ©2022 by Paul C. Cline, edited by Diane C. Cline

"Buddy L with His Trunk Turned Down" ©2019 by Paul C. Cline, edited by Diane C. Cline, for Great-Grandson Alvah

"Cupid's Big Day" ©2023 by Paul C. Cline, edited by Diane C. Cline

The Annals of Medicine

"A Compilation of Seminal Articles" ©2016 by Paul C. Cline, edited by Diane C. Cline

"Orthopedic Surgeons: The Beginning" ©2013 by Paul C. Cline, edited by Diane C. Cline

"Dermatology: The Annals of Medicine" ©2018 by Paul C. Cline, edited by Diane C. Cline

"The Early Days of Gastroenterology" ©2011 by Paul C. Cline, edited by Diane C. Cline

"Surgery: Eminence Personified" ©2018 by Paul C. Cline, edited by Diane C. Cline

"Dentistry: Colonial Times to Today" ©2021 by Paul C. Cline, edited by Diane C. Cline

"The Laugh-Booth" ©2015 by Paul C. Cline, edited by Diane C. Cline

A Skit

"Between You, Me, and the Lamp Post: A Musical Revue" ©2013, by Paul C. Cline, edited by Diane C. Cline

Acknowledgments

To turn around a well-known phrase, "All that I have met is a part of me,"—whether from family, friends, and acquaintances. They influence our thoughts and actions, and therefore our writing. Then there are family and friends who encourage or at least hold back their negative critiques. And there are those who are always there with encouragement and real practical contributions.

Specifically in my case, the first critique is and has always been done by my wife, Diane. After a book draft is completed, it is put together by our daughter Camille, who is also the publisher, and with the support of our daughter Alice and husband Bruce. Proofreading is performed by our grandchildren, Kemper and Jack.

To all of these members of the faithful, I am exceedingly grateful.

About the Author

Paul C. Cline was in his earlier days a printer's devil while in high school, summer worker in a paper mill while in college, and an Army private after law school. He spent time on a farm pitching hay and with his father hauling cattle. While having been born in a smaller city, his early life was influenced by his later living in a small industrial town and by the freedom of roaming the adjacent mountains. After law school and practicing law for a time he received the PhD and taught Government at James Madison University, 1961 to 1997, where he was the first chair of the Political Science Department. He has served on a city council and was a member of the Virginia House of Delegates. He has co-authored several books on American government topics and recently published *Second Fiddles,* about those who serve others but remain always in the shadows.

He has been married sixty-five years to the former Diane Chilcote, RN, and has two daughters, five grandchildren, and, as of this writing, three great-grandchildren.

Milton Keynes UK
Ingram Content Group UK Ltd.
UKHW010635040324
438885UK00001B/25